The water all around us

Lynn Michell

Published by Linen Press, London 2023

8 Maltings Lodge
Corney Reach Way
London W4 2TT
www.linen-press.com

A CIP catalogue record for this book is available from the British Library.

Cover art: Unsplash
Cover Design: Lynn Michell
Typeset by Zebedee
Printed and bound by Lightning Source
ISBN: 978-1-7391777-7-5

About the Author

I write and I run Linen Press, a small indie press for women writers: www.linen-press.com. It's a fine balancing act but ever since I saw *Elvira Madigan*, I've secretly wanted to be a tightrope walker.

My published books criss-cross genres and include a writing scheme for primary schools, a book recording the experiences of thirty people with severe Chronic Fatigue Syndrome, and the authorised biography of the super-realist painter, Rosa Branson.

Close to my heart is my debut novel, *White Lies*, spanning four generations and played out against the backcloth of the 1950s Mao Mao uprising in Kenya, and *The Red Beach Hut* about a fine but fated friendship between a man and a boy, both outsiders, both misfits, on a windswept English beach.

I have recently moved, after twelve years in southern France, to a remote croft in the Western Isles I live in a caravan with views of sea, seals and islands, and look after black and brown sheep.

Books by Lynn Michell

Fiction
2017 The Red Beach Hut. Inspired Quill
2015 Run Alice, Run. Inspired Quill
2011 White Lies. Quartet. Rights bought by Linen Press
1993 Letters To My Semi-Detached Son. The Women's Press

Life writing
2021 Rosa Branson: A Portrait. Linen Press
2013 Shooting Stars Are The Flying Fish Of The Night. Lynn Michell & Stefan Gregory. Linen Press

Non-Fiction
2003 Shattered: Life With ME. HarperCollins
1990 Growing Up in Smoke. Pluto Press
1987-1991 Write From The Start. Longman. A writing scheme for primary schools. Six illustrated pupils' books and two teachers' books

Anthologies
1997 A Stranger At My Table: Mothering Adolescents. The Women's Press
2022 Tabula Rasa: Poetry by Women. Linen Press

Praise for Lynn Michell's Writing

ROSA BRANSON: A PORTRAIT

'This wonderful book captures Rosa's great strength of character, her unquenchable passion to promote classical painting, her astonishing talent and her enormous generosity.'
– Heath Rosselli, Co-founder of The Worlington Movement

'Compelling and deeply felt. A narrative which has the intimacy and power of memoir.'
– Ali Bacon, author of *In the Blink of an Eye* and *A Kettle of Fish*

THE RED BEACH HUT

'Rare to find such beauty and language as crisp and refreshing as the seaside it so powerfully evokes.'
– Maureen Freely, novelist, translator and activist

'From the first pages, an atmosphere of such convincing threat that the reader's expectations are on red alert.'
– Jenny Gorrod. Dundee University Review of the Arts

'LOVED it so much. The characters are brilliantly rendered. I appreciated its subtlety in terms of how prejudice is handled. Structurally it works exquisitely, and the prose style is gorgeous.'
– Jess Richards, author of *Snake Ropes, Cooking with Bones, City of Circles, Birds and Ghosts*

'The prose is achingly beautiful…I doubt there can be a more poetic or lyrical writer when it comes to sea and shore.'
– Avril Joy, Costa and People's Prize winning author

'With poetic, melodious prose the narrative moves back and forth between characters, as well as across the ebbs and flows of time and timelessness.'
.– Joyce Goodman, professor of History of Education, Winchester University

'Lynn Michell writes a beautifully innocent and endearing tale twisted by the tainted gaze of society's perverse darkness.'
– Isabelle Coy-Dibley for The Contemporary Small Press

'A parable for our times... a sensitively written contemporary story and an intriguing book about secrets, assumptions, and consequences.'
– Derek Thompson, author of the Thomas Bladen thrillers, *Long Shadows, West Country Murder*

WHITE LIES

'A debut novel which possesses and is possessed by a rare authority of voice... It is the mother's voice that sings White Lies into unforgettability. Hers and Eve's. Their thoughts and writing ring like music.'
– Tom Adair, The Scotsman

'Gripping... with a bombshell of an ending.'
– Michele Hanson, The Guardian

'Credible and touching. Dramatic and tragic.'
– The Torch

'A first class read. Captures the time and transports the reader whilst exploring the reactions, feelings and fears of those who lived through the early stages of the Emergency.'
– Martyn Day, Lawyer for former Mau Mau against the British Government

'A wonderful evocation of Africa by an extremely accomplished writer. There are passages of extraordinary vividness and beauty. I love the sense, by the daughter, of unease at her father's painting of a golden era of colonialism, the spaces, the gaps that he is unwilling or unable to discuss.'
– Edwin Hawkes, Makepeace Towle

SHATTERED: LIFE WITH ME

'A timely and powerfully written book.'
– Bernard MacLaverty, author of *Cal, Lamb, Grace Notes* and *The Anatomy School*.

'Inspiring stories, not simply of broken lives, but of survival and hope in the face of terrible adversity.'
– Dr Vance Spence, Chairman of MERGE

'Shattered is a powerfully written account of life with ME – an unpredictable and devastating illness.'
– Tuam Herald

'The reader is kept on a steady and reassuring journey of validation and support. Identifying with the ME stories reminds us that we are not alone in this fight.'
– CF Alliance Newsletter 2003

For Ammie and Ella
who live on a croft with birds but who are not Finn.

Chapter 1

Beached

It's 07.30.

Julia sees the whale first.

The sky is cloudless, the air eerily still, but she knows that quiet dawns often foretell bad weather. Downstairs, she makes strong coffee before climbing to her studio at the top of the house, a short pause before the routines roll. On her easel is the sea-scape she began yesterday, the sky, sand and sea stretched end to end, bands of lime green washed with yellows. Yup, it couldn't be anywhere else but here, this ocean, this island, this bay, this beach. Looks like you could walk for twenty miles and not reach an ending. Good, she thinks. After her recent tight little compositions, the postcard-sized paintings, the stifled, shrunken emotions, she's painted something that's without boundaries. Fenn, who hates being told to colour inside the lines, will approve.

At the open window, she looks down at the sea and the stretch of white beach. No! Oh no! Hand to her mouth, she looks again. At the edge of the shallows is something enormous, something lumpen and dark, something beached.

Without doubt, a whale. Unimaginable, but there it is. Its size is hard to take in, even for someone who walks though life as an observer, recreating on paper what she sees. Of course whales are big, but the enormity of what's lying down there is a shock. It's a giant. There's not a flicker or shudder as thinning waves trickle over it, white on charcoal grey. The tide is on its way out. It will be high and dry soon, she thinks. In films she's seen them arching through oceans or powering to the surface to spin and sniff the air. Buoyed by the weight of water, they move with a balletic grace. Not this one. It's a shapeless collapse of blubber. A painful spill of dark, crusted flesh. Out of its element, its beauty has been stolen. She could never paint this painful image.

'Hamish!' Urgency makes her voice shrill. 'Quick. Come here.'

He's up, mug in hand, padding to her side. The tall man in faded t-shirt and boxer shorts hangs an arm over his wife's slight shoulders and looks where she's looking, expecting to see a sheep mauled by a fox or a deer caught and torn in the wire fencing.

'Christ! She was right all along.'

'Fenn! Oh heavens…she told us she heard a whale and we didn't take her seriously.'

'When a nine-year-old says she hears a whale when she sticks her head under the water, how do we take her seriously, Julia?'

'Hamish, she'll be distraught. How will she deal with this, a whale beached down there when she's talked about nothing else for days. This is too hard.'

For a moment Hamish is defeated. 'Aye, she'll be mad as hell at us. And heartbroken. But we'll have to deal with it.'

'Is it dead, do you think?'

'No idea.'

'It's not moving.'

'Means nothing. How can it move that much weight? What's the time?'

'Seven-thirty.'

'I'll phone the coast guard. Doubt I'll be the first. Crofters' eyes grow on stalks and for some this is mid-morning.'

'I'll get dressed. Make more coffee. Put out breakfast...' What can she do but retreat to the familiar because the new unknown is not fathomable. Downstairs, she moves like a puppet, stilted and stiff. Calm down, she tells herself. It's going to be a long, rough day and Fenn...oh my god, Fenn... Julia can't even finish that thought.

Hamish is gone and back in minutes. 'Boats are on their way. Someone's already phoned Sea Rescue. The harbour fishermen are driving round now. Our field's about to be a car park. I'll go see what I can do in a minute.' He looks wilder than usual, his curls corkscrewed, uncombed as always.

That's when Fenn appears in the doorway, one plait undone with zig-zagged fair hair falling to her waist. Hero gets out of his bed to wag his tail and lick her hand.

'You woke me up. Dad, you were talking loudly on the phone,' she complains, while Julia and Hamish exchange glances. She looks from one to the other. Picks up the vibes.

'Aye, well, something's happened, Fenn.' Hamish says, knowing it's inadequate. All words are inadequate.

'What? One of the birds? Which one?'

'No, none of the birds. Chickens, ducks and geese are all present and correct.'

'Dad! WHAT has happened?'

13

Julia puts an arm around her daughter's shoulders. 'Fenn, I'm afraid it's something awful. I'm so sorry but there's a whale washed up on the sand. Down there, on our beach.'

Fenn's eyes are wide-awake and round. 'A whale.' She repeats. What are they on about? 'What do you mean, a whale?'

'There's a beached whale down there.' Hamish says. 'I'm going down the now. See what we can do to get it back in the water.'

But Fenn has stopped listening and is running back up the stairs and into Julia's study where the window is still open, blowing in cold air. She stands on tiptoe. The shock makes her gasp, the biggest possible shock, and yet kind of what she has been expecting. Like, she knew. She really knew. No, it can't be. Yes, it can. Back and forth, back and forth go the contradictions until she tells herself that this is for real. Down there is a beautiful great whale who was out in the bay and now look at it...a hopeless wreck stuck on the sand. They must help it. Even as she watches, two men in waders are there, walking towards it.

'Dad...' she cries, tears streaming as she takes the stairs two at a time, 'Dad, we must go and help him. It's my fault. Jess and me...we are too late.'

'Fenn, calm down and listen to me,' Hamish says, holding his daughter until her sobs subside. 'One thing's for sure, it's no' your fault.'

'It is my fault, Dad. I heard him. I told Jess, and she heard him. I told you and Mum. You didn't believe me. And I wasn't quick enough.'

'To do what? To climb on his back and ride him back out to sea?'

'Dad, that's totally not funny!' Anger turns off the tears.

14

Her fists are clenched, ready to pummel him. 'Of course not! To get help. You know perfectly well what I mean.'

'How about we sit down and eat something and talk about what to do,' Julia intervenes, guiding Fenn to a chair, putting a glass of orange juice in front of her. She pops bread in the toaster. 'Then we get dressed, then…'

'Don't even think about telling me to go to school!' Fenn glares at her parents. 'Because I won't.'

'No,' Julia says, exchanging a glance with Hamish. 'I agree, Fenn. This is more important than school.'

'Phone Jess,' Fenn says. It's a command. 'She has to know. Now, Dad! She won't have seen it from her cottage or her beach.'

'OK. OK. I'll phone Jess. But here's the plan.' Hamish knows he's on very thin ice here. 'Fenn, there'll be a lot of folk down there soon, and not much you can do. I want you to be sensible and stay out of the way and…'

'Let the grown ups save the whale? No. I won't. I'm going to help too. I heard that whale, not you.' Tears well up again.

'Fenn, that whale weighs about forty tons, a dead weight out of water.'

'He may not be dead, Dad!'

'Stop jumping down my throat, Fenn.' His voice has dropped a notch. Enough hysteria, he is telling her. 'You know that's not what I meant. Listen, we're going to have to organise a team to move that creature.'

'Nothing can be done until the tide turns,' Julia says. 'How long is that? Two hours?'

'Aye. It's our only hope.'

'And until then we'll need to keep it damp…' Julia sighs at the enormity of it all. The whale. The situation. The despair she reads in her daughter's stricken face.

'I'll phone Jess. Then I'll go on down. I'll get some ropes...'
Hamish is gulping coffee and thinking out loud about physical
activity to solve the problem of a beached whale, his daughter
already fading into the background. As she must.

'We'll wait for Jess and follow,' Julia says. 'Fenn, eat your
toast. You need fuel.'

Fenn chews and thinks. Swallows and worries. She's calmer
now, thinking of the whale, not her own desperate attempts
to convince people that she knew he was out there. Only
one thing matters now. They have to save him.

It's 08.00.

They have been quick. Julia, Jess and Fenn are wrapped
in jumpers and anoraks, beanies and scarves, thick socks
and wellies because, as Julia predicted, the clear sky has
thickened to a dismal lid of overcast grey. She can smell rain
on its way.

At the top of the dunes, they stop and stare. Their first
glances take in its colossal size, its acres of cracked, crusted
skin, a fin trailed amongst seaweed, its slumped V-shaped
tail, its wide-open mouth. He should be in the ocean not
dumped out here, like a ship wrecked on the rocks. His fate
is terrible and wrong.

Fenn moves away to stand alone and to look at her
whale. Yes, it's her whale. 'I heard you,' she whispers, too
quietly for the others to hear, and anyway the wind is
whistling and voices rise in a babble from below. 'I heard
your song. I knew you were in trouble.' She concentrates
hard, beaming her words down to that magnificent creature
who is diminished. 'I heard you but I didn't get help in
time.' Then she bursts into tears and has to walk further
away from the others because she doesn't want their

sympathy or pity. 'Crying won't help you,' she says to the whale, roughly brushing away the tears. 'I'm coming. We're all coming. I promise we'll get you back into the sea.'

Julia and Jess are watching the commotion below. The news hummed along the village grapevine and brought fishermen and crofters in waders, and the curious who simply stare. Men in oilskins kneel by the whale. Others, further back, coil webbing and ropes and stack spades. Small kids race about. Older ones stand and gape, iPhones clicking double time. It seems no child from the village has gone to school today. A few reporters slung with cameras are snapping the stranded creature like an exhibit. In the bay, fishing boats putter back and forth, the skippers coiling more ropes for when the time comes. Others in inflatables are on their way; in fact anyone with any kind of sea craft has leapt in and pulled the whip cord to start the engine. Dunkirk all over again to save a whale. Or to be a nuisance and a voyeur. A spectator at a cruel sport.

Fenn moves back to her friend. 'Too much noise,' she says, looking up at Jess and scowling. 'He'll be terrified.'

'You can't do this silently,' Jess tells her.

'Yeah but most of them aren't helping, just staring at him.'

'They'll get organised soon.'

'Will they get him back in the sea?' It's the only question. And she has promised.

'I don't know,' Jess replies, unable to lie to this girl. 'Come on. Let's see what we can do.'

On the beach, Julia spots Hamish, tall amongst the stocky island men, and runs across the sand for an update, nodding to people she knows. No time to stop and talk. Hamish is in earnest conversation with a group of village youths, not even pretending to be cool. They are fired up and ready to help.

'Go and ask everyone to go home and bring buckets. Jimmy, organise it, will you? As big as possible but any size will do. Do that now please.'

'Hamish….' Julia calls over the talking and the shouting. The youths jog away and her husband straightens his back.

'Hamish, is the whale alive?'

'The vet's with him. Murdo. Says he's a young 'un. He's alive but must be kept cool and wet. That's all we can do for now. I'm organising a chain of people with buckets until the tide comes in.'

'What are the chances of rescuing him? Did he say?' Julia pleads.

Hamish frowns. 'Says it would be a lot easier if it were smaller.'

'But he's not, so what are his chances?'

'Yeah…well… he's weak…and his own weight is crushing his internal organs and he's drying out. We don't have long. Hours.'

'The whole village is here,' Julia says, unable to deal with this last bit of information.

'Thank god we're out of the tourist season or there'd be hundreds more of them. I've asked Callum and Jimmy to send away the gawpers.'

'It's not every day a whale lands on one of their beaches, Hamish.'

'I know. Can you go back to the house and get buckets?'

'Yup. I'll just tell Fenn first. About the buckets. Not the rest. She's desperate to help.'

'How is she?' he asks.

'Heartbroken. And angry.'

It's 09.00.

Murdo is shouting through a megaphone. 'Please don't come near the whale!' he hollers. 'I repeat, stay right away from the whale. You are not helping. Go back to the dunes! Or go home. Please keep your children away from the whale. We need space and quiet.'

A few people move reluctantly up the beach, but no-one sets off home. Mothers gather their excited children and settle them for a morning's viewing that's better than TV or Youtube. Dogs, wired by a new creature whose smell is alien, are rounded up and taken back to cars. Hero is dragged home by Julia who returns with buckets and blankets.

The whale lies with its head on the sand, tail flopped towards the sea. Those in waders are at the ocean's edge, willing the tide to turn. Others in wellies form a line on the wet, packed sand. Some, vetted by Hamish as calm and reliable, wait by the whale, glancing down with awe at its size and with sorrow at its desperate plight. Faces are grim but determined. Hamish shouts the command and so begins a dance of arms passing buckets from left to right. Down one side buckets go empty. Up the other side, they slosh full, swinging from hand to hand until they reach those close enough to throw. It's shoulder-hurting, arm-numbing work. After fifteen minutes, Hamish shouts, 'Buckets the other way.' The heavy work must be shared. Not wanting to disturb the creature who lies helpless, people bend and pour water with care, with respect, with kindness. Others step in to swap places with those whose arms tremble and pack in. All without words being spoken.

A hand tugs on Hamish's sleeve. He's been too busy to notice his daughter creeping to his side, step by silent step. She's holding the bucket she uses to feed the chickens, the red one. Jess and Julia are working in the line.

'Can I help?' Her earnestness is heartfelt.

Hamish knows not to refuse. 'Yes. Take your place near the whale, Fenn. Tell Jess to stand next to you. Pour water if you can or just smooth the water chucked by the adults. Use your hands. Stop when you get tired.'

A quick smile and she's off to tell Jess who steps out of line and moves in closer, woman and girl holding hands, and buckets. For a while, they can only stare. He's not black, more like charcoal, like cement, cracked and creviced. His pale underbelly has sunk into a trench into the sand. His eye is closed, as if he can't bear to watch. Jess doesn't want to cry in front of Fenn, but it's impossible not to. At her side, Fenn's shoulders are shaking.

'He's awesome,' Fenn whispers through tears, seeing his strength and power gone, his fate in their hands. 'I know you called to me,' she whispers, bending down, her back to Jess. 'I heard you. You told me you were out here alone. I wondered if you were lost. Now I know that you were. I heard your beautiful song. I heard it. Now we are going to help you. Hang on. Please hang on.'

'Amazing,' Jess replies, when Fenn stands back up. 'And he's only young.'

Fenn wipes away her tears and gasps. 'But he's huge!'

'He's a young male who has lost his family.'

'He lost his family and then he lost his way,' she replies.

Murdo, stethoscope round his neck, sits close, monitoring any change. The island's doctor squats by him. Jess has crept close enough to hear their exchange.

'I've spoken to Sea Rescue on the mainland,' James McLean says very quietly. 'They say it may be kinder to euthanise. A whale of this size.'

'Aye, I spoke to them too. And what will the islanders will say if we announce we're going to kill it?'

'This isn't about the islanders. It's about a suffering whale. Putting him out of his misery may be more humane.'

Murdo sits back on his heels. 'Aye, it may come to that. But not yet. The tide's on the turn so we should make one attempt to float him.'

'Even if you manage to float him, the odds aren't good. He can survive only hours out of water. His weight is already causing crush injuries to his internal organs. He may still die. He's weak. He's absolutely exhausted. Even if we get him floated, he may swim off and die somewhere else.'

Murdo sighs. 'I know that, James, but perhaps a quiet death at the bottom of the sea is better than the agony of lying here. It would break my heart to kill this mammal without trying to save it.'

'Well, it's your call. You're the vet.'

'Aye, a vet who knows a bit about sheep and cows and chickens...not whales. And thank god, it's not my say so. A team from the Rescue Centre is flying in. They'll be here soon. By the time they arrive, we'll know the chances of getting him back in the sea.'

The tide is breathing its way back up the beach. On the turn, it's slow, before it gathers momentum. The trickling waves will become rollers under the heavy clouds and in the quickening wind. Time and tide will decide the whale's fate.

Jess hears every word. 'Bravo, Murdo,' she says under her breath. And turns to Fenn, hoping she hasn't understood the big words, but the child is no longer at her side. Bucket abandoned, she has crept nearer, and sits close to the whale's head. Jess sees wonder and pity on the girl's face as she looks at his closed eye. Jess breathes out. Fenn is too absorbed in the magnificence of the whale, even a prone, helpless, collapsed whale, to bother listening to grown-ups.

It's then that Jess picks up the sounds. Soft and willowy. Oh heavens! What is Fenn doing? Humming? Yes, lying down beside the whale, her mouth close to his ear. The sounds remind Jess of pan pipes, thin and airy. Fenn is oblivious to everyone and everything except the creature at her side. As Jess listens, she hears Fenn settle on one musical phrase which she repeats in her high, clear voice, a small, sweet song of hope. And love. The whale opens his eye, a black pupil ringed with pale yellow, and looks straight at her.

'It's OK,' she whispers. 'We're going to rescue you.'

The vet has noticed the girl prone on the sand. James looks to makes a move but Murdo puts a hand on his arm. 'Leave her. She's not doing any harm. She seems to be singing to it,' he says with wry amusement.

Chapter 2

The Whale

The young whale calls. He sings his long signature note and feels its echoes leave his throat and hears them vibrate to a faraway point through the water. There is no reply.

Near the surface, amongst the floating yellow weed and the massed dashes of tiny shimmering fish, he swims within a small radius, his body moving smoothly and without urgency as he waits for the answering calls to guide him back to his pod. He has learned to speak the same language as the others, the same dialect of long calls, trills and clicks. Suspended in the water, motionless and with his head down, he runs through his repertoire and ends with his autograph note, a long arc of exquisite sound.

He knows, in the way that he knows and understands the ocean, that without the travelling notes of water-music, it will be hard to find his way. His eyes are tiny, his sight of little use, and anyway the ocean scatters light into fragments that flash and multiply their meaning. His sense of smell is better but the molecules that carry scent disperse in water, too dilute to help him. When the other whales left, they took their palest of scents with them. Sound is what he relies on so he waits to pick up the songs that will guide him back to safety. There is nothing to worry about. Not yet.

This is only his second year travelling long days and long nights with his family across oceans from cold feeding grounds to warm breeding grounds, and back again. He is tired but excited after that first circular journey, relieved that he was not one of the sad whales left behind because they faltered or grew tired or unwell. He saw them sink to the bottom. On went the others, he amongst them, the elders in the pod sending out signals of confidence as they navigated as surely as if following lines scratched in the sea bed. As they swam in loose formation over thousands of miles, they sent out their calling cards to one another. Keep together. Stay safe. That huge envelope of sound held them in its folds and kept them safe.

When one of them chanced on a patch of water crammed with fish, he summoned the others and they surged together to feed in a frenzy. We must eat, we must eat, they told one another as they hurried to the well-stocked sea larder. We do not know when we will eat again. He has a body-memory of them being here not long ago, the whole pod rushing through water thick with shoals of fish. They were close beside him, feeding, diving and soaring upwards, swimming through and under the shoals, their great mouths and throats extended to receive the gallons of fish-filled sea water that poured inside, rejoicing in the abundance.

One of the adult males began the ritual of a bubble-net feed, slowly circling the teeming fish while pushing bubbles from his blowhole. Others answered the signal and joined in until a multitude of fish and plankton, bewildered and disoriented, were trapped in a cage of froth. The pod traversed the net, mouths wide open. The feeding was easy. They ate their fill.

Whereas not long ago the young whale felt the push and shove of the others in water churned and murky by busy movement, now the sea is clear and empty. Not even the slap of a tail reaches him. It's a loud silence and a worrying one.

It was after the excitement of the bubble feed, when the others were swimming away to resume their journey, that he became distracted. On one of his whooshes to the surface, he had noticed out of the corner of his eye a fellow whale, a big one, some way off but near the surface. He had spotted the shadowy fin tail hanging below the water line. From above it came the high notes and throat noises of a language he did not recognise. Instinctively drawn to the shape and the sounds, he left the others and pushed forward to investigate. What was it? Was it a threat? And why did it call in staccato bursts into the air, not the water? He swam right up to it, but it didn't move, didn't flicker, didn't pulse. It was silent. The other sounds from high above had fallen silent too. He nudged and nosed the creature, perplexed by its rigidity and stillness. Then he dived underneath.

The sounds started up again, and in them he heard excitement. He heard the drum beat rhythm that was the stamp and scurry of feet on a wooden deck and the squeak of hands on wire, running along its length. In these sound fragments he picked up the adrenaline of fear and wonder.

It's a whale! It's massive!
As big as the boat. Forty-five feet?
At least...oh look, it's diving under the keel...oh my god.
Shhh...don't scare it!

Look, look, it's going under again.
What sort is it?
Don't know but it's huge...
Be quiet!

The whale swam under and felt the bump and hard scrape along his back and emerged puzzled on the other side. This static whale with its hanging tail neither sent warning signals to back off nor swam away nor sang to him. A trail of brown-green scum and barnacles drifted from the skin into the clear blue water. Not that he felt so slight a wound.

Is it hurt?
Oh I hope it's all right.
Look at that brown stuff trailing in the water.
They're scales. It's rubbed off its scales on the keel.
Or barnacles. His back is all crusty with them.
He's hurt himself on the boat!
Maybe not. Just scraped himself. I think he's OK.
He's come to see if we're a threat.
Maybe we look like a whale from down there.
Possibly, with our fin keel.

Back and forth, from one side of the boat to the other, the whale dived to understand the unknown sea creature who had invaded his territory but was lying in the water, unresponsive. He worried about the risk, to him and his pod. The hard rub on his back didn't feel like the rubbery softness of blubber nor the crusty surface of skin. This new creature gave no sign that it might attack, so his defences, raised to red alert, quietened. His aggression faded to curiosity. Curiosity cooled to indifference, but an indifference

26

edged with caution. He swam a short distance away to keep vigil. Surfaced. Stared back at the whale lookalike out of his small eye. Blew.

He's blowing!
Look at that plume of water!
He's OK.
Did he hurt himself?
I don't think so. Look, he's watching us.
I can see his eye.
Oh look...he's swimming away.
No, no, he's stopped again. He's still checking us out.
He's still not certain if we're another whale.

He watched and waited, with his ears and his eyes trying to pick up clues about a creature so like and so unlike his own. After his enquiring dives, his swooping crossings beneath its belly, he remained close, not letting it out of his sight in case it changed its behaviour. His waiting, most of all, was in case it called. But it stayed quiet.

Fixated on this puzzling creature, he forgot to monitor the changing colour of the sea as day faded into night and the sun slid down the sky and vanished into the ocean as it did in those latitudes, the transition to night sudden and fast. For far too long the whale had been unable to let go of a vigilance that anchored him to a radius not far from the boat as the light left the water. Round and round he went, pausing sometimes to check that nothing had changed. By nighttime, not a sound reached him from the thing that hung there. Maybe it was dormant or sleeping. He decided, finally, that his sentry duty was futile. There was nothing in this encounter to alarm him. Or his family. Not often called upon to take on a responsibility like this because that fell to his elders, he felt a certain satisfaction that he had done his duty and had survived unscathed.

With the target of his wariness offering no response, his adrenaline leaks away and he finally pushes himself out of his self-imposed vigil and returns to the present. The absorbing state of watching and waiting has taken too much concentration and has tired him. On watch, on guard, he has lost sight of his true purpose here, to be swimming beside the others as they continue their journey across oceans.

When he tunes back in the clatter and cry of the ocean depths, he finds the cacophony confusing. The sounds that play out in the ever-rolling swoosh of the currents feels like an onslaught, too loud and too overlapping for his weary brain to sift through and separate. A new anxiety replaces the older one. The fin-tailed creature no longer of any consequence, the whale tries different positions, different depths, and different directions as he searches for the one soundtrack that is missing. Whether the whale is unable to pick up the audio trail from his pod or whether the soundtrack is actually not there because the pod has by chance entered an area where sound carries less clearly, he will never know. Nor does it make any difference to what he does next. He chooses a direction and swims away.

Looping and turning in blackness feverishly illuminated by the sparks and flares of creatures who are neon-lit as they search for food, he surfaces, dives again, his weight of no consequence, and senses a long time passing. He calls often. A flick of his muscled tail holds him still while he listens keenly for the calls that always come even in an ocean that is a forever symphony of cries and slaps and gurgles. No whale song reaches him now. The family voices are silent.

Chapter 3

Fenn

Thank goodness that's over. It's been another annoying day and the term has barely begun.

Fenn stomps up the aisle of the school bus, ignoring the few empty aisle seats because the turned-away faces tell her she is not welcome to share. She throws herself onto a seat right at the back, rucksack at her feet, face turned to the window. Who cares? She needs to be alone. She needs to think.

She is fed up with being picked on. She gets good marks. She finishes her work faster than the others. Why does her teacher keep bitching at her?

'Concentrate, Fenn. Stop staring out of the window.'

'Stop your dreaming.'

'Get on with your work, Fenn.'

The teacher doesn't pick on the other kids but they've been at the school forever and she's the new girl like there's something wrong with that. Although her family moved to the island more than a year ago, she reckons she'll be the new girl for at least the next five years. Her dad told her to be patient, but it's so annoying being treated like an alien from outer space just because she wasn't born here. She didn't arrive from Iceland or Africa, did she? Just the mainland, a ferry ride away. She sighs.

And it's annoying when Mrs McCraig accuses her of dreaming when she's listening. She usually finishes her work quickly because it's easy, and then she tunes in to the sounds of the island because this wild place is rarely silent and she loves the jigsaw music of the wind and the sea and the birds. A lone corncrake's rusty krek krek broke into the first lesson, puzzling her because they usually call at night. That bird is up at the wrong time, she decided, or hasn't gone to bed yet. He'll be tired! Then in maths came an oystercatcher's hueep, hueep, and she could imagine the bird bob-bobbing across the pebbles and jabbing at shells with its sharp orange beak to extract the mussel inside.

Ignoring the over-loud chatter and laughter of the children on the seats in front, no doubt intended to make her feel high and dry, Fenn drifts back to the life she has left behind. She has a strong photo-memory of being very small and of sitting under a spreading tree in their garden, listening to the birds and answering their calls with chirps and tweets. But that scene moves on to later, annoying ones when her mother kept harping on about her amazing hearing and didn't know when to quit.

'I wish you'd stop asking me about the stupid birds,' she had snapped at Julia one day when she was older. 'I'm not four, in case you hadn't noticed. I don't do that stuff any more. And anyway there are only five kinds that fly over our garden.' Her mum didn't often treat her like an infant. They got on well and Fenn could talk to her about most things. Yes, she still watched the birds and listened to their

31

calls, but it was private. Between her and them. Time her mum caught up.

'Sorry,' Julia had replied, crestfallen. She tried hard to keep up with her fast-changing child. 'There'll be more birds on the island.'

Oh yeah. The island. 'I don't want to go,' Fenn said pointlessly. And predictably.

'I know you don't. But wait until we get there before you judge it. Give it a chance.'

'I don't want to leave my friends.'

'I know you don't, but you'll make new friends.'

'You don't know that, Mum.'

What Fenn didn't know was that Julia was having the same misgivings about them moving to a small Scottish island. Julia's conversations with Hamish, born there and already one of them, and stuff she had read, gave her concerns too about being an incomer.

'It's a good bet, Fenn,' was the best she could manage because Julia refused to tell lies. 'And your friends can come and stay.'

'They'll find new friends when I've gone.' Fenn had seen it happen. The kids left behind didn't pine for those departed but worked out how to survive without them.

'And so will you,' Julia said, the words out before she could catch them. Stop trying so hard, Julia. Let it go.

On the bus, Fenn has turned off the sound track of the other children chatting and giggling. She can do that. Tune in or tune out. Sure, her sharp hearing has its advantages now that she's older. She can pick up most of what is said through walls and keyholes, and hears what children whisper at nearby desks. But Julia was completely wrong about her making new friends. When she arrived, the other kids were already in tight little groups, having started nursery class together. They treated her like she was a foreigner. Or hard of hearing, because in those first weeks she couldn't understand what they said with their soft island accents and kept saying Pardon. Ha ha. So much for being the one with the good ears.

Now they're trying to make her feel unwanted and Fenn quietly fumes. Not that she'll give them the satisfaction of showing any hurt. Yes, she is lonely but she can deal with it. In school, she can escape to noises off stage. It stops the feelings of rejection getting to her. And anyway, listening to the sounds outside is more interesting than boring sums and the stupid colouring in. Colouring in! She's nine, for heaven's sake. Her mum, who's an artist, says colouring in is a total waste of time because you haven't even drawn the picture in the first place and what's the point of staying inside the lines? Julia says it's busy-work to keep children occupied and give the teacher a break. She and her mum groan together about colouring in. Then Julia, always ready to stop in the middle of her own painting, gives Fenn a big piece of paper and says, 'Here, paint something you want to paint and splash colour everywhere, inside and outside the lines! Go wild, Fenn.'

The rain is streaming down the bus window. From the leaden colour of the sky, she knows there'll be no let-up and she won't be able to run to the beach below her house. It's like she shrugs off all the hassle and hurtful nonsense when she runs across the field to the high sand dunes, then jumps and bum-slides down them at breakneck speed to stand and curl her toes in the white powder sand. She takes great gulps of salt air and watches the gulls swooping over the water.

Her heart beats faster as she races to the sea's edge and feels the ice chill of the frilly waves. There's never anyone else there and that's exciting. It's nothing like the loneliness of school because she doesn't feel alone on the beach. She feels free. This is where she belongs. This is her beach.

It took ages to persuade her parents to let her go without one of them tagging along and chatting. So annoying. She would finish her chores on the croft, then wait and wait for her dad to take a break from planting trees or for her mum to drag herself away from her painting. OK, eventually one of them downed tools and took her, some days, not every day, but it could be late and starting to get cold. And her excitement would be turning to impatience. She knew neither of them wanted to stand on the beach like sentries, Hamish glancing at his watch every two minutes, Julia longing to rush back to paint the colours of the sea and sky. She didn't want them wasting their time playing life guards. So she kept on at them, and when they got tired of her nagging and sulking, they agreed she could go after school, after she had herded the birds to their night time places. Julia agreed with a worried frown. Hamish agreed with one raised eyebrow which meant, Don't you dare let me down.

There were conditions of course. She wouldn't get her freedom without conditions. She had to promise to be back within an hour, to come home if the weather turned nasty, to paddle and swim only in the shallows, and never never never go out of her depth. Easy peasy that last one because when the tide was out, you had to walk a mile across the damp sand and another mile to get into deep water. The shallows stretched forever, palest green on sunny days, deeper blue under clouds. She'd watched others, the tourists in summer, and while scowling at their intrusion, she noticed how they hiked across the sand then bobbed on for ages in a few inches of water. Most then turned round and came back. Scaredy cats. Very few carried on to where the water was darker blue and deep. Give her one of Julia's crayons and she could draw the line where the sea plunged over a shelf. A few bobbing tourists kept going, torsos well above the water, and then suddenly their heads went under like they'd fallen off a cliff. From one second to the next, they were out of their depth.

One day she will fall off that cliff. One day, maybe when she's ten. Meanwhile, she can at least practise breaststroke and backstroke in the shallows because she's small and light and can float in a few inches of water without touching the bottom. Julia taught her ages ago, when she was small. Water sprite, she called her daughter. You must have been a fish in another life, she said. So it's fine for now, but one day she'll be old enough to swim to that line where the water turns a deeper shade of blue and her feet don't touch the bottom. She dreams of that first long swim. She'll put her head under because she can hold her breath for a long time, and there will be a whole new world of sounds to listen to. It will be awesome.

Fenn watches the watery landscape slide past as the bus continues on its predictable way. Because it is so flat, the trees having long ago given up their fight for survival against the battering wind, you can see far into the distance. She can see the intricate patchwork of lochs, a heron on a rock, sheep trustful enough to leave the fields and graze at the side of the roads, sudden glimpses of froth decorating the turquoise sea. The island isn't that big, about a hundred square miles, with maybe six hundred folk living on it. After more than a year here, she can draw an accurate map of the place and always she leaves it in monotone, colouring in only her beach in yellow and blue. She knows the route the bus takes along the main artery road that runs north to south. She could drive the bus herself. It takes little detours to drop children in small, clustered communities with their almost identical, one-storey white houses with small windows and washing blowing on lines. It loops along isolated tracks to crofts with parallel parcels of peat and crops, chickens and sheep. The island is more a piece of water with hundreds of lumps of land on top, she thinks, before she turns away from the damp contours to her own musings.

Damn that rain, she says, but not out loud. Swearing isn't allowed, not on the school bus nor anywhere else where grown-ups might hear. Her father swears, and worse words than damn. Anyway, the damn rain is damn persistent. September can be wildly unpredictable with days on end of knock-you-over gales and spiteful stinging rain that keeps you stuck indoors. But these late summer weeks have been good, fine enough to go to the beach almost every afternoon after school and warm enough to swim in the sea.

The bus is nearing home. It's quiet now with only a handful left on board. Only a few more minutes before it takes the road down the peninsula where Fenn's croft, and a few other cottages sit on a long thin finger of land that ends, a few miles further on, at the sea. People tell her it's one of the most beautiful places on the island, and one of the most remote. The beach below Fenn's croft forms a perfect half-moon bay, its white dunes higher than anywhere else on the island. My beach, Fenn thinks again.

Chapter 4

Jess

The rain is unrelenting. The sky was already steel-grey as afternoon faded into early evening and she joined the queue of cars waiting to board the ferry, but now she can't even see the massive bulk of the Caledonian MacBrayne rising up from the quayside. The official who stops at the side of her van to check her papers is in head-to-toe black waterproofs and rain drips steadily from the rim of his hood to his nose and chin. He doesn't wipe it away. Jess lowers the window a crack and slides out the forms for him to check.

'Awful weather for you to be out in,' she says, for something to say, and because she feels sorry for him walking the length of cars in such appalling conditions. It's late July, but she knows that July and August can be bad. This far north, there's no predicting what the climate will throw at her. She's not some naive incomer. She's done her homework and she will greet the inhospitable weather, the roaring gales, the endless stinging rain, with acceptance. They are necessary. Thinking otherwise would make a mockery of the whole plan. She goes willingly while carrying her sadness like a soft bundle in her arms, not ready yet to let it go. She has told herself it's like turning to a fresh page, or perhaps taking down a new notebook. By coming to this island, she has chosen the exact opposite of the technicolour canvas that is Lake Placid with its pretty clapboard homes against a mountainous backdrop of greenest pines. In between was England's flat south coast looking out to France, though that was never home. It should have been an exciting staging post instead of the saddest of endings. Don't go there, she tells herself.

'Ach, no' bad really,' the man replies, interrupting her meandering thoughts. 'Welcome to Uig.'

Is he joking or just bored with the same comment from every person in every car? In her old Ford van, crammed to the roof with her possessions, she flicks on the windscreen wipers to give her a few seconds of vision, then flicks them off again. Not much point really. It's just a line of cars and lorries waiting to get on board to make the two-hour crossing. The sea is rough today but the boat is plenty large enough to ride the swell.

It was a very long drive north, too far to make without an overnight stop in a budget hotel. This morning, she had woken to a rain-washed dawn which might or might not bring some light to the day. In the plastic-seated, brutally lit dining room, she was one of very few travellers. She took a mug to the machine that promised coffee but delivered something nasty and black. You don't get a cafetière and ground beans at the price she paid. At the counter, she reached across the lined-up mini packets of Rice Krispies and Coco Pops for two thick slices from a floppy baguette, a tiny wrapped pat of butter and a mini slab of jam. Out of the window, her van waited for the drive up through Scotland and to the bridge that would take her to Skye. The first of the two islands.

She felt no adrenaline rush of excitement. Her mood was one of quiet acceptance and that was good enough. After all, it has been two years. Her decision to up stakes and take herself as far away as possible was made soon after it happened. The incident. The accident. No name seems to quite fit. Since then, she has kept a close check on her emotions for any sign that the decision is misguided and wrong, a running away from something she needs to stay and face, a false move. But time has only brought certainty and clarity, and the recent weeks of cleaning and packing and paperwork have dulled the sharp stabs of sorrow that still take her by surprise. Her grieving can wait. She will deal with it. In this new place.

Car lights are being switched on. Windows are rolled down and hands throw out the dregs of a last cigarette. There's no smoking on the ferry. The driver in the car in front has turned on his engine, the tail lights glowing red, and Jess does the same. Their lane is moving now, and the cars roll slowly forward as Wet Man waves the vehicle at the head of the queue, then the next, up onto the tarmac strip that will take them into the bowels of the ferry. Inside, men in high vis vests do stop-and-start hand signals to bring each car almost up against the bumper of the one in front.

Jess heaves out her shoulder bag and locks the car. It's not just bitterly cold down here in the cavernous space under the steel girders, it's brutal. Surfaces are hard and shiny, the floor wet and dirty, the lighting ugly, and people bend their heads as they battle to the doors against the wind that whips through the open bow. The end piece which has been levered up to let the cars on is like a whale's jaw, Jess thinks.

Deck C. Bay 2. Chair 10. This small area, more like a wide corridor, is marked with Disabled stickers, but there's no-one else here. It's quieter than the big lounges where tired, over-wound children run and scream, and people around tables drink from their cans of beer and laugh. And laugh. Endless loud laughter disturbs her. Her problem, not theirs. She shuffles along the bench and leans her head against the cold, rain-splashed window. For a while nothing happens. Nobody else comes to sit here and Jess is relieved to have the space to herself. This journey is momentous, she thinks. This is a moment of transition. She catches her image in the dark window, and says, not out loud of course, But I feel numb.

When the deep throb of the engines start up, Jess feels the ships' vibrations in her bones and in her heart, a beat that will accompany her to another place and another life. The ferry is being backed away from the quay, its great bulk slowly manoeuvred to face where they are heading. As it writhes round, it churns the water into hectic waves that slap against the stern before readying itself in a moment of limbo. Then it heads out and rides the waves in what feels like a rocking movement, forward, up and over, forward, up and over. The strip lights inside, combined with the darkness beyond the windows, make it difficult to see anything out there. There is only water, fathoms of black water, and somewhere up ahead, her destination. A small island.

If she cups her hands round her face, she can just about make out the acres of dark water pushing past the boat, splitting into arching waves on either side of its hull. Lulled and drifting, she keeps her eyes on the sea, waiting and wanting to see her first glimpse of land in the distance. Don't be daft, she tells herself. You won't see a thing with a sky this full of rain. When the ferry docks, your first sight of the island will be a small industrial area exactly like the one you've just left. You'll see wet tarmac and rain falling across neon street lights. You'll see cars and vans and lorries waiting in lines separated by white stripes on the road and white tape that drips into puddles.

But out there, in the blackness, something does catch her eye and interrupts the limbo state that requires nothing of her. There's something moving, not very clear but not far from the ferry. Jess sits up and presses her forehead to the glass, looking past the pale, tired reflection that stares back at her. There are tiny lights way ahead, popping into view then vanishing again as the ferry climbs each wave and drops down the other side, a slow motion carousel, so they are nearing land. But there's something else closer in. The shape is blurred in the sheets of rain and flecks of foam, but Jess knows and trembles and turns away. No, not now, she pleads, her heart sinking. She is making this crossing to put miles of land and water between her past and her future, to erect a tall, strong barrier across the sea and to leave these painful memories where they began and where they should remain, in the sea and on the shore of a coastal town in England. Now, still, she has the same two options. She can look away and refuse to acknowledge what she sees. Or she can accept that this her grief is still showing itself in disturbing hallucinations. To look away is to turn her back on Dan, and she isn't ready to do that. Surely these flashbacks, conjured from her shock and sorrow, will go one day when the time is right. When her grief is a paler colour. She has no control over when that will be.

After it happened, they played everywhere, on the sea, in the street, on her bedroom walls, behind her closed eyelids. There are long periods now when she dares to think they have gone for good but then, when they do return, less frequently and always out of the blue, they take her by surprise. It's more of a shock when she's not on red alert, expecting to see them. It's been two years, she reminds herself. It's not about forgetting, she knows that. You don't forget your past. It's more like waiting for a colour photo to fade to sepia and to curl at the edges before she is able to place it face down in a drawer. And close that drawer.

In the approaching rowing boat that rises and dips through the waves, she can see the seated figure, as if someone is drawing him in while she looks. He is huddled in jumpers and fleeces and waterproofs and on his head, his red beanie whose scratchy feel and damp-wool smell she still knows so very well. At his feet is all the stuff he uses to aid and abet her: the tannoy to shout at her and tell her stupid jokes, the flasks of hot sweet tea, the rocket-fuel cereal bars and the chocolate. In his pocket is a flask of brandy, but that's for him, not for her ploughing through the water. The long pole and net he uses to pass her food and drink is folded in the hull. If he were to reach out and touch her, she would be disqualified but the rules allow her to take snacks from this daft contraption. Her channel-crossing must be absolutely solo and without support. In the prow of the boat is the life vest he will throw and the space blankets he will wrap her in if she gets into difficulties. A trained lifeguard and skilled coach, as well as her beloved husband, he is easily strong enough to haul her over the side and rescue her. They have practised it many times, ending up as a two-person wet heap in the bilge, laughing like kids as the boat rocked crazily from side to side, threatening to tip the pair of them out again. They have trained like this so many times.

That day, the day that plays on like a short Youtube horror movie, is the day before her longed-for channel-crossing. They've come out for a final training session in calm if dull conditions so that tomorrow she will be fresh and ready. There have been months of careful preparation, first in Lake Placid and now here. They are both eager and excited. They crossed an ocean in a plane for this momentous swim, rated by many long-distance swimmers as the most challenging.

Jess feels the ferry engines winding down to a slower, lower gear, and the boat pulling back its momentum, but she can't halt the movie that spools out on the water. It plays on. There is a bitter irony in the events that unfolded that day because all their months of training had been to protect her and save her if something went unexpectedly wrong. When you swim long distance in cold, deep water, you can take nothing for granted. The sea is its own place. Others have aborted swims because of freak conditions or sudden sickness or cramp. That very unpredictability is part of the challenge. But It won't be her who gets into trouble. It isn't her. What happened next was all wrong, inside out and back to front. A one-in-a-thousand throw of the dice.

She does not take her eyes off the rowing boat that bobs improbably in the swell kicked out by the docking ferry as the big boat continues to edge back. Don't look, she tells herself, and she looks. Turn away now, she says, and she doesn't turn away. It's enough to have to remember it, and to remember it in sharp detail every day, she tells herself. You don't have to watch this surreal replay that is constructed out of grief. Once she asked a doctor who told her it's a common response to trauma and bereavement. People are convinced they see their recently dead relatives behaving and speaking to them as if they are still alive. It will fade, he said. But it's been two years, she replied. He shrugged his shoulders. 'The mind is its own place,' he said. Like the sea, she replied, but not out loud.

It's not real, Jess tells herself now. There's no rowing boat out there. And still she watches. Each time, it's as shocking as the first time. Dan is bent over with one arm flung across his chest. It isn't Jess who is in trouble.

This is the point at which she stops watching. She closes her eyes or turns away or buries her head in a pillow, tears streaming down her cheeks. Is it because she presses Pause that it returns with instructions to see it through to the end? One day she will have to watch the ending.

Chapter 5

Hamish

It's 3.45 on the dot. Hamish clocks the school bus drawing to a halt at his gate and his daughter jumping down the steps. What he fails to note is that she doesn't stop to turn her head or wave goodbye but runs headlong down the muddy path to the croft. She slams open the croft door and rushes inside without a backward glance. He knows the routine but reads nothing into it. It will be a mad dash to her room to drag off her school uniform, fold it on a chair because that's the house rule, and to pull on her dirty cargoes, t-shirt and a hoodie. No time to twist them straight or tuck anything in. That will do. Neither he nor Fenn care a jot about clothes as long as they are comfortable and warm.

This tall man, with broad shoulders and a rain-darkened beanie jammed on his escaping curls, shakes his head with fondness and wonder. That girl! She still surprises him. He notes her familiar speed and what he correctly interprets as an eagerness to get cracking, to get stuck in, to be part of the place. What he doesn't see is her relief at getting away from the endurance test that is school and the loneliness that is her daily companion until she is back home. He leans on his spade, then bends again to his task of planting trees. So many trees. His attention is on them, not his daughter.

On her way, Fenn notes with a wry smile that her father is where he usually is at this time of day, down by the sea loch, planting saplings in what will one day be their very own wood.

'Dad, you'll be doing that forever,' she told him a few days ago.

'No matter. It's got to be done,' he had replied with his usual calm.

'Yeah…but three thousand, Dad!'

'The grant from the forestry commission comes with a deadline to get them in the ground.'

'Will you make it?'

'I have to.'

'It's hard work.'

'Och, it's no' too bad. The ground's soft.'

'I can help you when I've done the birds.'

'That would be grand, Fenn, but there's no need.'

'But you're always out here working on your own.' Doesn't ever seem to bother you, she wants to add. You never seem lonely. How's that?

Hamish heard only the words on the surface and to those he gave his reply. 'It will be a wind break. When they've grown, these trees will smother some of the gales before they break over the house.'

'Well, that will be good,' Fenn agreed. 'The wind can be a bit much.'

Hamish smiled at her understatement. The slamming noise of the wind could be a never-ending roar that drove them

46

all round the bend when it hammered its fists on the walls and windows of their cottage for days on end.

'Turn that bloody wind off,' Hamish would shout.

'Can't find the switch, Dad,' Fenn would shout back. It was their familiar refrain.

But despite the wind, and the months of endless rain, and the shortness of the dark winter days, this outdoor life suits and satisfies Hamish. His face is tanned and creased by the weather and there is more muscle on his lean frame. He has planted himself here rather as he is planting the saplings, his roots firm and deep. He is giving back to the land what it gives to him.

Born on the island, his youthful leaving, along with many others his age, never felt true though he stuck it out for too many years. At the mainland art college, he was not drawn to architecture and gave it up for labouring and landscape gardening. He was drawn to Julia, who was drawn to her fine arts degree, and was not giving that up. But neither could they give up each other. And so began a long waiting with him chipping away at her resistance to leave the mainland with its art galleries and exhibitions. For him there was no other choice. His soul waited on the island. In that waiting time, Fenn was born and started school in the city, too young to imagine this other wild place.

Hamish never fails to thank the fates that here he is, aged thirty-seven, a crofter because a croft came up for sale at just the right moment and he leapt at it. He is married to the woman he loves. He is father to a wonderful wild girl. He is breeding birds for their eggs and for their meat, building cabins for summer tourists, and planting three thousand willow trees to make his little parcel of land a more manageable, secure place. Every ounce of energy is an investment for future generations and for the island. Other islanders observe him at work, and he senses, at last, their growing respect. Hamish left, but he returned, and will be accepted back into the tight community. Many townies arrive here to start the good life and leave again after a year because they can't take the weather and the darkness and the dread monotony of the days. Why bother getting to know them, the islanders reckon, when they'll soon be heading back to the shops and cafes on the mainland. Not Hamish, though. Looks like he's staying put.

There are images and there are memories. Hamish is not one to dwell on the past nor to worry about anything that doesn't require an immediate solution. His thoughts are like stepping stones. You jump on them, land briefly, then leave them behind for firm ground.

Hearing a familiar bark, he smiles and lifts his head to see his daughter on her way back out of the front door. At her side, tripping her up and jumping on her in a frenzy of excitement, is their collie. You would think this familiar routine of the late afternoon gathering in of the birds is something unique and fabulous. Sounds and snatches of a one-sided conversation reach him as he continues his digging.

'Stop it, Hero!'

'I can't get my wellies on if you keep knocking them over, you silly dog.'

'Look, we're only going to get the birds in, OK? Same as always.'

Fenn is a blur of perpetual motion, shoving her arms into the sleeves of a fleece and then a waterproof, not stopping to pull the zips. With her woolly hat jammed on her head and long, somewhat unwinding plaits hanging beneath, he watches her run off, sturdy crofter's stock in her hand, dog racing in circles at her side, into a wind that nearly knocks her over before she steadies herself and leans into it. As she has learnt to do. The sideways rain stings her cheeks and soaks loose strands of hair, but on she goes. Hamish long ago told her not to complain.

'You work with the weather, Fenn, not against it. If we had good weather as well as the beauty of the place, this island would be a breeding ground for incomers and tourists, not birds. Be thankful. There are no' so many of us who get to live here.'

Taking her silence for agreement, he missed a girl's sigh that vanished into the wind and tears that could be rain stinging. It would take her a while yet to settle, that much he knew, and he thought no more about it.

The hens, ducks and geese are scattered around the croft but know the daily performance of the child who arrives to guide them to their nighttime places. At first they are flighty, gathering at her side to tease her with a false obedience before scattering again. She calls to the hens and gets them without much fuss into the wooden henhouse. They're the obedient ones, friendly, fearless and quite tame. The ducks are not too wayward either. There can be a game of chase but today the ducks slam down their yellow webbed feet in an orderly forward dance. Fenn holds out her stock while Hero lies down on the other side of the door. In they go. Fenn latches the half-door. The geese are bigger and more truculent. Girl and dog take up their positions and inch in on the birds. The procession continues, out of the garden and up the slope towards the blackhouse, a girl with wet plaits walking with purpose, a muddy collie and seven large white birds. The blackhouse, now roofless and crumbling, sits high on a ridge near the road. Long ago, the home of crofters, now it is security against foxes that prowl in the night. Some birds paid the price of freedom before Hamish saw the consequences and bitterly chided himself. Mellow Yellow was found by Fenn still alive but with her guts spilling out and her head barely attached. With one shot Hamish put her out of her agony. Fenn wept. And Hamish told her curtly that this is life on a croft. And death. Get used to it.

Work accomplished, Fenn will be back indoors, wellies shaken off and left on the floor to trip the next person who passes by, wet waterproof hung crooked and dripping on a peg. She'll be checking on the recently hatched chicks, holding one of the tiny, wispy birds under her chin. Then she'll run upstairs to her mother. That's the routine.

Hamish, having observed his daughter's efficient progress and lightning energy, has come in too, partly to acknowledge her good work, not that he's ever effusive with his praise, partly to check on the turkey eggs and chicks in the incubator.

'Well done,' he says, dripping all over the small hall. Not that anyone worries about a bit of mud and wet. This is a working croft.

Fenn glances up, eager for his approval. He doesn't know that school is where she marks time while home is where she finds security. He sees her content on the croft and looks no further.

'Nearly lost Madonna,' she says.

'There's always one.'

'The one's always Madonna.'

He nods his agreement. 'Another turkey chick hatched this morning, Fenn. That's two out of three.'

'Oh...let's see...'

Fenn turns and dashes off to what used to be a big walk-in cupboard off the hall before Hamish converted it into a warm hatching place with shelves holding three large incubators for eggs, and heated cages for the baby chicks' first three days of life. Sawdust spills out on to the floor. He comes up behind Fenn, one hand on her shoulder.

'So tiny,' she sighs, leaning over the cage, staring at the two fragile balls of fluff that have emerged from the broken eggs.

'You need to be quiet around these. They're not boisterous like hen chicks. These little guys are fearful and can get so nervous they forget to eat and drink. I've heard of them dropping dead from fright.' Hamish never minces his words with his daughter. There's no place for sentimentality when you rear birds and animals.

'Aw, no! Why?'

'Nervy temperaments. They should be OK if you don't scare them.' No need to give any further instructions. His daughter is quick to understand.

'Sure.'

Hamish turns on his heel to get back to work. So far north, there are almost endless hours of light left at this time of year and he's making the most of every moment, even if it is streaking rain. Fenn puts a hand on his arm.

'Look at the Duckwings, Dad. Aren't the grey chicks cute?' Fenn has moved to the heated cage and is whispering. 'Duckwing Araucana. It's a big name for a tiny chick. Do they really lay blue eggs?'

'So I'm told.'

'And Dad...'

Does Hamish not sense that his daughter is clinging to him as surely as if she had wound her arms around his waist and held him there. That since he uprooted her from the city, her world has shrunk to the three of them, Hero, and the birds?

'Guess what Mum said...' Fenn continues, to keep him at her side for a few more minutes, '...if we cross the ones that lay copper eggs, the Copper Marans, with the Duckwings, we'll get hens that lay bright green eggs! Won't that be cool?'

Hamish raises an eyebrow. 'Your mum is an artist who thinks in colours. I'm the one who raises the chicks so she has me to persuade about that.'

'But people already buy more of the blue and copper eggs. The Loyalty Box is full every evening now. Thirty quid last night.'

'We'll discuss it later, this idea of your mum's to colour eggs as well as paper. I'm off to plant trees. They're already green.'

Hamish may think all is well in the world he is growing and creating, but a backward glance at his daughter would show him a crestfallen face stripped of the mask she wears for others, especially him, not wanting to disappoint a father she loves and admires. You don't make a fuss. But the move from the mainland has left her stranded. If he turned round now he would catch her fighting back tears. And if, later, he followed her to the beach, he would see her sitting on the sand dunes, her head in her hands, her shoulders shaking with sobs she has held back all day.

Chapter 6

Jess

Jess has only one thought which is now on replay. I must get away. She has turned her face from the window and is poised to leap from her seat and run. Hurry up, she says, as she feels the vibrations of the ferry completing the mirror movements of its departure and manoeuvring back against the quay. Hurry up, hurry up. But the tannoy bleats the wrong messages.

'Do not leave your seats,' says the robot voice.

Come on, Jess says, frantic to be gone from here.

'It is not safe to move until the ferry has come to a complete halt.'

It's not safe to stay here, Jess replies, not if I value my sanity.

Then a bell rings and everyone is released. Jess is on her feet pounding down the wet metal steps, pushing past other passengers without apology to get to the lowest deck. The floor is soaked and shining and her boots squeak as she runs towards her van. Inside, it is safer. Inside, there is nothing to see but other people opening other car doors.

For god's sake, Jess, pull yourself together. Get a grip. This is no way to arrive on the island.

Yeah but no-one told me it would follow me here.

OK, but you're here now. Let it go.

Why can't it let me go?

Maybe it's telling you not to run away.

I'm not running away. I'm starting over.

You can't start over while you cling to the past.

I'm not clinging to the past.

Her pointless monologue for two voices is interrupted by the grinding noise of the whale jaw being cranked up. The loading area outside is exactly like the previous loading area, the rain and low-hanging cloud obliterating everything beyond the parking area. She takes slow, deep breaths. Puts her hands on the wheel. One of the first to roll on, she will be one of the first to roll off. The few drivers in front of her turn on their engines and rear lights glow red. One by one they are waved out by the men in the dripping waterproofs and high vis jackets. The small creatures leave the belly of the giant fish.

The lack of light gives no clue as to the time of day but it is late afternoon and Jess has only a twenty-five minute drive to her cottage on the peninsula. She has calmed herself and is monitoring her breathing as if it's a self-conscious act. Now it's her turn to cross the line from the ship to the land, from the past to the future. Another border. Another threshold. Will it hold? she asks herself.

Following the exit signs, she is quickly on her way on the only main road on the island which runs from the southern tip to the north then circles back down the other side. Here there are two lanes and she can pick up speed. All the other roads are too narrow and when drivers approach from opposite directions, one must pull into a passing place before they meet. The locals lift a middle finger from the wheel to acknowledge this etiquette and as a friendly gesture. She must remember to do that, not wave. Tourists wave, or ignore a car approaching and then have to reverse. The locals know almost every car. Almost every driver.

After twenty minutes, she spots the sign to the turn-off, in Gaelic she can't pronounce, and drives three miles inland along a good track dotted on one side with small crofts, each on its own long strip of land. Lights burn in their windows. On the other side of the track are sloping stretches of rough grass which lead to the sand dunes, the beaches and the sea.

She came over just the once, the previous spring, on a flying visit to view and buy the cottage after she had seen it advertised online, reduced for a quick sale. There was never any doubt that it was right. Would be right. Sitting on barely half an acre of land, it had lain empty for a long time, not attractive to locals wanting to keep sheep or start a working croft because it doesn't have enough land. The agent told her the islanders would be pleased that the cottage is sold to someone who will live on the island all year round because they don't take kindly to wealthy incomers purchasing holiday homes they occupy for three weeks a year. Cottages like this one would once have made a home for a young islander but second homes and buy-to-let have pushed prices beyond their reach. This is a working island, not a tourist centre, they tell one another, though hikers and nature-lovers are welcome in the summer months because they bring in an income. They worry that the island will become a second Skye, a place whose spirit has departed along with most of the islanders.

On the evening of the day she came to view the house, the air had been as crisp as green apples and the early sunset glowed with the surprising colours of sherbet sweets, reflected again and again in the water mirrors of sea and fresh water lochs and the glittering expanse of ocean. A heron stood on a rock below the cottage and she heard the raw cry of gulls and curlews winging their way back and forth from the beach. It was magical. It is magical. This island is a watery, fairy-tale place where land and water curve around one another in sweet protection. The light changes from moment to moment from a tropical brilliance to the excluding grey of lashing rain.

The immediate certainty took her by surprise. Like a sense of recognition. It flowed in her veins and out to her finger tips when she reached out and stroked the rough surface of the old stone walls and touched the lichen that flowered in crevices. No-one had loved this house for a long time and its longing mirrored her own. As did its strength, bravely perched up here facing violent storms and gales. It had endured, and so would she. Together, they would face the future.

Jess notes, with relief and satisfaction, a fizzing excitement and a smile playing on her lips as she drives slowly along the final stretch of the track, admiring the patches of land and sea and fresh water lochs that fit together like a difficult jigsaw. As she nears the far end, the rain stops like someone has turned off a tap, and a pale violet light sweeps in from the sea to shimmer on the wet roofs of the squat white houses and in the puddles on the road ahead. The wind drops just as abruptly. The place is utterly still and quiet. Sheep with fleeces heavy with the recent rain raise their heads as she drives past. A solitary black horse shakes his mane, making a halo from jets of water. Jess slows down because from here on she can catch glimpses of the sand dunes on her right, a short walk away through rough grass, and between them she can see a sea that is still topped with white horses after the wind. And there is her cottage, last but one, a child's drawing of a house with a front door and four small windows.

Jess turns in, parks the van in the driveway, gets out and stretches her arms to the sky, mauve now with torn rags of purple where the rain swept through such a short while ago. There are tears of happiness in her eyes as she spins round and draws a sharp breath at the impossible beauty of the place. It is epic and elemental. That sky that stretches huge, open and never-ending. Nowhere else has she seen a sky that reaches so far away into the distance. Under this enormous protective roof, surely her grief will shrink to something more manageable. Even now, she feels ashamed of her earlier overwrought reaction. Perhaps it came from being too tired from the journey, too wound up. This sky puts things in perspective.

With calm, soft movements, Jess reaches in her bag for the keys and walks up the path, step after deliberate step, and over the doorstep into her new home. The front door leads straight into the big kitchen at the front. It is a simple dwelling, two up, two down. Living room at the back facing the sea. Upstairs are two small bedrooms and a bathroom with sloping roofs in the eaves. The walls are very thick. The windows small. The house stands squat and solid and brave against whatever the weather throws at it. The previous owners have left a peat-burning stove in a corner of the main room and an old Aga in the kitchen. The islanders build and furnish their homes for warmth and practicality, not prettiness.

From the living room window, Jess stares across the grass to the high domes of the sand dunes spiked with marram grass sharp enough to cut fingers. After a bit of a struggle, she gets the window up, and with her first breath she rejoices in the salt and seaweed tang drifting up from the sea. It is close. From her previous visit, she knows that below the cottage is a small, untidy, rock-strewn bay that is also the secret and unmarked entry point to a five-mile beach of extraordinary beauty. That beach is hidden behind a promontory that marches a long way out into the tidal sea, but last time she was here, Jess walked round it and, shoes in her hands, walked barefoot along the icing sugar sand. This is the Atlantic side of the island where the white beaches stretch forever and the ocean takes its time to roll in long, shallow waves to the seaweed fringes that mark high tide.

Tears prick her eyes again and she lets them fall as the flip side of her neatly planned future life comes into focus. There will be no more swimming in the limpid blue depths of Lake Placid. No more competitions. No more marathons. No training. Without Dan, what would be the point? For a few moments she falters, her defences down, as she considers whether there could still be a point, a purpose, because she is that same long-distance swimmer who has broken records and held trophies. She could resume where she left off, alongside her swimmer friends. You're running away, they have told her. You will heal on this side of the Atlantic. Come home.

Jess shakes her head, banishing the already rejected possibility. Stupid to even think about it when she is here now. She'll swim, but in a way that is natural and free. Look forwards, not backwards, Jess, she chides. There are other beaches and other waters. Deliberately, because it's a bit of an effort, she imagines her feet racing over the white sand that is just around the headland, her feet high-stepping into the froth of the waves, then the head-first plunge into breath-taking cold and heading out, arms slicing through the surface, legs pushing her forwards until, to someone on the shore, she looks like a dot on the water. In an ocean this big, she will feel small and humble, and that's soothing. These feelings are too big to process and that's all right. This sea will allow her to be here and she will thank it. I don't want anyone else to swim there, she thinks, smiling at her selfishness. I want it all to myself. From what she's heard, albeit not a lot, the islanders think anyone who goes into the water for pleasure is insane.

Rain is falling gently again as the night clouds gather, the kind of rain that glistens on the twisted-wire coats of black-faced sheep and hangs in twinkling dew drops from deer fences.

Chapter 7

The Whale

Troubled by time passing and still unable to pick up the reassuring calls of his pod amongst the constant chorus of water noises, the whale again sings his song, a ringing stream of sound that lasts six minutes and ten seconds, but there is no reply. With a shrug of puzzlement expressed not out loud of course but in a resigned swish of his muscular tail, he swims on in a direction he guesses is the one the others have taken. But the distraction of the immobile whale has disoriented him. His navigational skills, still immature and tentative, falter and the direction he chooses is off track and wrong.

Through days and nights, the whale swims on, always seeking the others, sometimes surfacing to flap his long wing-like fins to call attention to himself in case by some chance the others can see or hear him. Otherwise, worried but not yet afraid, he noses forwards through the tons of water, feelings its wash over his crusty back and across his paler underbelly. Just as he did when he was secure amongst the others, he arcs and dips, rises and falls, travels high to surface feed, sometimes slides down to take it easy near the seabed among the bottom feeders and the shellfish. He crosses a great distance in a short time with isolation as his companion.

The questions accompany him and roll around him. Where is his family that always swims close by? Where is the pod that moves as if choreographed? Where are the friendly bumps and nudges against his solid blubber? Where are the glimpses of fast, shining shapes trailing streams of bright water as they leap out, arch and dive back? He swims with echoes and memories of a group travelling together, each aware of the others in front, to the side, following behind. As one of the younger whales, his place was mid-field or towards the rear, following the older males who took turns to lead the pod. Like his companions, he has learned not to crowd the others and so they spread out in easy formation, free and flowing. Looking to his left, to his right, and turning in circles, he peers hard through reeds and seaweed and shoals of smaller fish, hoping to see a creature like himself, massive and bulky, streamlined and fast. Turning his head this way and that, he listens for the criss-cross of calls that will tell him that his troupe is somewhere close by, perhaps in front but heading in the same direction. Nothing reaches him except the busy soundtrack of the ocean. His solo swimming feels physically empty and increasingly upsetting.

When he swam his first migratory journey the previous year, he laid down in his memory the early tracks of a musical score that he and the others followed and would follow in subsequent years, like a reliable and trusted sound map. The humming and shrill beeps came to him like notes along a wire that stretched from one side of the ocean to the other, a trail which the older whales followed with absolute sureness, and he followed the older whales. But because he was young when he first made the crossing, the notes he has retained are elusive, unconnected bits of the whole, and he cannot use them to find his way. Now he stops, trying with every fibre of his being to hear that journey's tune, but he only hears the ocean's unreadable cacophony made by scurrying fish and slapping weeds and other loud noises which seem to come from on top of the water and which he does not recognise. The signposts that would guide him safely on his way are absent.

On he goes, calling again and again, but as he twists and turns, starts and falters, nothing reaches him except the turbulence of currents and the slaps and splashes of a thousand other species. I am alone, he thinks, without words but with growing alarm. I am wrongly, worryingly alone in water that goes on forever.

Using too much energy, he soars up and breaks through the surface to see if there are any clues out there, in case he can catch a glimpse of the others. After the push to the top, he tilts his body to the vertical, holds his head out of the water and flaps his tail to hold himself in position. He wobbles there for a while, listening. Round and round he goes, revolving like a mighty spinning top as he surveys the landscape with his small eyes. Is there a shoreline? Are there other whales? But there is nothing to help him here. He is in the middle of endless blue, bemused that the others can't be found. This sky– hopping is tiring so he takes himself down again to the dark depths and glides on, passing eels and sea turtles and the blue and white flashes of merlin, passing through invasive shoals of menhaden, not that he knows any of their names. The miles slip past and soon he has covered another great distance. Once more he stops to look, listen and take stock.

Summoning up his flagging energy, he sings his calling note with a new urgency and holds it while it ripples out through the blue.

I am here, here, here.

Where are you?

Call to me.

Sing your songs.

The first time it reaches him, it is like a tingling against his skin, a current that is not water, more alive and racing through the ocean in streaks and starts. The vibrations loop over and around his body in circles, and he curls inside the net of fine bright lines. He stops and holds himself still. Twists. Tilts his ears, and realises that he is mistaken. The current that plays around his body is in fact sound, a filigree pulse of song unlike anything he has heard before. It reaches him as a thin silver thread with high notes that carry tenderness with blue notes of longing not unlike his own. The silver and blue come in waves until the colours pool and he hears the sounds clear and close. He can't be sure but perhaps another creature is calling to him. It's not a whale. These sparkling notes are nothing like the epic calls of his family. Nothing like any other water noises.

Who are you? He calls.

Where are you?

Are you calling me?

Can I reach you?

Mesmerised and thrilled after days listening to a turbulence of noise that has no meaning, he turns towards the direction of the sounds. Listening to them and reading them, he wonders if he is at their ending, their stopping point. The silver notes are faint and faded, just a trace, like the see-through drops of water that fall last into the ocean after he has jumped and plunged. Still bright, they are also a long way away. Across an ocean perhaps. It doesn't matter. He is young and strong and vigorous.

Excited, he heads towards them.

Chapter 8

Julia

Like her husband, Julia is primed to listen for the school bus as it comes down the track to stop at their gate with predictable regularity. She tries to extricate herself from whatever she's doing a few minutes before her daughter arrives like a whirlwind. Today it's not hard, in fact it's been a while since she felt that all-consuming energy and a burning concentration that closes her off from the real world and leaves her walking inside it like a temporary ghost.

'Mum...Mum...' Fenn calls, taking the bare stairs two at a time, and heading for Julia's study at the top of the house. Julia sends out signals when she is busy, the loud swish of the brush and the scrape of a pencil, to tell her daughter in the nicest possible way not to interrupt. Fenn knows the drill and will turn round and head back down. Today, Julia sends out streams of silence.

'Mum, are you busy or can I come in?'

They have an agreement that Fenn can interrupt Julia if she isn't working or if she's invited or if it's something terribly urgent that can't wait. This third condition, Fenn has told

Julia, is not fair because sometimes she thinks something is urgent but her mother demotes it to not urgent, or not at all urgent, the minute she voices it. And then Julia points to the door and tells her to come back later. In the nicest possible way of course.

That won't happen today. Having heard the rush of feet, Julia sighs loudly, not at the prospect of her daughter's arrival because she looks forward to Fenn's starburst interruption, but at what she has to show for a whole day's work. The painting is the size of a postcard and shows half a chicken's head facing sideways, just a bright eye and a collar of fluff. Yes, it's exquisite. Yes, the details are true. Yes, the brushstrokes are many and tiny, like threads of finest cotton. And the colours are wild, which is what Julia does. The iris of the eye is a streaky purple and the day-old fluff is crazy shocking pink. Julia, she scolds herself, it's not hard to see where this has come from. You've been obsessing about breeding a hen that lays grass-green eggs. And you haven't even broached the subject with Hamish. He can seem severe, she thinks, and that's what the world sees, but under that stern exterior, he feels things keenly. Inside that huge frame, a tender heart beats, but the mask he wears is well stuck on. On an island like this, men are strong and silent and mostly in charge. After blotting his copy book by leaving it, Hamish has taken pains to fit right back in. He thinks a lot but says little. Julia shakes herself free of this train of thought as the footsteps reach her door and a skinny arm pushes it open.

'Hi, Mum!'

'Hi, Darling!'

'It's raining. I can't go to the beach.'

Julia has indeed observed the rain, all day long, rivers of

it running down the windows, stopping her from wandering out in search of something new to paint.

'I know. But we've had a lot of good days recently. For the island. I do sometimes watch, you know, from my spy hole over there and I do see you racing to the beach.' Julia nods at the window.

'Hey, Mum, why are you painting a chick?'

'Why not?'

'Like...don't we already do enough with chicks? You could think of something else.'

Julia laughs. 'You're right, Fenn. Our lives our full to the brim with chicks. It's quite ridiculous. How about we get on a plane and go back to Edinburgh and live in an ordinary house in an ordinary street again without geese and turkeys and hens and I can paint the people we pass in the streets?'

Julia regrets the stupid words the minute they are out and she sees a cloud pass over her daughter's neat features. She wonders, not for the first time, if her daughter secretly harbours a wish to do just that. Return. As she herself does sometimes, not that she is going to admit, not to Fenn, perhaps not even to herself. Early days, she tells herself. Must carry on. Give it a fair chance.

'Are you serious?' Fenn asks, her smile gone.

'No. Not really.'

'What do you mean, not really?'

'Oh well, on a day like today when the rain has been so loud it has stopped me from finishing a single thought and the sky is hanging just above the roof and I don't want to venture out for a walk, I might be forgiven for being a bit sentimental about Edinburgh. Warm cafes with internet and coffee, little boutique clothes shops, art galleries, no chickens...'

'Mum! Are you kidding me?'

'Yes. I'm just going through a bit of a blue phase and all this rain has shrunk my paintings.'

'Mum, the chick looks pink to me and I think it's you who've shrunk your paintings.'

'How right you are. What would I do without you to put me straight.' Julia hides her smile. And the tears that prick her eyes. Heavens, pull yourself together, she tells herself.

'But the pink chick is cool.'

'Thank you.'

There's a beat of silence while Fenn shifts topic, like moving a painting to look at the one stacked underneath.

'Why have you stopped doing those big paintings?'

Fenn is looking up at the studio walls where Julia has hung paintings of island skies and beaches as big as bed sheets. The colours are watery pastels with blobs of surprising yellow and purple and green. Julia follows her daughter's gaze and sighs.

'When we first moved here...' Julia begins, leaving the sentence hanging. She hesitates because she doesn't want to burden her daughter with feelings that recently have been, well, a bit wobbly. And anyway, she is still not sure herself why she wakes up some mornings feeling unsettled, nor why her paintings have shrunk to postcards. She'll have to find a plausible answer, quick, because you can't bullshit Fenn. It's not just her hearing that is acute. You have to be careful because she knows when someone is papering over emotional cracks. That girl has long, delicate antennae that wave in the wind. Julia worries about her.

'...you were always walking on the beach and then you used to come back and paint those huge paintings.' Fenn finishes Julia's sentence. Waits for her mother to answer.

'Oh, I don't know, Fenn. This island was such a wonderful surprise. I fell in love with the changing colours of the sky and the sea. I had to paint its bigness, those white beaches that stretch for miles with no people on them.'

'So did you get bored with painting beaches, Mum?'

Too near the quick and a bit wide of the mark. 'No... no...not bored.' Julia doesn't know what bored means, not while she holds a pencil or a paintbrush. She considers Fenn's question a moment too long.

'Mum?' Louder this time.

Julia turns back to her daughter, sees the ripple of worry on her forehead, and summons up an answer that she hopes will suffice.

'I suppose the early excitement when you first move to a new place always fades a bit. That's all. Like you scream your head off the first time you go on a Ferris wheel but after ten times it's not quite such a thrill.'

'I'd still be screaming after twenty times. But Mum, you do like living here, don't you?'

Too near the quick. What has her daughter picked up when she's been so very careful to hide her doubts? 'I do, Fenn.' It's not a lie. More a truth inadequately white-washed over. 'What about you? Are you happy here?'

There is a beat of hesitation which Julia doesn't miss. 'Yeah, I like it here. I like the croft with all the birds. It's cool.' Another pause. 'I like having a beach that's my very own and going in the water.' She stops and Julia waits for the other words, unsaid. No, best not make a fuss about nothing. About the teacher and the kids at school. And then it slips out. 'I'm fed up with Miss Murdoch picking on me,' she says.' And the kids being unkind. Don't say anything about that. That's for me to deal with, not my mum.

Julia snaps into the present, alert, her daughter's words a shock. 'You've not said anything about this before. You say she's picking on you?'

'Yeah, sometimes.' Fenn is rolling a pencil over Julia's table. Up and down. Up and down.

'What about?'

'Oh...she says I'm always dreaming. I don't concentrate.'

'Wait, Fenn.' Julia's hackles are up, perhaps because she's feeling unsettled herself. 'You're doing well at school. I've seen your work and the marks you get. When did this start?'

'Sort of from the start of the year. Miss Murdoch doesn't like me.'

Fenn drops the pencil and fiddles with a piece of paper. Picks up a crayon and starts to draw stick men while Julia gathers her thoughts. The thing is, she and Fenn have collided here, her own doubts not so unlike those of her child. The timing is uncanny. Or is it? Maybe this is just how long it takes for the first rose-tinted impressions of a new place to wear off, for a grown-up and for a child. The pink chick who started this train of thought has a lot to answer for.

'Some teachers are just not much fun. Hard luck! I bet she picks on some of the others too.' Julia hears her own lies. Fenn, after all, is not one to make a fuss or make things up. She is finely tuned, yes, but also made of stern stuff. Her core is steely. There is some of Julia in her daughter, but also a lot of Hamish.

'It's only me she picks on.'

There's a leaden pause. Julia is thrown back to feeling unsettled and wonders if Fenn is thinking what she has been thinking. No, no, that's nonsense. You're colouring Fenn's simple complaint about a teacher with your own adult uncertainty, she tells herself. Fenn is nine. Nine-year-olds don't compare island versus city living. Or worry about being treated as incomers. Or the meaning of belonging. Or do they?

'Look, let me talk to Hamish this evening. He knows Miss Murdoch. She's been a teacher in that school...'

'Forever,' Fenn finishes. 'She's at least seventy.'

'Hardly seventy, and age isn't a crime. But, Fenn, if it's troubling you, we can make an appointment to see her.'

'No, Mum!' Fenn is up out of her chair and shouting. Not like her, Julia thinks, alarmed at the outburst. What is going on here?

'If it's upsetting you, we need to do something about it.'

'Honestly, it's nothing. Some teachers don't like some children. I hit unlucky this year. It's not a big deal. Forget it, Mum.' Fenn shrugs her shoulders and Julia can see her daughter wanting to take it all back. That child is fiercely independent and likes to work things out for herself.

'That's true,' Julia says with deliberate calm. 'And maybe that's all it is. But we could have a quiet talk to her.'

'No! I don't want you to make a fuss. You'll make it worse.' Fenn takes a deep breath and rambles on. 'Anyway Primary 6 next and we get Mr Bridle for our class teacher. He already takes us for art. I like him. He makes jokes and he makes sculptures out of stones and dried seaweed. We might get to do that.' Julia hears the attempt at a cover-up and knows not to push any further.

'It's rather a long wait, Fenn. You've not long started Year 5.'

'I suppose. Well, maybe Miss Murdoch will retire or drop dead or something.'

'Fenn!'

'Sorry. Only joking.'

'That's not funny.' But Fenn looks less tense and is edging towards the door.

'Sorry.'

'I know Mr Bridle,' Julia continues, deciding to underplay this whole worrying outburst. For now. 'He takes art classes at the Wave Arts Centre. I was going to ask him about maybe doing some teaching myself. OK, don't worry, I won't dash over to the school, but I will talk to Hamish.'

'Can I go now? I think I'll go on the trampoline 'til tea time.'

'In the rain?'

'Doesn't stop me bouncing.'

'You'll be soaked.'

'I'll put my gym things on and take them off afterwards. Mum, you're not trying to stop me getting some healthy exercise, are you?'

'I'm not stopping you! Off you go. And Fenn....'

'What?' Fenn is hopping from one foot to the other, an eye roll happening of its own accord.

'Thank you for telling me. It's important.'

'Fine.'

Her daughter gone, Julia sits for a long time, not trying to pick up her painting where she left off but replaying the conversation with Fenn and then allowing her own questions to roll back in. When Hamish wore down her resistance to returning to the island, she knew exactly what she was signing up for. It's hard to put her finger on what is troubling her now, a year down the line. No-one is rude to her. People nod and smile and say, good morning. So what's bothering her? Sure, she can go days without speaking to anyone but solitude comes with the territory and she's fine with her own company. Come on, Julia, say it. OK, so she has decided, after a year here, that either you are an islander or you are not, and that never changes. And she does not belong here. But you knew that before. Well, yes, but knowing and living it is different. The next question, she can't begin to answer. Why does it matter? And because she is struggling to work it all out and because she doesn't understand her own conflicting feelings, she has retreated to the constraints of tiny paintings of tiny objects because they ask less of her. Into the early landscapes, she worked hope and excitement, the big contours containing a nascent sense of this new place which one day she might call home. Now she sees that as false. And so she has turned her gaze to what is manageable. Three shells. A chick's egg. A fallen magpie's feather of iridescent blue. She puts her confusion to one side, and says nothing. When she talks to Hamish, she will only talk about their daughter.

*

On the bouncy black mat, inside the mesh, Fenn is flying up as far as she can go, with as much energy as she can summon, because she's mad at herself. That was really dumb, she says angrily as she soars upwards and catches the briefest glimpse of the beach. There was no need to make Julia worry, she tells herself as she comes back down, bending her knees to cushion the landing, before shooting up again. Especially with her mother seeming a bit off colour today too. Off colour, she repeats. A painter who is off colour. Her mouth twitches towards a smile. Her worries shrink and float way as she jumps, legs together, legs wide, legs in front, legs bent. Up, glimpse of white sand coloured grey in the rain. Down. Up, glimpse of turquoise sea darkened to navy blue from

73

the rain and mottled all over as the drops still fall. Down. Don't ever mention stupid Miss Murdoch again, Fenn! She's just nobody.

Her grin is wide as she bounces her biggest bounce yet, and holds herself like an outline of a girl against the sky. Watch it, Fenn. Don't let it eat you. No point going loopy because of some dumb teacher and some dumb kids. I've heard some people go bonkers living on tiny islands.

Chapter 9

Jess

Most of the unpacking is quickly done because Jess has brought so little with her. She and Dan had lived lightly, much of their time together spent in hotels and guest houses, or competitors' accommodation on the shores of lakes and rivers. The sea was their home more than any building. In some ways, it still is. She has yet to make the transition from water to land.

This cottage with its thick walls will be her physical refuge, bricks and mortar, a base that's always here, waiting for her above the beach. Will it suffice? Will it mean something more than a roof over her head? How long will it take before she gives it the name home? But, she tells herself, stopping dead in the middle of the room because the thought arrives with its familiar stab of pain, that rootlessness did contain stability. Dan was her rock in a sea of changing places near water waiting to be safely crossed. Now Dan is not at her side. He is not here to lean on. You have to move on, she tells herself. Meaning what exactly? Eyes bright with tears, she bends to the boxes left unpacked from the previous day. Without thought, she lifts books onto shelves, and throws bright cushions on the sofa, and stocks her kitchen cupboards with the unfamiliar ingredients for baking unfamiliar bread and cakes. Baking? Really, Jess? At the moment, perpetual motion seems to be the only way to carry on. She is an automaton, going though the movement of making a house a home, but feeling nothing. One foot after another. Do, don't think. Upstairs, in the bedroom under the rafters, she unpacks the quilt bought for the bed she would share with Dan when they finally bought their own home. Its downy softness unsettles her all over again and she lets the tears fall. Sobbing, she runs her fingers over the hand-sewn patterns, stares at the turquoise and the dusty pink. She buries her face in its folds.

Cross with herself, and roughly brushing the back of her hand over damp cheeks, she forces her attention back to the squat white cottage. It will protect me, she tells herself for the tenth time that morning. Not for a moment does she doubt her choice, but will it ever be anything other than good thick walls and a roof over her head? Wandering from window to window, unable to concentrate on finding homes for objects, she listens to the cry of the birds overhead. Out of the windows, she can see rabbits feeding and scattering, ears twitching forward and back as they monitor danger. And from the distance comes the sea's voice, a fixed soundtrack as it advances and retreats, a frothy whisper on calm days, a loud call over shifting pebbles when the wind roars.

Some time later, Jess wraps up and goes out. Here you can leave your door unlocked. It's a few minutes walk across the tufted field and she's standing at the top of the sand dunes, looking down on the ocean. She has noted the way its colours shift with the light and the weather. It is an unlikely iridescent turquoise. It is a flat blue sheet topped by the colliding and collapsing crests of the waves. It is a flat grey that swallows the horizon, and blurs sea and sky.

Days pass and the routines calm her. She may feel numb but step by step, Jess is quietly walking her way towards a tentative possession of this place. She starts with the rooms of the house, pacing from one to the other, noting where the light falls at different times of the day and positioning a table or a chair to catch the sun's movement across the sky as the light flashes on and off in its game of hide-and-seek with the clouds. On grey days, she turns on the lamps and burns in the stove.

Outside, she circles the cottage in ever-widening rings on her small patch of land, treading the gale-flattened grass and planning where she will plant roses close to the house and where she'll put up a strong poly tunnel for vegetables and flowers. She will hang deep-toned wooden wind chimes from the tree because here, without doubt, they will sing. She plans to work on a small garden of hardy wild plants tucked around found and made objects. Sure, the soil here is not exactly rich and crumbly, not a place for pretty borders and delicate flowers whose petals will scatter in the first gust of wind. She has noted how few people on the island have bothered to create gardens, making do with a few pots of red geraniums in the summer. But that's the challenge. With Dan, she visited Prospect Cottage and the garden built by Derek Jarman at Dungeness. His wooden house sits on a swathe of shingle beach and, in that inhospitable ground, he planted poppies, wild orchids and water lilies which grew and flourished until they became wild shapes and natural sculptures blowing in the sea breeze alongside his circles of flint and pieces of driftwood. Hers will be gentler, more feminine, more suited to this landscape, but he cheers her on when doubts trouble her. She has begun drawing. She has made lists of plants. She has found online sites that sell wild flower seeds. She will spend the rest of this year hoeing and digging in compost, and in the early spring she will plant.

As she walks her ever wider circles, each footfall claiming the place as her own, she reaches the vertical, wind-ironed dunes and skitters down to the small horseshoe bay below. It's a messy kind of a beach, rocky and strewn with slimy brown seaweed. The rocks are wedged in crammed clusters at the back, letting you hop from one to the other. At the sea's edge they lie as flat, round stones, their once-jagged edges washed away by a million tides. Shiny black from the spray and slippery under foot, it would be a bit of a clamber to walk over them to get into the water, but not impossible. She considers it, day after day, but holds back, not ready yet to take the last step, the final plunge. Jess stays firmly on dry land. Today her circle takes her along the length of the beach, back up the sand dunes at the furthest point, and then back to her house. Some days, instead of stomping in circumferences, she lingers on the sand to pick up sea glass and shells and driftwood for the garden she plans. She meets no-one. Others don't walk here. Not even a man and his dog. And perhaps because of that unbroken solitude, she starts to feel it right to call the house hers and the beach her own, as much as one can ever own a part of nature.

It could be a Saturday. Jess isn't counting. She doesn't know if it's days or a week since she drove here from the ferry. Time is of little consequence. This day, she wakes from deep sleep to a sky painted in streaks of lime green and palest blue as if someone has run across it with a large, loaded paintbrush. The light, if it lasts, will be amazing. The breeze is gentle and slight. She makes ground coffee, fills a bowl with home-made muesli, adds almonds, yoghurt and seeds, walks from window to window, watching the expanding colours as the sky lightens from the east. The morning will be clear and luminous. As she pulls her wellies over thick socks and zips up her anorak, she decides that today is the day for a bolder, wider circle outside the boundaries she has already marked as her own. The promontory to the right of the beach below her house stretches for a quarter of a mile into the sea, a headland that hides everything on the other side. Getting round it can only be done in a small time window at low tide, but even if she miscalculates the rush and crash of the returning flood, she can climb the sand dunes that fringe the next bay and then walk back along the road.

It takes her fifteen minutes to jump over the rocks and walk out to where the sea is waiting to turn, holding its breath at low tide. The sand, so soft near the dunes that she sinks up to her ankles, changes gradually to a surface that is hard-packed where she can run and jump in a sudden rush of energy. She heads out to where the cliffs fall into the sea in a muddle of wet and broken rocks and stones, and carefully picks her way over them. And on, to the place that is hidden.

Once round that screen of a cliff, Jess stops in her tracks. She saw this beach last time she was here, spoken of by the locals as one of the most beautiful on the island, and there is plenty of competition, but seeing it again takes her breath away. It is a half-moon of a bay, perhaps five miles long, stretching far into the distance to another headland. It is a perfect curved sweep of salt-white sand edged by a sea of long, wide waves. They roll in threes and fours, regular, unhurried, as they make their quiet way up the beach. At the back, all the way along, are straight-sided sand dunes, their high-rise sides swept as smooth as a giant iced cake by the winds that blow in from the Atlantic. Little drifts of powder blow off and float down. It is a long, sheer drop from the top of the dunes to the beach but Jess can see a few narrow tracks where people have raced and slid. Not that many do, Jess imagines. Not out of the tourist season. The beach is deserted. Not a soul claims it. Looking up, Jess can just make out the green of fields atop the dunes and not far away, the roof and one dormer window in a white-painted croft.

Here heart is beating faster than it has for a long time, or so it seems, as she walks along the biggest beach by the biggest sea under the biggest sky. Hers are the only footprints that mark the pristine powder of the sand. She is small here, a humble part of a much greater whole. She understands that the place is on loan to her and she gives thanks. And promises to cherish the gift.

Half-way along, she stops because the ocean draws her, a liquid magnet, salt water, not iron. She heads down to where the waves curl in with a comforting inevitability, inch by inch, to the wavy line where driftwood and seaweed scrawl the tide's finishing line. How long is it since she stepped into the sea? Never mind, she's sitting on the sand, untying her trainers and wriggling her toes into the grains that are too numerous to count. Up again, and jogging to the water's edge, she enters the clearest of shallows and feels the pebbles shift beneath her feet. Soon she is wading in, jumping the slow-trickling waves. She registers a pure clear cold and laughs at the rogue waves that knock crookedly and soak the hems of her jeans. Soon she's taking long strides right along the shore, kicking up the water. She wishes she had a dog to keep her company and to bark with crazy excitement as each wave breaks on the sand. She must get a dog. She stops again, pushes up her sleeves and dips in her arms, happy that her jumper is wet now as well as her jeans. Shivers run down her spine, of delight, not cold. Jess is pretty immune to cold. A larger wave bumps up against her legs and sends salt spray into the air and onto her face. Tears join the droplets of salt water on her cheeks. The feelings, absent for so long, come fast and strong. She wants to go further, she wants to be in it. She wants to be submerged. She wants to feel cold water washing over her body, calming her, thrilling her, holding her. She wants to swim and swim with crazy energy until her arms and shoulders ache. She wants to head towards that faraway horizon, pretending that she is swimming away, never to return. She wants to float on her back and stare up at the enormous, redemptive sky. She will start swimming again. Tomorrow. Here. The wait that has been part of her grieving is finally over.

This need to be one with the water has been held in check. Since the accident, the lid she hauled over her emotions has been heavy and hard to budge. And it has served its purpose. By edging it off, Jess knows she is opening herself to more feelings of sorrow but also perhaps feelings of peace and acceptance. She is ready.

Having reached the smaller headland at the other end, she turns and walks back, head down, eyes on the trickling waves, drinking in their peaceful progress up the beach. She doesn't notice the figure at the top of the dunes. Only when she raises her head to see how far she has to go, does she spot her. A child. A girl of maybe nine or ten in a bright blue fleece and a beanie. Hands on her hips, head on one side, the small person stands stock-still and stares down at Jess. Or so it seems. The pose suggests indignation but that, Jess tells herself, may be her over-charged imagination. The islanders have not been hostile, merely over-curious and very nosy. On the other hand, this girl is definitely not holding up a welcome sign. Jess has a hunch about what is written in the speech bubble above her head.

Who are you?

What are you doing on my beach?

You are trespassing.

You are not welcome.

Then there's a stirring at the girl's side and a big pale dog is running in circles and jumping on her and barking. Then, clearly impatient with its immobile mistress, it races down the dunes and arrives in a flurry of sand at Jess's feet. She offers her hand which he licks.

'Hey, Fella! I was just thinking I need a dog.'

The dog runs in circles, tail wagging, then starts to dig, cascades of sand spewing out in all directions.

'Your mistress doesn't seem to be joining you,' Jess tells him before she resumes her walk back.

Nor does the girl move from her vigil-like position until Jess is a lot further along and has begun her trek back up the steep dunes to the fields above. As if she has been waiting for the coast to be clear. With Jess out of the way, the small figure jumps and slides down the dunes and races along the sand to crouch down by her dog who has by now dug almost to Australia. Turning her head, Jess smiles at his boisterous greeting, as if the girl has been gone for weeks.

High above the beach, Jess stops once more to stare back at the wide sweep of the bay. It is astonishingly beautiful. The dog is where it was, the hole bigger, the piles of excavated sand more mountainous. But where is the girl? Near the dog is what looks like a pile of something with a big stone on top. Clothes? Then a movement in the water catches Jess's eye and there she is, twenty yards out from the beach, thin arms doing a careful but rather rapid breaststroke, head poking out of the water like a turtle. She stays exactly parallel to the beach.

Goodness! Jess thinks. No wonder she wanted me off the beach. That stance was clearly proprietorial. Perhaps she comes here regularly. She watches for a while, knowing the girl can't concentrate on staying afloat and at the same time scan the cliffs for intruders. She's young to be swimming alone. I presume someone knows she's there, but I can't see anyone keeping an eye on her. Whoa, Jess! So she swims by herself. It's none of your business. Islanders will not welcome you prying, let alone interfering. Jess notes that the girl doesn't attempt to go further out. Then another thought strikes her. What on earth will she think when I start swimming from this beach too? It's probably the last thing she wants. This will call for some diplomacy. I hope it isn't going to be a problem. She watches for a while longer, always interested in how others navigate the water. Good little swimmer though! With a few small changes to her posture... back needs to be held higher, head lower, she'd be more efficient and streamlined and she needs to slow down and breathe more slowly...Stop! Stop right there! You do not coach young swimmers anymore. And nobody coaches you. That's history. You will swim, like she swims, for the simple pleasure of being in the water. If she doesn't mind, and if you can negotiate the sharing of the place, you will swim from this gorgeous beach. You will swim alone. Period.

If she spoke out loud, Jess would manage to sound certain and final but the mask is only paper-thin and will go soggy with the first splash of water. She's mislaid her steely core, her backbone, that got her across lakes and along rivers in some pretty filthy conditions. If she spins round and closes her eyes, she's standing in her red racer bathing suit on the shore of Lake Placid, thigh-high in water that waits for her, clear and deep and invigorating. Behind the lake rise the mountains and rivers and streams of a seemingly endless wilderness. On the lake, there is Dan in the rowing boat, oars dripping, waiting for her to get into the water. Come on, L'il Jess! We haven't got all day. Lazing on the shore after their own training, some of the team wave her off and shout nonsense about trying not to drown. Jess grins as she takes a deep breath, plunges in and does an elegant crawl under the water until she surfaces right beside Dan. She's smiling as her head bobs up. Water all around her, what better life could there be?

Chapter 10

Julia and Hamish

This far north, at this time of year, the island barely sees darkness. Hamish and Julia go to bed in the light and get up in the light, wondering sometimes if there ever was a minute of true pitch black in between. In mid-winter, it's a very different story. The sun begins its sluggish ascent well after nine and hangs half-heartedly above the horizon for a few hours, casting Giacometti shadows everywhere, before it slides back down. By four, it's dark again.

It's cold tonight, even though the sky has finally cleared after twelve hours of hard-hitting rain and, in the living room, the peat fire smoulders dark red. As he always does at the end of a day's hard graft, Hamish nurses a glass of single malt and ticks off the tasks he's accomplished while Julia finishes tidying the kitchen and lining up shoes and wellies ready for morning.

In the living room, her touch is everywhere, lifting a fairly ordinary croft parlour with traditional small windows into a space of texture, colour and surprises. Twisted round one of her paintings on the wall, one end left hanging, is a tangle of fairy lights. Threaded through a small forest of succulents and spider plants on a low table is another shimmering string, gold here instead of silver. Hamish teases her for her childish love of sparkly lights, and asks her if it's Christmas, but he appreciates the mood she has created even if he doesn't always notice the details. On the old saggy sofa are mismatched cushions in tangerine and blue. On wooden shelves are sculptures which she has exchanged for paintings over the years, and pieces of driftwood shaped like birds and animals. Over one armchair hangs the softest alpaca throw in colours like heather, a birthday present from Julia's mother before she died. There are plants on every surface and hanging from hooks on the walls, all in pretty pots. Julia won't buy a new plant or beg a cutting unless she has first saved up for a decent place to house it. Plants in plastic containers are a crime against aesthetics and doomed not to thrive, she told Hamish long ago, receiving for a reply a raised eyebrow of amused acknowledgement. This living room couldn't be more different from most of the other dwellings on the island which stay stuck in a time warp of heavily patterned carpets (different in every room), bulky furniture, net curtains and single ceiling lights. It's functional. It works. Grand Designs hasn't yet reached this island.

'Pleased with your day's work?' Julia asks, climbing onto the sofa and tucking her legs under her.

The flames from the fire illuminate her husband's fine features and hewn angles. Other women comment on his looks, on the symmetry of his face, his straight nose, his deep-set navy blue eyes. Not that she would repeat any of that to him. This is a man who doesn't possess a comb: That's what fingers are for. And who rarely looks in the

86

mirror: I can only see from the neck down to my knees. Julia loves his total indifference to his appearance and his lack of vanity. At Christmas, you don't give aftershave to this man. Maybe a new hacksaw.

'No' bad,' Hamish replies, which Julia translates as 'pretty good'.

'You were soaked out there.'

'I can't turn off the rain.'

'Could you not do indoor work when it's bucketing down?'

'I'd rather finish. Once the trees are in, I can start on the fencing. The deer are about their destroying again.'

It's a superhuman task, Julia always thinks, but Hamish is comfortable with larger-than-life projects and possesses a dogged determination and hearty stamina. Since returning to the island, he has taken everything it has thrown at him without a word of complaint, without ever admitting that he is exhausted, though he does sometimes fall asleep halfway through his after-dinner dram.

'Have you lost any more saplings?' she asks.

'A few. Bark chewed. So I must press on.'

'And there's the deadline.'

'I'm no' worrying about that. It's the damn deer.'

If you were to cut and roll back a slice of Hamish's head, Julia thinks, like peeling open a tin of sardines, and if you were to peer inside, you'd see an exact map of a water-logged landscape, willow saplings stacked by the thousand waiting to be sunk into the ground, miles of strong fencing, plans for two eco cabins for tourists, birds in various stages of hatching and growing, and away on the horizon, rare breeds of goats and some llama which will be part of a modest children's farm. Does this man think of nothing else? They've owned the croft for more than a year and he has thrown himself into the project like his life depends on it. Well, his livelihood does depend on it since this is how he has chosen to keep a roof over their heads.

But wait, this is casting the project in an unfair light, as if it were all his doing. When they lived in the rented cottage, they sat at the kitchen table and talked and drew plans into the night. They looked up breeds of chickens and turkeys and ducks. They did homework on growing vegetables in poly tunnels. They visited and checked out other timber-frame cabins which bring in an obscene rent in the compressed months of the tourist season.

'I'm excited,' Julia had told him. 'But I want you to be able to stop working yourself to the bone. How many jobs are you doing? For others?'

'Aye, but bit by bit. We'll need the income until the croft starts to pay for itself.'

'But, Hamish, you work so hard looking after Jen's cows and helping build Alastair's byre and you'll have so much more to do on top of all that.'

'And how else can I earn enough to keep my family in the style it likes?'

Julia smiles at his irrepressible optimism. 'I know. But I would just love you to be independent.'

'In time, Julia. And what about you? What will you do?'

'Oh I'll dust the furniture and sew curtains and put meals in the freezer...'

Hamish throws an arm round his wife and kisses her on the cheek. 'Dearest soul, don't give me that bullshit because I happen to know my wife rather well. She will be wandering on the beach below our croft and picking up shells and bits of wood and she'll forget to come back in time for her daughter arriving on the school bus.'

'Hamish! I have never forgotten to come home in time for Fenn!'

'Close shaves, then,' he says, before changing the subject. 'Anyway I love your paintings.'

But those exuberant energetic landscapes started to grow smaller until now she is colouring in little pages from a sketch book and rarely is so engrossed in the shifting colours of the sky that she forgets all about the time. There's been a sea change which she herself can't explain. Her mood is blue. How true is that saying? And she was already feeling unsettled before Fenn dropped her own little bombshell about not belonging. So, nothing for it. She must knock on the door of her husband's overfull cupboard of a mind and ask him to find a little space for a few more items. And he's a bit reluctant to make room for personal stuff, unless it's really important. But this is important, Julia reassures herself. There's Fenn, that's important. And to a lesser extent, there's me. Or maybe I shouldn't trouble him with that. Julia has tried and tried to deal with her own malaise without bothering her always-busy husband, and the result is a pile of painted postcards. Well, she can always sell them at The Wave and in her online shop.... that was always part of the plan. She hasn't really veered off course.

She waits a few more moments while Hamish refills his glass. He usually stops at one.

'Can I bother you?' she asks.

Hamish turns to his wife, and smiles a rare smile. 'As long as it's no' difficult.'

'I can't promise that.'

Hamish puts down his glass and moves closer to Julia, his arm flung over her frame. 'What?' he asks quietly.

89

'Well, first there's Fenn and then...'

'Ah now, you didn't say you'd be bothering me with more than one thing.' He's rubbing her knotty shoulders, tense from painting, the muscles of his fingers knowing exactly where to press and knead.

'I'm serious, Hamish. Let me finish.'

'I'm listening.'

'OK, Fenn told me today that Miss Murdoch picks on her. She was fed up.'

'First I've heard. Picked on for what?'

'Dreaming. Not concentrating.'

'Being a normal nine-year-old, then? And a very normal Fenn.'

'Quite so, but Fenn says Miss Murdoch doesn't pick on the other children.'

'As far as she knows. Or chooses to report.'

'She's observant, Hamish. I think she'd know.'

'Is Fenn upset?'

'A bit. More cross than upset. She doesn't like unfairness.'

Hamish is silent. Then, 'Does she want us to go and talk to the old biddie?'

'Hamish! You're worse than Fenn. Absolutely not.'

'Then that's an end to it.'

'But if she says anything else...'

'We'll think again.'

Subject closed, Hamish reaches for his glass and takes another swig. But he gets no nod of agreement from Julia. No smile wiping out her frown. 'Is there more to this?' And when Julia doesn't answer, he adds, 'You're not just bothering me about grumpy old Miss Murdoch, are you? Go on, Julia.'

Julia takes a deep breath, rather wishing she had left

herself out of this conversation. It's not really pressing. 'Um... this is hard to say because I don't want to exaggerate, and I don't want to appear neurotic, but I've been wondering lately if we are really welcome here, Hamish.'

Hamish twists round to look at his wife. 'What? Where has this suddenly come from?'

'It's not a totally crazy thing to think.'

'You think Miss Murdoch is picking on Fenn not because she's staring out of the window but because she's...hmmm?' He pulls himself up short, deliberately leaving unsaid the other reason, not wanting to give it substance.

'It crossed my mind.'

'Surely a teacher wouldn't single out a child?'

'I wouldn't have thought so.'

'If it's true, and I very much doubt it is, there's not much we can do. We can't call her out.'

'I know. The islanders would close ranks.'

'I don't know about that, but more important, it wouldn't help Fenn.'

'I think Fenn can deal with it, Hamish.'

'Fine. Leave it.'

In retrospect, Julia knows she should have left the talking there. Enough.

'It's me too...' she ventures.

'Who's been bitching at you for dreaming?'

Julia ignores the feeble joke. If she were Fenn, she would roll her eyes. 'Oh, it's just the same old thoughts about belonging. Or not belonging.'

'In that case, let go of the thoughts, Julia. We're incomers. I can't say it less bluntly. It will take the islanders a while to get used to us. People come up here and stay for a year and run away back to the mainland. Why make friends with new people when they only disappear? That's how things work. You knew that before we came.'

'You're not an incomer.'

'I use the term loosely.'

'No-one treats you like an incomer.'

'I was born here. My parents and grandparents lived here. I blotted my island copybook because I went away for years but one day the elders may forgive me. And you're only half an incomer because you're my wife.'

'I don't want to be a half-incomer. It means half-accepted.'

'It's a manner of speaking.'

'I don't want to be half-accepted.'

'Better than half-rejected.'

'It means I'm not one of them.'

'You can't be one of them.'

'OK, not one of them, but I'd like to feel welcome.'

'And who says you're not welcome?'

'No-one. It's just a feeling.'

'Like Fenn has a feeling that Miss Murdoch is picking on her?'

Julia knows not to rush Hamish. And she also knows that however flippant he may sound, he'll think about this long and hard in his own time. Heaven forbid that his wife and daughter are not content on his island. And he'll find a way to put it into proportion. He's good at defusing things that have got a bit out of hand.

'Mebbie this is about time passing,' he says now. 'We were all running on adrenaline when we came. We made our plans and we waited our chance, and now here we are with a croft of our own and birds multiplying. Mebbie the hard graft of the past eighteen months has taken the shine off things a bit, but we are making progress. Good progress.'

'I know. You may be right,' Julia says, while not fully believing it.

'End of the list of things to bother me with?'

'No.'

'So three worries? I charge extra for three.'

'It's not a worry, Hamish, unless you give me the wrong answer.'

Hamish glimpses a twinkle in his wife's eyes and notes that the dark cloud is blowing over. Julia is an outgoing soul, his brave and wise companion. This little episode is out of character, but understandable if it was triggered by her daughter's upset. He wonders what's really got into Fenn.

'So what next?'

'Well, I've been thinking about eggs. If we were to cross a Duckwing with a Copper Maran, we'd get chickens that lay bright green ones!'

'I've heard a rumour about this.'

'Ah...Fenn again. Well, what do you think?'

'I prefer my scrambled eggs yellow.'

'You spoil sport. The blue eggs and copper eggs sell within hours of me putting them out and I get a silly price for them.'

'Green may be a shade too far.'

For a moment, Julia looks disappointed, though she admits this isn't exactly a matter of life or death. Then she catches the way Hamish is looking at her.

'Dear soul, if birds that lay grass-green eggs will make you happy, then that's fine by me, but don't even think about making me an omelette with them.'

'It's a deal,' Julia says, kissing him.

He kisses her back, his love for this unconventional woman undimmed by the years they have been together.

And Julia wonders if her loop about islanders and incomers, teachers and dreamy kids, is nothing more than that, a tape jammed in the player. Then she laughs at her old-fashioned image. Fenn would roll her eyes. Catch up, Mum. Streaming and Spotify, she'd tell her. Julia is hopelessly behind the times and will need Fenn to drag her into the technological present. Meanwhile, she can at least turn the volume down.

Chapter 11

Finn

They had agreed to make it look very casual. Under a returned sun, on damp land covered with puddles that shine with yesterday's rain, Hamish is hammering together long planks to make a raised bed for herbs and vegetables. It's destined for what was once perhaps a front garden, but is now a wide moat around the croft with squelchy mud in winter and dried and caked mud in summer. Here, the chickens, ducks and geese waddle and peck freely until Fenn arrives home to persuade them to their shelters for the night. The raised bed is strictly temporary. After he has planted the saplings, Hamish will build a poly tunnel for all their vegetables and espalier fruit trees.

'Don't forget, space for flowers for picking too,' Julia says, gazing up at him with an exaggerated pretence of a flirty smile. 'David Austin roses and peonies and passion flowers.'

Hamish raises his head. 'It's not a heated conservatory, Julia.'

Julia gives a resigned sigh. She is sitting on the doorstep, pretending to draw the hens, or maybe she is drawing them while her mind is occupied with a nine-year-old on her way home with a worry.

'We'll just ask her how things are,' Julia says for at least the third time. 'Nothing more.'

'Aye.' Hamish looks sceptical. He's had his arm twisted hard. He'd wanted to draw a line under all of this.

A few minutes later, Hero's ears prick up, and the birds shift a gear and are fighting one another for space near the gate, which means the school bus is close. Of course Hero knows when it's bus time, but Fenn swears the birds can tell the time too because they start to gather and flap and squark minutes before she arrives home. Or maybe they have sharp hearing like she does. Sure, a few slope off, too proud to show they care about this small human, but others give her a noisy display of welcome that can include some sharp pecks.

'Stop biting my ankle, Runner Bean!' Fenn scolds as she squeezes inside the smallest possible opening, careful not to let any of the birds escape, and clicks the gate shut behind her. She is up to her knees in a sea of feathers and eyes and beaks, with a large collie in their midst vying for her attention with yelps and leaps. 'Hero, get down! Hilda, budge! Let me at least get in the gate.'

Up to now, she hasn't noticed her parents. She stops and stares at them. Shifts her gaze from one to the other, a wry smile threatening to spoil her nonchalance. It's so totally obvious something's up, and she has her suspicions.

'What's this, a welcome party? What are you two doing out here?'

'I'm drawing the chickens,' Julia says.

Really? Fenn thinks.

'You can see what I'm doing,' Hamish adds.

'Yeah but how come you're not planting trees, Dad?'

'A man needs a change now and again.'

Fenn looks from one to the other. Shakes her head ever so slightly and raises her eyebrows. 'Looks suspiciously like you're waiting for me. You aren't about to ask me how I got on at school today by any chance?'

There's a too-long silence while each parent fails to find a convincing reply.

'How was school?' Julia asks brightly, ignoring her daughter's warning words.

'Fine.'

'Um…was everything OK today?'

'Yes. Fine.' Fenn knows the game and is not playing.

'Fenn, I talked to Hamish last night and…'

'I'm fine.'

What's up with her parents? They are usually more cool. 'I need to get the birds in. Have you looked up at the sky today because if you do, you'll see puffy white clouds and that means the beach after the birds.' There is an unmistakable lightness in her voice as she literally turns her back on her parents' concern. No, Fenn, say nothing about the woman who has appeared on your territory. It's really annoying. But one worry blurted out yesterday was a big mistake. Just look where that got her – her mum and dad standing guard, pretending to be doing stuff in case she comes home in tears or whatever. She certainly isn't going to give them anything else to worry about. Some things are best kept from grown-ups.

'Fenn, we just need…' Julia's last feeble attempt goes unfinished.

'No need,' Fenn replies, squeezing past her mother on the step, and vanishing into the hall with Hero running circles round her heels. From behind the door, they can hear the dog barking and Fenn telling him to calm down. What they don't hear, or see, is a child with acute hearing listening to the whispered conversation outside with her hand over her mouth to stop exasperated sighs escaping.

'What did I say?' Hamish says to his wife.

'Silly of me. We look a right pair.'

'Yesterday is history when you're nine.'

'I'm not sure about that. I think she's decided she can deal with it.'

Hamish throws down his hammer. 'I'm away to the planting. I won't be expecting a phone call for a further audition as a concerned father then?'

'No, because you weren't one bit convincing.'

'And you were? Sitting on the step drawing a chicken?'

Julia pulls a face.

'There's no grass growing on that one.'

Julia stands and collects her drawing things, shamefaced, and Hamish takes pity on her. 'I don't see a very worried child,' he says before he wanders off. 'In her head, she's already on the beach, already in the water, Miss M and school forgotten.'

'I got it wrong, Hamish.'

'So stop worrying, Julia.'

Julia brushes away a rogue tear, but he's away, striding down the slope, and Fenn is doing a superwoman transformation from school kid to young crofter. Now is absolutely not the time to start on her own upset again.

Back in her studio, Julia pins a large piece of paper to her easel and chooses a thick, stubby brush. You have to try, she tells herself. Fenn is an example to you. There she is, not very happy at school but not making a fuss. Her first expansive brush strokes are accompanied from below the window by the refrains of a girl chasing and calling to birds, and birds squawking after a girl, intermittently interrupted by the excited barks and howls of a collie. It's the same every day, come rain or shine, gales or storms. They had given Fenn her own stock as a welcome present when they moved to the croft, not knowing quite what to expect, and she took to her chores like, well, a duck to water. How long, Julia wonders, will her childish enthusiasm last? Will an adolescent Fenn still rush out to put the birds to bed?

With the birds safely in their night places, Fenn climbs the stairs two at a time and places her stock in the corner of her room. She strips off, drags on her swimsuit and pulls her clothes on top. She finds her towel. Then she is on her way again, Hero at her heels, barking with joy because he knows exactly where they are off to next. She hears the rough scrape of a large brush on paper through the half-closed door of the studio and hopes her mum has moved on from tiny pink chicks. Fenn knows. While Julia was listening carefully to her daughter's worries yesterday, Fenn was tuned in to her mother's subdued mood. Julia tried to help but her talk of fading excitement and Ferris wheels didn't convince. I wonder why mum is unsettled, Fenn asks herself, as she jumps the stairs. Perhaps she's too much on her own now that Hamish spends his whole life planting trees. Perhaps she needs a friend to do fun things with. But who know what grown-ups want?

Let it go, Fenn tells herself. Leave it at the croft. Her mum will work it out. Her mum is strong and doesn't let things get her down. Anyway, she's always thinking about her painting, even postcard-sized ones. This mood will pass.

Fenn sets off at a crazy headlong pace with Hero ecstatic at her heels. Run, run and leave it all behind. Forget Miss M and the stupid kids because you don't have to think about any of them until tomorrow. Here you are free. Here is where you belong. Bent double to catch her breath, Fenn is soon at the top of the sand dunes, knowing it is there, as it should be, waiting for her. When she straightens, she blinks. The sand is so white when spot-lit by bright sun that she's dazzled by the dancing daggers of light. That's when she sees her. Damn. Blast and damn. She lets out a huge sigh and frowns. Her mood, restored by her run to a bright balloon, deflates to a shrunken bit of rubber. That woman is there. She's in a blue swimsuit, her clothes in a pile, sitting at her end of the beach, near the promontory. Why doesn't she stay on the other side of it, for heavens sake? Fenn takes in every detail, the hands pressed behind her back on the hard-packed sand, the raised head staring out to sea, the stillness. Pretending I'm not here, Fenn thinks. She knows perfectly well I can see her, and she knows perfectly well I don't want her here. She'd better stay put on her own patch and not come any nearer. Anyway why isn't she swimming? Why doesn't she hurry up and swim and go home? Then Hero is at the woman's side, doing his friendly dog act, licking her hand. Damn dog! Unfaithful hound! Fenn scowls, and stomps down the knee-deep sand. Well, she can't stop me swimming. She turns with a deliberate swerve in the opposite direction and walks a long way from the other figure on the beach.

Fenn hunkers down against the sand hills and waits. And hangs her head. I will not look in that direction and I will not give her the slightest hint that I know she's there. She even snaps at Hero, who has returned with a wagging tail, and tells him to leave her alone and go and dig somewhere else. The misery of yesterday, which she tried to hide from her parents, today comes down like a shutter caught by the wind. I mean, do they really think it will all get better overnight? she asks herself. Like the other kids will all suddenly be friends? What were they expecting me to say when they stood there in the garden like a stupid committee? They may want to hear 'Oh yes, I'm fine' so they don't have to worry, but I can't give them that. So, if it's not much fun at stupid school then I totally need this place to myself when I get back, she says, furious at having to wait for that woman to get up and go. It's not much to ask. I only get an hour, and then they'll be worrying that I've drowned as well as worrying I'm not happy. Is it that much to ask? I want this sea to myself.

As she fumes, she catches a movement out of the corner of her eye, not that she's looking of course, not that she's taking the slightest notice. The woman is picking up her towel and making her way towards the headland. And around it. She doesn't look back. And Fenn is on her feet and racing towards the sea and throwing herself into it, screaming at the shock of the cold, screaming at being released from guard duty, screaming at being finally alone in the element she loves. The pale-green water washes over her body and holds it afloat. Fenn breathes out, long and hard, and begins a slow breaststroke out to the bay, but of course not out of her depth. The day's tensions dissolve in the water and seep away.

The sound comes from far, far away, the thinnest ribbon of song, faint and fine and fragile, the colour blue. Like the vapour trail of a plane is no more than a scratch in the sky so this is just a fleeting current through waves. Whether it reaches her by bouncing over the water or streaking along below the surface, Fenn does not know. What she does know is that the mood music is very much like her own. Something else out there is not sure and not at ease. Fenn stays there, lying on her back, held by a cushion of water, listening to a blue silken thread of a song. She is dreaming again, free to dream and make of the sound the shape she wants. Something or someone a bit like her.

Chapter 12

The Whale

Days and nights stream on as does the young whale, weaving his way through an underwater world that is unfamiliar and full of surprises. A sixth sense, maybe memory remnants of his previous journey, tells him what is normal and natural in the depths of the ocean and what is jarring and wrong. His song may not reach the others, but it echoes around the shapes of other creatures and the vegetation that crowds the ocean floor. It rings around the tall flowerings of slippery reeds, collides with crusted walls of coral, pushes through shoals of a thousand different kinds of fish who swim to feed, feed to survive, as he himself does. The whale calls, not with the hope of reaching the others because that wish is fading, but to give himself a sense of where he is and what is happening around him. How deep is the water? Is there land in the distance? Is it warmer here? Is there plentiful feeding or are the fish in short supply?

This is such a different journey, with loneliness his phantom companion. Last time, he swam without hesitation or fear as he followed the others through the ocean, playing a small part of a bigger whole. He was surrounded and contained by his pod, unmistakable shapes soaring and diving, sometimes nudging him in greeting, sometimes all of them jumping in arcs for joy, and always he heard their streams of sound accompanying them and spreading out into the ocean as they travelled onwards. It felt effortless. It felt true and real. It felt right.

He has swum on without any sense of direction but he knows that he has arrived in a different kind of water space because his skin registers warmth from the sun and the deep, black water has lightened to a dark blue. It is soon apparent that all is not well here. Around him, the creatures start and stir in a maelstrom of frantic motion. The shoals of smaller fish are sparse and skittish, their eyes round with panic. On red alert, they dash away before he can get anywhere near to scoop them up into his open, brush-filled jaws. Although he lunges to the surface again and again, the fish and plankton scatter and evade him. What's wrong with them? The frequent trips to feed sap his energy but give him scant nourishment. For long periods, he swims by himself, hunger in his belly, in a blueness that lacks depth, and where his dives to the seabed are brief and shallow. Feelings of unrest are all around him.

What reaches him next, from far away, is a cacophony of noise, dull and burdensome and grinding. It grows louder as he covers mile upon mile. The sounds jar his senses and are nothing like the liquid ocean noises and the taps and trills he knows so well. No creature of the sea interrupts the ocean's mood with such discordance. Twisting round and round and peering out of his tiny eyes, he sees that above him, the surface is troubled, a disturbed mass of bumping waves and rising ripples as enormous dark shadows criss-cross back and forth, back and forth. The jagged, grating noises come with the shadows and the water froths and seethes around them. What are those creatures that churn up the water.?

There is no getting away from it either because the continuous deep throb drowns out the other water sounds and spirals down to the depths where he swims in circles of puzzled annoyance and anxiety. How can he pick up the calls of his fellow whales when he is deafened and disorientated by this interminable din? Swimming onwards, he hopes to escape it but the shadows with their brutal noises still pass directly overhead, moving towards him then moving away, each time sending a turbulence of water spiralling down. Up there are noises for which he has no names.

Nervous and wary, he stays still and peers upwards for a long time. As each shadow falls across the water above him, huge and hulking, it brings a temporary darkness as it blots out the light of the sun. For a few minutes he is blinded, and has to wait until the light leaks back down. They are cumbersome, these creatures, and take a long time to approach and retreat, so unlike the powered swimming of his fellow whales. Each time one passes overhead, he hopes it is the last. But here comes another. And another. There is a never-ending procession of creatures that throb and vibrate as they ride the surface, disturbing the natural world below. The whale holds himself still with slow swishes of his tail. Here comes the pointy front end of another flat underbelly, and on it goes, on and on. Its incredible length is bigger than any whale in the ocean, but they are hard to see other than as dark shapes because in their wake comes water that is thickly sand-filled and opaque. He blinks away the dust.

He peers through the murk. Smells the alien oil. No wonder the shoals of fish are scurrying away in terror. No wonder the coral reefs are empty, the creatures who live there having moved on. Who would want to stay here with that racket overhead? As he waits and watches, he can piece together a general picture of perpetual movement and aggressive noise, but he can't understand it. The sea is churned up and occupied and busy, he thinks. There is no peace here. We have lost the gentle rhythms and the natural ways of the tide and the currents, of bright day and dark night. What are those things that have invaded our habitat?

The whale has stayed down in the depths for too long, overawed by the almost hypnotic movements above that cover the seabed with shade and rattle the fishes with their rumbling. He needs to find out if it is safe to move on which means taking the risk of breaking through the water's surface. But what if he emerges into the path of one of those monstrous things? He would stand no chance. It would bear down on him and crush him. Be brave, he tells himself. Find out what is crashing across the water. Assess the danger. Look for a way to escape. It takes a surge of energy to soar upwards, and already his reserves are depleted. But he gets there. A slow spin through three hundred and sixty degrees shows him what his view from the shallows could not. These moving things rise high above the water, the size of more whales than he can imagine, piled one on top of the other. They are wide too, like many whales laid side by side.

He is astonished by their monumental size, bigger than anything he has ever seen, and knows he risks his life as they roar past him much too close. Can they see me? he wonders. Can they see my head sticking out of the water? Do they attack? Will they come after me? He monitors them travelling in opposite directions, sometimes passing one another side by side in bumping waves of foam and froth. Of course he doesn't know that he is watching cargo vessels and container ships moving along a busy shipping lane. He does not know that the stage is set for frequent and deadly collisions between his own kind and this never-ending traffic. He does know that he is far too close to objects that travel with a terrifying momentum, and considers only for a second what it would feel like to be ploughed underneath one. A cold dread shivers across his skin. His poor sense of smell brings him traces of oil and dirt of a kind he does not recognise. From the odd behaviour of the fish all around him, he senses that other species are haunted and hunted too. The smaller fish are darting all over the place, falling out of formation and turning in hopeless loops and circles. There is no order. The ocean is thick and distraught with unnatural sounds.

The whale remembers the place where his journey began where he swam with his pod through gentle quiet seas that were transparent and luminous near the surface, comfortingly black in the depths, and where all their songs could pour forth without obstruction. How can I hear what I need to hear? he asks now. My song is drowned out, and the songs of the others won't reach me through this blast of sound. This worries me. I am afraid. His song is indeed coloured by new, fearful emotions and is muffled and curtailed. It will be difficult for it to penetrate the other frequencies that crowd the water.

This is the first story that the whale takes with him as he continues on the wrong course. There will be more. The stories will be washed with the emotions built from colours and patterns absorbed through the whale's small eyes and his delicate acoustic system. These colours he carries with him as he swims on. And on. The further he goes, the darker are the colours.

Chapter 13

Jess

Her comings and goings have been noted. She knows that people are talking about the woman who has turned up on the island with a small van of belongings and has moved into the shabby cottage towards the end of the peninsula. She was told by the agent who sold her the cottage that there was no resentment, but he warned her that the islanders' curiosity will be peaked because anyone new is a novelty. Jess comes with no reputation and no known past and so far not even the busiest of busybodies has been able to uncover her back story.

Jess has been living out of the tiny supermarket at the end of the track, on the main road, and notes that conversations suddenly stop each time she arrives at its doors. People stare. When she's choosing vegetables or leaning into a freezer, there is someone right at her side, and out come the inevitable questions. She gives her practised answers.

'So how are you settling in then?'

'Oh, fine, thank you.'

'How are you liking it here?'

'Very much, thank you.'

'And where have you come from?'

'America,' Jess replies, watching eyebrows shoot up and other questions lining up behind this one.

'That's a very long way away.'

'Yes.'

'And what brings you here then?'

This is more tricky but Jess is good at skidding away from the questions without giving a thing away and without appearing rude.

'Oh I came here as a tourist years ago and loved the place. I decided to move here.' Lies, shocking lies, but she isn't going to pour out the truth to someone she doesn't know while taking a packet of oatcakes off a shelf in a corner shop.

'And is there someone coming out to join you?'

Oh, how they long to ask outright, 'Do you have a husband?'

'I live alone,' Jess always replies. Nothing more.

A few of the older folk don't mince their words. 'You'll be a mite lonely, all by yourself?'

'I have plenty to keep me busy.'

'You do know what you've let yourself in for, do you, lass? The winters are terrible harsh.'

'Oh I don't mind the weather,' Jess replies truthfully. It's the least of my worries.

'Aye, the island's bonny enough, but it can get you down in the dark months.'

'I'll be fine,' Jess says.

Or will I? Yes, it could all be a terrible mistake but this isn't the time or the place to air that.

'If you're no' going to croft, what will you do here?'

And so it goes on.

Jess thinks she might as well climb onto one of the shelves, write herself a label and let them give her a prod to see if she's ripe. Instead she nods her head, shakes her head, and smiles a lot. She twists the conversation back to the island and the islanders, gives bland answers and reassures everyone she talks to that she loves the place and is staying a long time, because that's what's at the bottom of all of this. Is she going to stick it out for six months, realise the error of her ways and flee back to the mainland like so many that come here to try the good life and find the isolation and the weather intolerable? Or will she stay the course and settle in? The gatherings in the shop wind down when she supplies no further information, and she becomes simply the new American woman in the cottage on the peninsula – alone, eccentric, but so far harmless.

The islanders continue to take note of her movements. When she's out walking in all weathers, pushing forwards into a wicked wind or with her face turned up to drenching rain, net curtains twitch and fall. Crofters working on their land and tending their animals raise their heads when she passes by and nod a minimal greeting. How many see her running along the beach and up and down the vertical sand dune? She imagines the gossip.

She's very fit.

Very active.

Always on the go.

Strikes me she's running around like a headless chicken.

When is she going to settle down?

Aye, but she's still new. She'll calm down. She's American, remember, and they're different. She has to get used to our ways.

And they have no idea, no idea at all, that rushing about is this new woman's way of coping with a grief that is too big to contain and too overwhelming to live with. They do not know that there are many days when Jess sets off on yet another walk in torrential rain and asks herself if it's all a terrible mistake?

What the hell am I doing on this godforsaken Scottish island when I could go back to where I belong? I could catch a plane tomorrow and be back in the Adirondacks the next day. My friends will welcome me back. They think I've taken leave of my senses. The lakes are waiting for me. I know how to live there. But, and it's such a big but, do I know how to live there without Dan?

When she starts swimming from the stony little beach below her cottage, Jess doesn't bother to ask herself what the islanders might say. They'll lose interest eventually. Who cares? What the hell does it matter if the old women talk about me? She will carry on as she pleases and if it raises eyebrows, so be it. Those who live here do sometimes go to the sandy beaches for an afternoon out or to chat and drink tea from a thermos in the shelter of the dunes. Some of the adults, women usually, paddle along in the shallows with their trousers rolled up while their kids race screaming in and out of the water. But it's just a half-day trip to the beach and they don't stay long. Soon they're walking away up the sand dunes for their lunch or their tea. Jess, on the other hand, swims most days, in all weathers, and stays out in the bay for a very long time, by their standards. She's in the water on cool days, on rainy days, on days when everyone else stays sensibly indoors.

Jess deliberates long and hard about swimming from the next-door beach with its wide sweep of bay. She knows that as far as the girl is concerned, she will be trespassing. There are other coves and smaller beaches, but this long horseshoe curve of white sand has a formidable presence – peaceful, powerful and utterly compelling. Far out in the bay, islands are layered in mist and coloured in pastels. Behind the beach are sand dunes higher than anywhere else, great mountains of sieved icing sugar, their sides squared off neatly with a palette knife and decorated with stiff grass. They tower over the beach, protecting it and blocking out the nearby crofts, all except the one window in the house where the girl lives. Occasionally the black and white face of a sheep peers down, then turns away, thinking better of risking that steep drop.

The first few times Jess swims from the beach, she chooses to go in the mornings, and she knows she'll be alone. The girl will be at school so she needn't worry about feeling like an intruder. After her long abstention, she wants to concentrate simply and purely on the sensation of being back in the water. The sea here is perfect, the waves long and widely spaced so she is barely disturbed by them and soon she is far out, doing a steady, effortless pace half a mile from the shore. The jagged edges of her grief are smoothed by the swoosh of the water. She surges on, stroke after stroke, the rhythmic kick of her legs pushing her further out and the cold water washing and embracing her. It is exhilarating. It is invigorating. It clears her head like nothing else can. After the swim, her limbs are loose, her muscles tight, her skin tingling. It is a rite and a ritual, a baptism by water, a way of becoming herself again.

But swimming in the morning feels out of kilter. Jess soon establishes a routine and a rhythm to her days which have their proper ending and wind-down in the water. Keeping busy is her only way of coping. A fixed pattern of work and walks divides up her days and gives them a structure, albeit it a shaky one. Even so, she is often ambushed by grief and there are mornings when she has to force herself out of bed to face another day alone. I must get a dog, she tells herself, blinking back tears. But it's hard. It is always so hard, and she wonders if life will ever have any real meaning. Will she always be going through the motions of living, feeling little except loss.

After breakfast, eaten at a small table by the window where she can watch the birds winging over the sky, she settles to paint and decorate the driftwood she's collected for the garden she plans. After lunch, she switches to domestic mode and paints a wall or organises drawers or moves around her few treasured belongings. It's nest-building time, and that's important. By late afternoon, she has run out of steam and her grief comes closer, threatening to halt her in her tracks and fell her. Nor does it let up as the days pass. There's nothing for it but to go out and walk and walk in all weathers until her legs ache and her heart pounds and the tears stop streaming down her cheeks. And then, of course, the ocean calls and her feet take her to the beach, either round the peninsula or along the road and across the field. It's not an option. It's a necessity. Her arched dive into the shallows is an act of separation, a way of slicing off the feelings that follow and smother her. A fast crawl is her way of leaving it behind on the shore, at least for now, at least while she is buoyed by this mass of water that puts things somewhat in perspective. The ocean is its own vast place, and she relishes the thought of herself as a tiny insignificant speck, of no consequence to its tidal comings and goings nor to its changes as the weather calms and smoothes it or whips it into turmoil.

But she needs to solve the problem of the girl and her antagonism sooner rather than later so that it doesn't nag at her and spoil the only part of the day that brings her some small pleasure. The next day, she waits until the school bus has passed her gate, then heads for the beach. It's mild, though not exactly warm. Thinking about it afterwards, Jess smiles as she replays the awkwardness of the pair of them, like two bad actors in a bad play. She sits on her bit of the beach, then swims, then heads home. The girl messes about on a bit of beach further away, pretends she isn't watching, waits until Jess has headed off, then stalks down the beach and into the water. She tosses her head as if to throw off an unwelcome presence and seize what is hers. At last! she seems to say. Good riddance!

The conundrum for Jess is how to befriend this girl who sends out messages of annoyance that are so loud she might as well shout them through a tannoy. Her small, slim body is all angles of anger and taut fury. Jess feels the tension across the expanse of sand when the two of them occupy their own spaces as clearly as if they have drawn the words in the sand. There are Danger and Keep Off signs. She watches the girl stomp off to sit in the sand dunes, elbows on knees, chin high as she stares at the sea, until Jess swims, picks up her towel and leaves. On a couple of occasions, Jess has lingered and peeped between the barrier of rocks. She's seen the girl run with a furious energy into the sea where she hurls herself into the water, as if to say About damn time.

And so it continues. Stalemate. There are, Jess acknowledges, fair reasons why she should stay away, and she understands the child's resentment. But this bay of white sand and quiet rolling sea is exactly the right place for someone battling demons. Apart from that, it has its own wild beauty that is irresistible. No doubt the girl feels the same. While staying well apart, Jess watches her and reads her fierce attachment to the place and to the creatures who live here. Like a small sentry, she stands guard and keeps watch. It is obvious that her feelings are fierce and constant. One day, Jess sees her find a gull washed up on the beach after a night of storms, unable to fly and horribly smothered in sand as it tried, and failed, to flap away. The girl picks it up with exquisite tenderness and carries it to the water where she cleans its head and wings. With the edge of her t-shirt, she wipes the sand clotting the bird's eyes. Having wrapped it in the folds of her hoodie, she walks up the sand dunes, probably carrying it back to the croft, holding the bird close and warm. Perhaps the bird flew free. Perhaps it died. If so, Jess guesses that she cared for it to the end and buried it with a loving ceremony. Maybe a little wooden cross or wildflowers. Yes, Jess knows from observing her, the girl's quiet confidence and... how to describe it...a deep sense of wanting to be here. Of feeling she belongs right here on the beach. Her roots go into the sand and hold her securely.

In return, and to give back something, Jess keeps a watchful eye on her, just in case, because accidents happen in isolated places, near water, even when you are careful. And this girl is careful. She spends no more than an hour on the beach, splashes in the shallow water and jumps the waves, and only very occasionally, on warm, quiet days, ventures in for a short swim. Jess notes that she always stays parallel to the beach and never ventures out of her depth. Wise child, she thinks. She has earned and deserves the trust that's been given her. Jess knows too that the sea stays shallow for a very long way out so there is no danger of her suddenly finding herself out of her depth. It is later that she learns that the girl's mother also keeps watch from the only window visible above the sand dunes. She has her freedom, but she is never out of sight. Jess would love to befriend this girl who is half-wild herself, but as with any wild creature, it will be one tiny careful step at a time or she will fly away.

Meanwhile the sea is her refuge, on a good day when she breathes softly, a blank blue canvass that waits for her and demands nothing in return. It is itself, a constant presence. It flows up and down the beach and shifts the sand and rattles the pebbles at its edge. It says, I am here, I am eternal and you do not disturb me. She is light, for now empty of her hurting past and unsettled present as she travels lightly towards the line that separates sea and sky. The sea contains and holds her. Her sleek, stream-lined strokes barely break the surface, as insignificant as drops of rain. The sea is all around her.

Chapter 14

Fenn

Fenn used to race to the beach, relieved to shed her hours at school like so many garments tossed off and left on the ground. Damn them. She welcomed the rain and the wind because they washed away her resentment and she welcomed the sun because it ironed her frowns and scowls. She so badly needs to be alone at this time of day. She is alone at school, but being alone on the beach is not the same thing at all because she has the sea and the birds and the other creatures for company. She catches scurrying crabs in the pools between the rocks, touching their crusty backs before she lets then go, and laughs when her first steps in the shallows interrupt shoals of tiny fish. She swears they give her a resentful glance out of their tiny eyes before dashing away. I won't hurt you, she tells them. I will hardly disturb you. I like you.

She can cope with the occasional tourist or walker but she absolutely does not want that woman sitting on the sand like she owns the place. Worse, she doesn't want her swimming in her bay. What a damn cheek! She doesn't even know until she reaches the top of the dunes and looks down whether she will have the beach to herself. Or not. Having reached that vantage point, she either gives a loud whoop of delight followed by a mad, joyful scramble down the dunes, or her heart sinks. Hero mirrors her mood, an emotional sponge at her side. Either his ears droop and he gives a little groan of sympathy, or he bounds down the dunes, kicking up fountains of sand and sometimes howling with the canine equivalent of relief.

Oh no! Today she's there. Sitting on the sand like she's taken up residence. Oh, it's so unfair. Sighing loudly, Fenn picks her way down the dunes, one step at a time, making sure her back is turned and the woman gets the message that she is an intruder. You're not wanted here! Why can't you get that? GO AWAY! Fenn shouts ever so quietly. Kicking the sand with every step, head down, she heads for a spot a long way away and plonks herself down, knees bent, head on her arms. And there she waits. And waits. Why on earth doesn't she hurry up and swim and go away! It's so annoying. Why should she share her bay with this newcomer? Meanwhile, Hero has turned traitor and is bounding over to the woman's side. Oh for heaven's sake, he's licking her hand and she's stroking his head. So much for his loyalty.

Not that the woman exactly hangs around, Fenn has to admit that. Out of the corner of her eye, she keeps track of her every move. Fenn may sigh her way through what seem like hours, but it's only minutes before the woman is up and running across the sand. The girl notes her speed, the way she sprints down the beach, plunges head first into the sea, somehow able to do that even in the shallowest water, and is off, powering across the bay until she is only a moving dot in the distance. For a moment anger fades to a grudging admiration as Fenn notes her strength and ease. She can certainly swim. With the woman too far away to know she's watching her, she lifts her head and admires her fast, neat crawl. She's miles out! She doesn't even stop to float and get her breath back. I wish I could swim like that. Watching her swim isn't half as annoying as watching her sitting doing nothing on the sand. Then she's on her way back, not slowing, not breaking the rhythm of her strokes. Fenn adopts her previous pose, head down, pretending not to take the slightest notice as the woman sprints back up the sand, gathers her things and disappears round the rocks, towel wrapped around her waist, fleece shrugged on. It doesn't occur to Fenn that this high speed performance is perhaps because the woman knows perfectly well that she is not welcome here and is telling her, Sorry. Sorry to upset you. Here, have the place to yourself. I'm off now.

That evening, Fenn's resentment simmers. And boils. And spills over. It's just not possible to put on a brave face and pretend life is hunky dory. The image of the woman sitting on her beach plays on. And because it nags away at her, she forgets about moaning to Julia about Miss Murdoch and forgets her vow to keep all further worries to herself. And so, defences down, she sits at the table while Julia gets dinner, scowling and giving one-word answers to her parents' silly questions about school and other stuff she doesn't want to talk about. What's up with them, pestering her when they can see she wants to be left alone. Fenn sees Hamish and Julia exchange glances. Here we go, they're about to start asking more questions. Just quit!

'What's up, darling?' Julia is the first to break down. What happened to the cheerful girl who was so eager to get to the beach?

'Nothing.'

It's the expected reply. 'Doesn't look like nothing,' Julia persists but gets a glare in response.

'Is it Miss Murdoch?' Hamish asks quietly.

'No!' Fenn shouts.

'Don't be rude, Fenn. I'm only asking.'

Her father's piercing glance can't be ignored. She sighs. 'Nothing to do with Miss Murdoch. It's just that there's always that woman on the beach now and I don't want anyone else there.'

'What's all this?' Julia asks gently. 'You haven't said anything about this before. What woman, Fenn?' First it was Miss Murdoch. Now it's a woman on the beach. My daughter is going from one crisis to another. This isn't like her.

And out it all comes before Fenn can bite it back. 'That woman who's moved to the cottage, she keeps coming to my beach and she keeps swimming, and I have to wait for her to go in the water and come out, and she swims for ages, and then I have to wait for her to go away before I can have the place to myself. And I only have an hour because that's the rule. She can swim from her own beach. Why does she have to swim from my beach?'

'It's no' your beach, Fenn,' Hamish says firmly. 'Better get that straight.'

'It was until she came along.'

'She has the same right to be there as you.'

'But it's below our house not hers.'

'Don't you go on other beaches?'

Why can't he understand? What if someone started planting trees just along the way from him. He'd go mad.

'I like it empty.'

'It's not exactly full.'

'I like it quiet.'

'And exactly what noise does she make?' Hamish raises a querying eyebrow.

Fenn considers his question and strains to find an answer. The woman runs hard on the sand so that the oyster catchers in the shallows bob away. Gulls take off in whirling circles and call to one another in annoyance, or so Fenn has decided. No. Better not say. Hamish will come down on her like a ton of bricks. She hears his annoying need to tell the exact truth. She can't hear the unspoken soundtrack in his head. He understands only too well his child's wish for solitude, for doesn't he seek it out himself, but he has to discourage any belief that she is somehow the proprietor of the beach. Fenn hears his disapproval, not his sympathy, and feels her cheeks burn red.

'Anyway the beach is right below our croft...' Not beaten yet, Fenn veers off with a different argument.

'So?'

'There is a beach right below her house, Dad.'

'So?'

'She could swim there.'

'How long is the beach below our croft, Fenn?'

'Yeah, yeah, Dad, it's miles and miles...but why does she have to swim in our bay?'

'It's not our bay. Not your bay. Not hers.'

Fenn shrugs her shoulders. His twitch of a smile goes unnoticed, as does his empathy with his feisty, independent daughter. Julia reaches out a hand, but Fenn throws it off. Her mother hasn't given her any support either. They've ganged up on her.

'OK,' she says. 'Sorry I spoke.'

'Look, sweetheart,' Julia says, 'we understand that you love to be down there by yourself. I'm sorry you're not happy. Maybe she'll find somewhere else.'

Fat chance, Fenn thinks. They just don't get it. 'OK,' she replies. 'What's for pudding?'

The woman doesn't find anywhere else to swim, not so far as Fenn knows. She's still sitting on the sand or already in the water most days when Fenn peeps over the sand dunes, and her heart plummets. But you can't keep being furious because it's tiring and it's hurting her and making her miserable and it's not having the slightest effect on the woman, so her anger morphs into a sulky, grudging stalemate. She still pretends, pointlessly she knows, that she is the only person on the beach and stays well clear of any possible contact or conversation. She fills invisible sandbags and wears her tin helmet. It occurs to Fenn that the woman is canny and does know how she feels, so doesn't do anything really dumb like trying to talk to her, for that at least she is grateful, but she's still there. Fenn bides her time. If the woman turns her head and catches Fenn's eye, Fenn ignores her, spins round and gets on with drawing in the sand or whatever.

The next move on the board game played out on the sand is that Fenn gets fed up with being forced to sit still. Why am I sitting here like a moron? she asks herself. Like I'm letting her stop me from walking about? That's really dumb. She decides she won't be constrained by the woman's presence so she wanders off to the rock pools to stir them to life or chooses shells from the thousands that crunch underfoot. Even so, it is as if woman and girl have drawn an invisible boundary and the rule is to stay inside your bit of territory. Don't go over the line! Like colouring in, Fenn thinks, and laughs, despite herself. If one goes in the sea, the other stays on the beach. And vice versa.

It is an uneasy truce, like storm clouds that hang in the sky but neither darken and burst into rain, clearing the air, nor blow away to leave uninterrupted blue.

Impasse.

There's another thing. An important thing. All this upset and distraction has chased away all thoughts of that magical moment when she had imagined sounds like none she'd ever heard. That day, she was by herself, knee-deep in the sea, and had stood there for ages, as if in a dream. She imagined, while telling herself it wouldn't be true, that something out there was trying to reach her. To tell her something.

Now that the woman has gone, at last, and good riddance, Fenn steps into the frilled edge of the ocean and stands very still again, poised, alert, listening. Don't think about the woman, she tells herself. Concentrate on the sounds out there. Fenn is herself. The self she was before. She is the girl with sharp hearing who is never a threat to other creatures, however shy they are, however ready to flee, however uncertain. They have come to accept her as she accepts them.

It comes. Faintly, like a raindrop in a puddle, like an echo in a tunnel, like the brush of a feather. The thread of notes is coloured silver and as fine as silk. It could be birdsong or wind whistle. Does it come over the bright bay, bouncing on the blue glass surface of the water, or does it come from underneath, released like a whisper to tease her as she stands and waits? It doesn't matter. It comes, a thin line of sound, almost imperceptible, but with notes of loneliness and longing. I hear you, Fenn calls back, cupping her hands. I can hear you. And I feel the same.

Chapter 15

Jess

It's Jess who makes the first move.

She gets up and starts her walk to where Fenn sits and scowls, and crosses the invisible boundary between them. Heavens, it's like a war zone down here. She'll be filling bags with sand and wearing a tin helmet next. Time to make peace, if I can. The girl gives no sign that she's seen anyone approaching, if anything she tucks her head down further and stares through her knees at the sea. It's like she throws an invisible circle of barbed wire around herself. Danger. Don't cross.

'Hi.' Jess says, halting a few footsteps from the hunched little figure.

The girl glances up. Glares. If looks could kill, Jess thinks. Waits a few beats.

'I'm Jess. I live in Gull Cottage.'

Fenn looks up again, a fleeting glance which reaches Jess's knees. 'I know.' It is without intonation.

'Do you have a name?'

There's an eyeball roll and a sigh before she gives an answer. 'Fenn.'

'That's unusual. Nice name.' It is.

Fenn ignores her.

'Look, Fenn...I know you are angry with me for coming here so I wonder if we could just talk about it? I'd like to explain.' Jess bobs down next to her where they can at least have eye contact once the girl has stopped looking far out to sea and pretending there's no-one anywhere in sight. Oh my goodness, Jess thinks. I think I've underestimated just how fed up and cross this child is. 'OK, Fenn, let me be straight with you. You don't like me coming here, do you?' She asks the question quietly and without antagonism.

'No.'

Jess accepts and appreciates the directness. 'You look pretty cross, sitting here. I do know.'

'I am cross,' Fenn replies, a flash of anger in her winter-grey eyes.

'I'm sorry if I disturb you.'

'Then why do you come?' Wow, the girl doesn't mince her words.

Jess waits a moment. How to edge forwards? 'It's very special, this beach. This bay. Kind of magical. It pulls me, probably the way it pulls you. Those sand dunes are like cliffs protecting the beach.'

'It's the same below your house.'

Has she seen my beach? It's tiny and covered in rocks. Of course she has. 'Not exactly. No, it's not the same. It's the same sea and the same sand, but it's not so dramatic and there's a different mood. Maybe some wouldn't notice it. Here...the scale is completely different. The sand and sea and sky...they're huge.'

The girl frowns, and glances up again. She looks like she's giving the words some thought, not shutting Jess out. 'I suppose.' She casts another quick, sideways glance. 'But this is my beach. You do have your own beach.'

'Yeah, but as I said, it's just not the same.'

'Like...does it matter?' Hurray. The girl has asked a question.

'If I tell you a bit about myself, Fenn, you may be less cross. OK?'

'Whatever.' The girl sighs long and hard. Like, get on with it then.

'OK. Well, I'm American.'

Another whiplash glance, the girl's eyebrows rising up, same as the women in the shop. But she says nothing. Jess knows she's not going to get the slightest help here.

'I'm a swimmer. Long-distance. I used to swim in the lakes back in Lake Placid near New York where I lived. I swam marathons.'

Silence. But Fenn is listening, the look on her face softer and more attentive. Jess meets her stare and holds it. Feels her interest.

'Something bad happened. An accident. I've come here to start over. Like turning a new page.'

'Oh.'

'And yes, I planned to swim a lot from my own beach, and then I found this one, and I suppose I fell in love with it. Can you understand that?'

'Yup.' More silence. Jess waits it out.

'But this is my beach. I've been coming here for ages. I like to be by myself. Swim by myself. You've spoiled that.'

Heavens, this girl sure is hard to win over. 'Look, I'm sorry I'm trespassing on your patch. And I do understand your wish to be alone...I'm hoping we might come to some... um...arrangement. A deal.' Jess waits.

The girl shrugs her shoulders, then shakes her head, then abruptly changes the subject. 'You haven't been on the island long, have you?' she asks, a drop of venom squeezed into the question.

Ah, the familiar dig. 'No. But I'm here now. And I intend to stay. And you live back there?' Jess turns and stretches her arm towards the almost hidden croft.

'Yup.'

'How long have you lived there?'

'Bit more than a year.'

'And before that?'

'A rented place. For a while.'

Ah...so an incomer just like myself, if we're talking island ways. 'So neither of us has been here that long. Where before, if you don't mind me asking?'

'The mainland. Edinburgh.'

'So you do kind of belong here. You're Scottish. More than an American anyway.'

'I suppose.'

'Do you like living on the island?'

Fenn gives an eye roll. Stupid question, Jess tells herself. Bad move, Jess. Don't treat her like a kid.

'OK, stupid question. I can see that you do. I do as well. It's...special, isn't it?'

Fenn doesn't deign to reply. They both stare at the sea. The emotional temperature has risen only a few degrees from its icy start.

'And you always come to this beach by yourself.' Jess says.

Another eye roll. 'Hero comes with me.'

Jess smiles. 'Great dog! I can imagine he looks out for you.'

'He digs.'

'And your parents?' Jess ventures.

'Dad's busy on the croft. Mum's a painter and used to come to draw things. We used to come together.'

'Why has your mum stopped coming?'

Jess senses a shutter coming down again, like that topic is out of bounds. 'Oh, she's painting other stuff. Anyway I'm allowed to come by myself cause Mum can see me from her studio window and I'll soon be ten,' Fenn replies, and at length compared to her other answers.

Jess loves the neatness of her arguments. 'I've seen how sensible you are in the water. That's good. We have to respect the sea.'

Fenn nods. Looks up for longer. 'So you are a real swimmer?'

'Yeah. It's what I do. Well...did.'

'Why did you stop?'

'As I said, there was an accident.' For a moment Jess is the one to look down, to gather herself, to not pull this girl into her personal tragedy. That wouldn't help one little bit.

'That's sad,' Fenn says, looking at Jess, not flicking her eyes back to the sea or the sand.

'Yeah, it was sad. And that's why I said I wanted to tell you a bit about myself. I swim here because it's peaceful and it gives me...um...some peace. I'm not explaining myself very well.'

'So it's not peaceful from your own beach?' Fenn asks, very straight.

'Not as peaceful.'

'I agree. It's not. I know your beach.' The layers of caution are finally falling away and Jess senses the girl there, at her side, fully engaged. Strike now, she tells herself. 'I've watched you in the water, and you are pretty good. Look, as I said before, I've come to strike a deal. Don't say anything please until you hear me out. I wonder if you'd like to swim with me…sometimes…and I could…um…teach you a bit of what I know. Maybe. If you'd like that.' Jess is crossing her fingers behind her back, hoping she's not misread the signals. This girl is a swimmer in the making. She loves the sea.

Fenn looks like she's considering this offer. Nods her head, and doesn't immediately speak. 'I'm only allowed to swim in the shallows,' she tells Jess, almost conversational now. 'Even though I do know the place pretty well. I know the tides and the currents. I know the sea's shallow for a long way out though I don't know exactly how far.'

'Well, that's all very useful.'

'But I don't know what it's like to swim out there. Where it gets deep.'

Jess hears the wish and sees the crack in the girl's armour. 'Look, here's my suggestion which you can accept or ignore. How about we swim together and I can take you further out.' It is tentatively suggested, but Jess sees the thrown back shoulders and the spark of interest that flashes across the girl's face.

'Really?'

'Sure. I'm a strong swimmer. I'm a qualified teacher and lifeguard. You'll be safe with me.'

'Like…we'd swim way out in the bay?' Fenn asks.

'Yeah. Once I've taught you a bit more technique.'

'Oh. Yes. Maybe.' It's said quietly. 'I'd like to swim better. I'd like to swim further out. I've never been out of my depth.'

'I've seen. You're absolutely right. But yeah, we can go way out once you're a bit more confident.'

Fenn nods. 'I want to hear what's under the water,' she

says, in a tone that speaks of secrets. 'I listen to the birds here. In the shallows I can hear the tiny fish rushing about... but way out...'

'Oh, a whole new world,' Jess agrees, and sees that she's played her trump card.

'Yeah. OK,' Fenn says, with a ghost of a smile.

'Of course I'll need to check with your parents first.'

'No need,' Fenn replies. 'I'll tell them.'

'I'd prefer to ask them myself. How about I come back with you one day?'

'Cool. How about now?'

Fenn is up on her feet and whistling for Hero who has been very busy some way off removing a ton of sand from a very deep hole. He comes when called, tail wagging, nose covered in sand and encrusted with a few tiny pebbles, and pushes his face into Fenn's waiting hands. 'Let's go,' Fenn says. To him and to Jess.

With Fenn striding in front, the three of them head back and climb the sand dunes. Jess is amused at the sudden urgency, after the days of stalemate and the hours of hostility. And maybe there's something extra for her in the bargain, not just the end of hostilities but the chance to do what she does well. Sure, she'll keep the girl company out there in the bay, but she'll also teach her what she knows. Yeah, she really does have a swimmer's build: skinny, long-legged, straight-shouldered. Just a matter of giving her the techniques so she's stronger..

But as they walk back towards the croft with its black-faced sheep peering over the fence at them, Jess's mood halts, shifts and wavers, turning on a coin from light to dark, something that happens often these days. Her hard-won victory strikes her as not quite so clever. With every step, her triumph leaks away like water in a trusty bucket that has sprung a leak. Pull yourself together, Jess. Now you have a girl to swim with. Tick. Now you can swim from the beach without her resentment. Tick. Now you have to go in the water even on days when you can't face it. Cross. Is this whole plan too rash? she wonders now. Too soon? Too ill thought out? C'mon, Jess, she chides herself. Spit it out. Say what's really bothering you. Yeah, OK. What if the flashbacks come back when I'm out there with the girl? They walk on, Fenn skipping along with the dog at her side, while Jess wrestles with the worries that crowd out her recent triumph. Just another mood swing like so many that taunt her when she least needs them. She can't take back her promise. If the past returns to trouble her, she must deal with it. Flashbacks are a just a sign that your grief hasn't healed, she tells herself for the hundredth time. They are normal. Deal with it. Jess searches for her happy face as Fenn pulls open the garden gate and turns to give her the warmest of smiles. Together they wade through the sea of feathered, pecking, scrabbling creatures that gather to welcome their girl.

Chapter 16

Julia

Julia alternates between brushing paint onto a canvas full of black-faced sheep, for who can resist their bemused expressions, and jumping up to check on her daughter down on the beach. It's turned blustery out there. The clouds are massing, dark with unspilt rain and a squall line is pencilled on the horizon. She'll come back if the weather turns nasty. They have drilled it into her. On the other hand, she is only nine. Or nearly ten, as she insists. Not quite a rebellious pre-teen, though signs of its imminent arrival are there in the sighs and slammed doors. There will be more of that. But her daughter will never shed her respect for the ocean, not even when the advice of parents is so very has-been. Yes, apparently that's the new word for anyone over twenty-five.

That woman is down there, Julia notes. Sitting by the rocks near the headland. Fenn has headed off in the other direction and her hunched little body, even from this faraway look-out post, exudes fury and frustration. Look at the way she's banging the sand with a stick and staring out to the horizon. Bad timing after her outburst. But what to do? Hamish is right that the woman has as much right to be there as Fenn herself. Julia sighs and goes back to the sheep, adding yellow ears.

So now what's happened? More time must have passed than she realised, as is often the case. Five minutes somehow becomes half an hour when you are painting black sheep with yellow ears. Amazing! The woman and Fenn are together, one sitting hunched and the other crouched at her side. And they seem to be talking to each other. Oh well. She'll no doubt get a report later. Back at her easel, Julia adds flowers for the sheep to munch, considering first what kind and what colour, and by the time she jumps up again, a human yoyo, two humans and a dog are heading in the direction of the croft. The woman, her head crowned with short, sand-coloured spikes, is bending down to the one with the long plaits.

'Hi!' Julia is on the doorstep, wiping her hands on her smock, unable to hide her look of surprise. With a quick head-to-toe inspection, she judges the woman to be about the same age as herself, strong, muscled, with pink cheeks and eyes the colour of a winter sea. She's in leggings and a thick fleece and looks immune to the weather. At her side, Fenn certainly doesn't look cross. Far from it.

'Hi! I'm Jess,' the woman says, offering her hand.

'Mum...Jess says she'll teach me to swim properly,' Fenn blurts out, eyes sparkling. 'And then I'll be able to go out of my depth. I can stop messing about in the shallows. You will say yes, won't you?'

'I must give you my qualifications first,' Jess adds quickly, exchanging a look of amusement with Julia. 'After all, it's asking a lot of you... a stranger turning up out of the blue

134

to suggest she takes your daughter swimming...I'd want to know a lot more.'

'Oh you're not a stranger,' Julia replies, intrigued by this surprise request after Fenn's endless complaints. 'I've seen you about, I know where you live, but our paths haven't crossed yet. It's remiss of me. I've been rude not coming to introduce myself when you're not far away. I apologise.'

'No...you are busy. You're a painter. Fenn has told me.'

'That's no excuse,' Julia smiles, warming to this woman's easy manner and generous spirit. 'But when I'm on guard duty at my window, I do see you in the water. You go miles out. You're a strong swimmer. I'm impressed.'

'It's what I used to do. Long-distance swims.' Jess leaves further explanations for another time.

'Well, do please come in. We don't have to discuss this on the door step. How about a glass of wine? I was about to knock off. Hamish will be back soon from his tree planting.'

'I'm all sandy,' Jess warns.

'And I'm covered in paint. Don't worry one bit.' And Julia is pulling off her smock and leading them into the kitchen.

It unfolds slowly, but without effort, the two women with their glasses of wine talking about simple things, feeling their way and not demanding too much, too soon. Fenn moves away to get a book about birds, but listens in.

'We got the croft about a year ago,' Julia is telling Jess, and Fenn has heard it all before so tunes out, but she can read and listen at the same time so is ready to jump back in when they get round to the swimming. Adults are so slow. 'We're rearing rare birds and selling their eggs,' Julia continues while Fenn rolls her eyes. 'We hope to build two cabins for tourists and that will bring in an income.'

'What about your paintings?' Jess asks.

'Oh...they bring in nothing. I'm not exactly famous.'

'Is that yours?' Jess asks, pointing to a big landscape that is recognisable as the beach they've just left.

'Yes. I started big, then my paintings shrunk.'

'Postcards!' Fenn flings into the conversation. 'Mum's painting postcards of pink chickens.' Then she turns back to her book.

There's a loose note of tension, of something unresolved, which hangs in the air. 'I want to build a garden,' Jess says, partly to change the subject. 'I make things out of whatever I find.'

'So you make sculptures? You're an artist too?'

'No, no,' Jess cuts in, shaking her head. 'I just mess about with driftwood and paints. I'm reading up on what might grow here and kidding myself I can do something with the land close to the cottage.'

They talk on for a while, neither venturing too far below the surface, not at this first meeting, knowing to keep things light and untroubled. Julia senses an easy assurance about Jess, as if she is comfortable in her own skin and feels she doesn't have to try. But she also hears an untold story, one with darker notes, and is curious.

'If you don't mind me asking, and I bet everyone asks you the same question, why have you come to the island?'

Jess puts down her glass. Breathes in. Breathes out slowly. 'It's a long story. I'm starting over. And this seems like a good place to do it.'

The blue notes are back, loud and clear. If she were painting Jess, Julia would reach for black, navy and darkest purple. 'So something happened?'

'Yeah.' Jess seems to gather herself closer, the brightness

of her conversation now tarnished and dull. 'Yeah, there was an accident. I've come here to forget, if I can. Or at least… get it in perspective. Hard to explain. To make a new life. If that sounds hackneyed…well, it is, but that's what I hope to do.'

'I'm sorry,' Julia says, seeing the speech bubbles above Jess's head that say, Please drop it now. This is not the time. But whatever could have happened?

'It's a harsh place,' Julia says tentatively, not wanting to cast further doubt on a plan that sounds as fragile as egg-shell. 'The winter months are difficult and dark.'

'So everyone says. Like the weather is the worst thing I'll face. But it's not.'

Julia picks up the warning. Again. 'Well, I'm glad you're prepared for it,' she says. 'The days can be very long and the sun struggles to rise.'

'You manage,' Jess says, tossing the cable back to Julia.

'Some days,' Julia replies.

Julia gets up to fetch the bottle from the fridge and refills their glasses. The two women exchange a look that speaks of acknowledgement and of something exchanged.

'Mum…' Fenn says, judging her moment well and jumping into the silence. 'Jess has come to talk about taking me swimming.'

'Oh sorry, Fenn. Sorry, we've been talking about all kinds of things.'

'I know. I've been listening.' And it's been really boring. 'But can we talk about swimming?'

Jess smiles at Fenn. 'Yeah. About the swimming,' she says. 'Seems we two might have fun in the bay together and I can teach this girl some technique.'

Not long ago, Julia thinks, Fenn was telling us she wanted

this woman confined to her own patch of sand, if not banished from the island, and now she's welcoming her with open arms.

'You can trust me to take care of Fenn,' Jess is saying. 'I'm a trained lifeguard as well as a strong swimmer.'

'I do trust you,' Julia replies. 'I know an excellent swimmer when I see one. It's a gift of an offer for Fenn. She's been fretting to get lessons because she's bored and making little progress. We've been very strict about her never going out of her depth, after all she's only nine.'

'I'm nearly ten.' Fenn says, on cue.

'And she respects all of that,' Jess says. 'I've never seen her do anything even slightly risky. She's very sensible and she's a natural in water. She'll be easy to teach. I'm looking forward to it.'

'Yes, Fenn is solid. I wonder if it's because she's an only child.'

'Or a well-behaved one.'

'Why are you talking about me as if I'm not here?' Fenn asks the two of them.

'Sorry,' Jess replies, pulling a rueful face. 'I guess I'm not very used to kids. Other than to teach. Adults, huh? No manners at all.'

'Sorry, darling,' Julia adds, putting an arm around her daughter's shoulders. She turns back to Jess. 'Thank you. I'd love you to give her some lessons.'

'So I can swim with Jess?' Fenn asks, looking from one to the other. It's taken them forever to agree something that's dead easy.

Jess is gathering her things, knowing to take her leave now that things are agreed and above board. She smiles at Fenn. 'Hey, kid, I'm a strict teacher. You may regret this.'

Fenn grins back. 'I won't.'

'Let's meet again some time, and you can report progress,' Julia says.

'Sure. I'd like that.' And to herself, And we don't always have to talk about Fenn.

When Jess has gone, Julia feels lighter and less troubled. It's been a pleasure to sit down and have a conversation with someone. She and Hamish walk in the same tracks, follow the same routines. Is Jess someone who just might be a friend? Way too early to know, but Julia's spirits lift. Other than her husband, she has no-one to talk to. Certainly no-one to confide in. Jess is an incomer like me, she thinks. Neither of us belongs here. That's a good place to start.

As soon as she has the answer she's been waiting for, Fenn excuses herself and runs off outside with Hero to check on her father's progress down by the loch.

'How many now?' she shouts as she reaches his side.

'One thousand, six hundred and forty, at a rough guess.' He puts down his pick axe which he finds more useful than a spade. At his side lies an enormous stack of saplings.

'Not many to go then,' Fenn grins.

He punches her lightly on the arm. 'Very funny.'

'Here, I'll help you,' she says, picking up the smaller of the two spades that lie on the ground and starts a fresh hole. 'We'll get the last thousand in before tea.'

'Did I see someone up at the house there?' Hamish asks, having bided his time, not wanting to interrupt. And not wanting to break off from his work.

'Yeah. Jess. Came to talk to Mum.'

'Who?'

'Jess. The woman who swims on our beach.'

'She's come to complain you've put the hex on her?' Hamish keeps it low key and hides his interest.

'No, no…I haven't, Dad! Jess is cool. She's going to teach me to swim better.'

Well, here's a turn up for the books, Hamish thinks, but of course he says nothing. Julia will tell him everything. Later.

Chapter 17

Fenn

At school, the clock on the wall ticks with spiteful slowness through the long hours. Fenn stares out of the window to watch the restless cloud formations, to check on gathering grey, to monitor the patches of blue that teasingly grow and shrink and grow again. Hey sky, stay blue! Bigger bits of blue, please. Bigger! The incessant staring out of the window inevitably invites Miss Murdoch's wrath but Fenn no longer cares. This is important. Dividing by seven isn't. She can do that. She plays the game, Fenn Against the Weather, as she wills and tugs it into the right shape. She knows how it can change from drenching rain to sun and back to rain in the space of an hour. She knows about gales that batter the place for days without respite until you wake up one morning to an eery silence where only hours before winds had howled round the house like banshees and rattled all the windows.

At last, at last, the bell rings and Fenn is racing away from the place that holds her with the thinnest of threads, then tapping her impatient feet on the floor of the school bus, and finally, finally she is allowed down and set free. A whoop of joy, and she's at the gate and the birds are gathered at her feet. Still she greets them all with affection and kindness, strokes a head, picks up a wriggling weight of feathers, and doesn't skimp on her task of getting them all to their bedtime places. This too is important. There's her dad digging holes in the same spot, and on the stairs in the house she can hear brush-on-paper noises from her mum's room. All is well. All is as it should be.

Fenn and Jess make no definite arrangements about days and times because each senses, rightly, that the other is happier with an agreement that is as fluid as the sea. Some days, Fenn finds herself alone on the white sand. No sign of Jess. The reason doesn't matter. It's not a problem because that's how it used to be and she steps backwards easily into that other time. There are rock pools to search, terns to watch while she sits very still with her back to the dunes, maybe a buzzard or an eagle circling further away, a moving dot on a big blue canvass.

Today when Fenn reaches the dunes and peers over, there is Jess sitting on the sand, her spiky fair hair already wet. So she's been in. My turn next.

'Hi,' Jess calls, fountains of sand preceding the stamp of a girl's feet and the skitter of paws. Hero is at her side first, licking her hand and shaking more sand all over her. She closes her eyes. 'Hey, stop! I can't see. Go and dig somewhere further away.'

'Hi,' Fenn says. And before she has even sat down, 'Can we go swimming?'

Jess laughs. 'Hello, Fenn. How are you? How was school? Yes, I'm fine, thank you. Yes, we can go swimming. Some of us have already been in.'

'Now?' Fenn asks, ignoring the teasing, stripping off her

fleece and clothes to reveal her blue striped swim suit. 'And the same as last time, can we? Just a bit out of my depth?'

'Hey, not so fast. The swimming coach decides on the programme. It's one tiny step at a time, you know, or rather one tiny stroke.'

'But we can go swimming...' Fenn is hopping from one foot to the other.

'Sure, whenever you are ready,' Jess relents. 'No point waiting until it clouds over, is there? Last one in is a sissy!'

Wow she's quick, that Jess, on her feet and pounding down the beach like she's in a race, Fenn already left behind despite a head start and her long-legged determination to keep up. How can she do that? Fenn wonders, stopping breathless and half bent-over in the first waves that roll up the shore. Five strides into the sea and she can dive like an arrow into the water. Anyone else would bang their head on the bottom.

'C'mon, Fenn!' Jess calls, powering on out. 'I'll wait for you where it's not quite out of our depth.'

'Coming,' Fenn shouts, and strides on, kicking up spray in sparkling bursts, a lot of space still between her and the woman who seems to be more fish than human.

About thirty metres out, they stop and move close together, Jess up to her shoulders while Fenn has to bob up and down to keep her head out of the water, and they smile at each other and Fenn catches the twinkle in Jess's eyes. She seems to feel the same as me. This is such fun.

'OK, time for lessons. Time to be serious,' Jess smiles.

'Ready,' Fenn replies, pulling down her smile.

'OK, same as last time. First, I'll hold your head while you let all your weight go and you float. And breathe. Remember?'

Of course she remembers. Fenn allows Jess to enclose her head in her firm hands, then kicks away her feet until her body is floating, floating, and above her there is only blue sky.

'Relax a bit more,' Jess instructs her. 'Flop. Breathe out. Shoulders less tense, Fenn. Spread out. The water will hold you and never let you go.'

It's easy, the way Jess tells it. The way she does it. It's like lying on a great big water cushion and she can be heavy and still and think of nothing much at all. The water is all around her, holding her, keeping her safe.

'OK, I'm going to let go of your head very slowly, and you stay exactly as you are. Good. Excellent. Excellent, Fenn. The water is solid. It can hold your weight easily. Trust it.'

Fenn squints just a bit to the side, sees Jess twist onto her back too, and the two of them are lying side by side, smiling up at the blue.

'Wow! Well done, Fenn. OK, I'll count to five and then you lift your head and put your feet down, Ready? One... two...'

And so it continues, the two of them inching further and further out, Fenn floating without help, both of them floating side by side.

'You see, it's important,' Jess tells her. 'You have to trust the sea. If you ever get into difficulties, you have to know you can do this...lie on your back...get your breath back... wait until you are ready to set off again.'

'But you couldn't stay like that forever?' Fenn asks.

'No, but you can float to have a rest. To take time out if you need it.'

'You don't.'

'I've done a lot more swimming than you, and I do float

on my back if I need a break. Or if I just want to look up at that enormous sky. OK, Fenn, I don't want you getting cold so how about we do some breaststroke before we head back?'

Fenn nods, thinking, 'This is awesome. This is the best thing that's ever happened,' while Jess starts to talk about rhythm and about being slow and sleek.

'I hope you're listening, Fenn,' Jess says, poking the girl in the ribs.

'Ouch. Course I am. You said, Push your arms straight out as far as they'll go then cup your hands and round and back, round and back...'

'And at the same time, the frog legs scrunched up, then around and kick!' Jess finishes. 'Start! Off you go! Slower, Fenn....slower...good...now you're getting a good rhythm. Trust the sea like you trusted it when you floated. Never fight it.'

Anyone watching from the tops of the dunes would see, at this point, a woman and a girl, swimming in formation, doing a slow breaststroke that seems to be effortless. They cut through the smooth water, on and on, until the woman says something, turns and starts to head back. The girl follows. And if the person watching has a pair of binoculars, she will see the grin on the girl's face and the smile on the woman's as they smoothly enter the shallows and carry on until both are bumping along the seabed in only inches of water.

'Awesome!' Fenn calls, her feet trailing in the soft sand and pebbles, her arms propping her up so that only her head is above the water. Two wet plaits hang down below the surface.

'Hey, well done,' Jess says. 'That was good work, Fenn.'

As if reluctant to leave the ocean, they stand and look out to where they have been, not that there is any way of knowing the exact spot. Then Jess puts an arm round Fenn's shoulders. 'C'mon. Out now. Can't have you getting cold. You're shivering.'

'Wait!' Fenn says, catching a whisper on the breeze, a ripple through the water. It's there. It's come back. She can hear it. 'One more minute, Jess. Please. You go on. I just want to remember where we went so I can think about it tomorrow when school is too awful.' Is that convincing?

'One minute,' Jess says firmly, and starts to walk up the beach to where Hero is still digging his hole to another part of the world.

The trail of notes that find her are as blue as the ocean is blue, as deep as the ocean is deep, a knotted thread of sound that is like nothing she has ever heard, not on the land nor in the sea. I didn't hear it when I was further out. Maybe I wasn't listening. I was concentrating on what Jess said, on what Jess told me to do, and I wasn't paying attention to strange sea sounds. Next time, I must somehow do what Jess tells me and listen. Hey…that'll be hard. Fenn shakes her head. Maybe impossible. I can only hear the creature who calls when I really really concentrate. Jess is calling from the beach but Fenn stays put to finish her train of thought. OK, stupid to try to do both together. I can only hear the blue notes when I'm alone and really really listening. So…I need to go swimming by myself. Next time Jess isn't here. I'll go out as far as I need to.

And then Fenn grabs an invisible knife and is severing this thought because Jess is shouting firmly, and beckoning, and Fenn must leave the sea and run up the beach and say nothing about hearing weird stuff out there.

'Coming,' Fenn calls, not wanting to cross Jess, and pounds up the sand. She's shivering but maybe not just from the cold.

And while Jess rubs herself dry, Fenn peels off her sticky swimsuit and imagines being with Jess much further, way out where the blue notes will travel over the water like skimmed stones, barely disturbing the surface, but holding the weight of the distance they have travelled. Then with a skip and a jump they'll be gone. They'll be clearer and louder out there. She's told no-one because who would believe her? She turns to watch Jess tugging leggings over damp skin and shrugging on her fleece. Jess gives her a broad smile. Yeah, she's my friend. She's cool, Fenn thinks and feels the bond that comes from their shared love of the ocean. But will she believe my story about a creature who sings to attract my attention? No, she won't believe me. Not even Jess will believe me. There's no-one I can tell. I'm the only person who knows that something out there needs help. That he's in trouble.

Chapter 18

The Whale

This is only his second migration but he has laid down memories of that previous journey in his skin and in his muscles. Stored away are the maps composed of bounced-back sounds so he knows for sure that he has left the arctic ocean far behind. Through slate seas with stripes of darker indigo, sometimes he swims alone. The water itself is different, empty and hollow-sounding. A place of shadows and ghosts. In the cold water of the arctic seas, a thousand species of fish and mammals swam alongside him and around him on their own life journeys and he was one of so many. The ocean was crowded and with every thrust forwards, he had company. Not so here. Small shoals of tiny silvery fish rush past with frightened eyes and are gone in a trice, before he can open his great mouth to swallow them. The seabed seems to be incomplete. Where have all the fish gone? he wonders. Something is not right. The sounds of the ocean are off key and out of tune.

He swims on for days and nights until he finds himself in water that is still shallower. He calls, letting the answering echoes tell him he is not so many miles away from small masses of land rather than a single, solid barrier. He does not know the word for island but he can create its shape and contours, its heights and depths. Clever at negotiating his way round land clusters, he changes tack again to put them behind him and at a greater distance. He must get no closer. He has swum round islands before on his previous migration, but not here. None of this is familiar. The signposts are missing. He swims on without the soundtracks of other species and the calls from his pod that would embrace him with notes of reassurance.

Even in these light seas, there is noise, though thankfully not the full throat clamour that bore down on him in the busy shipping lanes he has left behind. The sounds that accompany his swimming now are more of a rattle and buzz. Small moving things whizz over the water's surface making sounds that are metallic, shrill and high-pitched. And those same non-fish voices he heard before call out above the surface. He recognises their high pitch and the jerky rhythm. Sometimes a darkness rolls across the water above, blotting out the light and bringing a long silence, apart from the calls of the non-fish voices. Puzzled, and hunkered down in the depths, he turns his small eyes upwards and watches. It comes floating down gently, creating barely a splash, something huge and light, spreading ever outwards until a lot of water is covered with a criss-cross layer that floats and bobs with every wave. It doesn't block out the sun but breaks the light into a pattern of tiny squares on the seabed. He has no idea what it is. There is no-one to tell him that the clicking sounds he heard earlier are the engines of small fishing boats that make their way back and forth across the bay, the fishermen spreading their nets and returning the next morning to haul them back in, fish-filled and heavy. With uncanny insight, he knows that he must stay away from that stringy stuff on the water because how could he possibly make his way safely through it? How could he sky-dive without getting caught in its ropy folds? How could he set himself free if one of his fins or his tail became entangled?

Anxiety and fear hang heavy in this place. He can taste it on his tongue and smell it in the metallic and oily notes in the water. He hears it in the harsh click-click rattle of the moving things on the surface and in the silence and emptiness below where almost nothing swims. Dread lingers here. And a way of being that feels unnatural. That thing that floats just below the water's surface looks like it could lure and catch many creatures who would swim into an unnatural death. Death he knows as a part of the life cycle because he and others prey and feed off one another to survive. His kind can live for half a century but he has seen his fellow whales die before their time. Some, who are old and weak, sink to the seabed and lie there, a dead weight. Some are young but hurt and wounded, or unwell, and can't keep up with the others. There is nothing to be done. The other whales move on and leave behind their dying friends. What he senses here is a different kind of suffering and death. As he swims on, he sees more criss-cross shadows covering the surface of the water, and knows to keep away. There are many smaller fish and shelled creatures caught in those black squares. They are not yet dead, but flick their tails and thrash, trying in vain to get away, until their energy is spilled and they lie in the web, still and spent.

Needing to get away from an ocean mood that he would call sad, maybe ominous, if he had human words, he swims on, and for a while nothing momentous happens. With enormous grace, he arcs and falls, rises and dips, his body a coiled spring of fluid strength that takes him onwards without tiredness. The emotion that accompanies him is called loneliness but he does not know that name. On he goes.

He's nosing along in the depths, quite close to the seabed, taking it easy and diving gently after his energetic rush away from the place that seemed out of key when, up ahead, amongst the thin shoals of small fish, he sees a bigger, oddly moving lump that lists from side to side and sways in slow circles. What is it? It flails and twists in the water, floating up only a few inches from the seabed before falling down again. There it stays, and there it struggles, a living creature like himself, but wrapped up and contained. He swims up to it because surely it can do him no harm, stops and holds himself still in the water, nudges it with his nose, goes up close and stares into its eyes with his own tiny ones. He sees panic and pain. At once he understands its plight and is saddened. With slow shushes of his tail, he circles this fellow whale and smells that she is young and female. She is packed inside that thing he saw spread on the water, her fins and tail sticking out of its coils, the rest of her body encased and held tight. The smell that seeps from the pores of her skin is fear. And defeat. And helplessness. Along with the blood.

She cannot tell him her story. She can only show him its tragic ending. She is a young whale like himself, perhaps not wary and careful enough, perhaps misunderstanding the abundance of caught fish as free and floating and ready to be eaten, so she swam right into the net as it hung just below the surface. At first she snapped at the fish, content to eat.

151

She soared and dived back down. She did little leaps and arcs to catch the fish and eat her fill. But soon she too was trapped and all around her were walls of rope. She stopped feeding and searched for the exit but the more she twisted and turned, the more the rope tightened around her and held her fast. Terrified and desperate, she spun in faster, more frantic circles, flipped and flailed, snapped at the string as if there was a chance she could bite her way through it. But she was truly caught. Her energy gone, the trap of string and rope and small cork buoys pulled her down to the seabed, alive but soon to die. Every few minutes, she repeats the same futile movements, thrashing her bound tail towards inevitable and exhausted defeat.

When the fishermen pull up their nets the following morning, they will find her, exhausted and with cuts in her skin from her last futile efforts to get past the rough, scraping thing that holds her. She has struggled for ten hours, her movements serving only to further tighten and injure her, and she hasn't long left to live. Her breathing will be shallow. Her acceptance of her fate – for what other option does she have – will be complete.

The whale finds her in her final hours before she is hauled to the surface. All he can do is stay with her for a while, circling her and calling his messages of shock and sorrow. It grieves me that you are dying so young. It grieves me that you are dying this way, ensnared and in pain, cut and torn, alone and frightened. But I cannot help you.

Then he swims away. The shock of what he has seen stays with him, as does his failure to help her. Nor can he tell her story because his whale song can't detail man-made net traps nor the horrific deaths of sea creatures caught in them. What he can do is absorb the tragedy and take it onwards because he needs to warn the others, when he finds them, that new dangers lurk in the oceans. He will tell them in his own way. He will speak of a story that is a nightmare.

For now, dispirited though he is, he swims on and calls his signature notes, the same song he has sung over hours and days, across hundreds of miles, for what else can he do? His song is his own, its shape and pitch settled and fixed, but with some slight leeway for variation. This time, the part of the melody that dips into a minor key is more dominant, and louder. It is a subtle change, but a significant one. There is only so much adjustment he can make, but anyone with sharp hearing will hear that his song is a tone darker, a deeper shade of blue.

I am lost, he calls.

I am saddened by what I have seen.

I swim in waters that I do not know. They trouble me.

Can you hear me?

Are you listening?

Chapter 19

Jess

So far, so good, Jess thinks, as she gets ready to head for the beach a few days later. It's a relief to have broken through the barbed wire fence, waded through the trenches and made friends with the enemy on the next beach. She doesn't need that girl's anger and antagonism. It's enough of a challenge to get through each day with an ever-present, critical observer at her side, a second Jess who watches and waits for her to stumble. Oh stop following me about! Jess says. Go away and leave me alone. The move to the island feels neither good nor bad, not yet; in fact, it doesn't have much reality. Like the edges are still blurred. She's here, but that's about it. She sighs, then pulls herself up sharp before the critical one can jump in to register her glum mood. C'mon, Jess. There's a keen girl waiting for you on the sand. And she does look forward to being with Fenn. In the water, she slips back into the skin of the woman who spent her days in clear lakes, sometimes swimming for miles, revelling in her strength and fitness, sometimes training others to do the same. The echoes of her past are positive ones and that helps. Today, Fenn will be fizzing with excitement because she promised they would go further out into the bay. Oh to be nearly ten and thrilled about swimming out of your depth. She gathers her things and heads to her own beach, taking the route round the headland because the tide is far out today.

The tall skinny girl in jeans and a blue hoodie, dog cavorting at her side, appears at the crest of the dunes and comes sliding and skidding through fountains of sand. Plaits flying, she races over the packed crust to where Jess waits halfway up the beach, a smile on her lips at the child's predictable exuberance and energy. Hero gets there first though and gives Jess a licked greeting before he runs off to dig again. Hero digs. He doesn't do swimming.

'Hey!' Fenn calls, plonking herself down at Jess's side.

'Hey! Good day?' Jess asks.

'OK.'

Jess knows school is not Fenn's favourite place and that her real life happens on the croft, on the beach, on the island.

'Ready for the big dip?'

'Yeah, of course,' Fenn replies.

'Better get going then. We have perfect conditions. Calm as a mill pond,' Jess says, pulling off her jumper and joggers, folding them on top of her towel, and searching for a big stone to anchor the lot. She stands tall, stretches her arms and rolls her fine shoulders.

'Way out of our depth?' Fenn asks, as she too strips to her striped costume and folds her clothes just as Jess has done. 'Yeah?'

'Yeah.'

'Awesome!' Fenn replies.

'Last one in's a sissy,' Jess calls as always, and they're off, racing down the soft sand, and then jogging across the packed damp sand that seems to stretch for miles.

'Tide's way out,' Jess calls, not even out of breath. 'On we go!'

And finally they are at the edge of the tricking sea, still and lazy in that in-between waiting stage before the tide turns.

'Keep walking, Fenn. Let's head right out. No need to spend time in the shallows today. I can see you're ready for the deep stuff.'

'Awesome.' Fenn says again. It's obviously a favourite word.

From the slight change in the sea's colour, Jess knows exactly where the shallows run straight over a steep, vertical ledge but chooses to let the girl discover it for herself. She watches her with amusement, blithely bouncing along, toes touching the seabed, and then suddenly her head goes under. Like falling off a cliff only under water. Jess is ready, and alert, just in case.

'Hey! You didn't warn me!' Fenn splutters, as she surfaces, plaits soaked and face streaming. 'I wasn't expecting that!'

Jess is right beside her, treading water, ready to put out an arm to steady her, and laughing. 'Tread water, Fenn. Good. Yeah…like that. I thought I'd let you find out for yourself. You said you wanted to know where the water becomes really deep.'

'Yeah…well I thought I'd get some warning!' Fenn is grinning.

The girl has taken it well, and that's a good sign. 'I was watching and was right here,' Jess says.

'It was fine,' Fenn replies, quickly saving face, and changing the subject. 'How far out are we? About fifty or sixty metres?'

'And some. When the tide is out like now.'

'And the same right along the beach?'

'I guess so. Certainly in all the parts where I've swum. It's what you'd expect. The seabed runs downhill in an almost vertical dip parallel to the shore. From here on, you're out of your depth. Just remember that. But you can quickly get back into shallow water so there's no need to panic.'

'I'm not panicking.' Fenn replies, indignant.

'But listen, here the ground vanishes under your feet, and the trick is to predict it happening, and be ready. Ride the transition and move seamlessly into swimming. Don't be caught off guard.'

'OK, but let's swim,' Fenn says, already pushing off, and Jess hears her wanting to shed the lecture. But the girl has to know the sea is not always safe. She stays at the girl's side.

'Fine, we'll do breaststroke, slowly and steadily like I showed you so that you conserve your energy.'

'But we can just...like...swim?'

'Isn't that what we're doing?'

'I mean...no lessons...I mean...you sound like...you're giving me a lesson.' Fenn is finding it a bit hard to swim and talk at the same time, and her words emerge in little bursts.

'Hey, what's this? Are you tired already of me putting you through your paces?'

'No, of course not...I love all that stuff...only today...I just want to swim and swim for miles.' She stops to take some deep breaths and steady herself. 'Like there's no stopping ever...like we're the only creatures...in the whole wide ocean.'

'Sure. That's the plan,' she says. There's some subtext here that she can't quite pick up and interpret. Fenn's voice has a tiny edge of eagerness, even neediness, which she's trying hard to hide. Jess hears a request that if refused would cause her more than disappointment. She wonders why a long swim is not just fun but important, but decides to say nothing. Who knows what goes on in a nine-year-old's mind?

Jess is absolutely fine, swimming beside this eager child, her worries cast off and left on the shore like her garments, and then. And then. And then it's like someone suddenly changes the scenery, and she's in the next act, and it's not a fun swim with a kid at all but a woman moving towards a line on the water where her own demons hide and taunt her. Don't be stupid. That's much further out, she tells herself. Why are you thinking about that now when you're still so close to the shore? She will cross that line later, on the water. She will deal with it. Don't think about it, she tells herself. Enjoy being with Fenn.

The two swim on in a long silence broken only by arms slicing into the water, Jess more streamlined and sleek than the girl at her side who sometimes kicks and splashes, but she sorts out her limbs and carries on. Jess can see how determined she is to do this properly. And well. The girl is taking it seriously, and that's what matters.

'This is wonderful,' Jess calls, as much for herself as Fenn, still calming her own worries.

'Awesome!' Fenn calls back. Then, 'Jess?'

'Yeah...what?'

'Can we go on? I'm not tired.'

No, not at this very moment, but you will be. 'Sure, we can do that. What do you have in mind? Five miles?' Jess tries for her usual teasing manner, kicking away her upset as she kicks back the water from under her.

Fenn throws her a grin. 'You're not serious, are you?'

'This sea is not very well marked, is it?' Jess calls back. 'No rocks or buoys. Just blue water and more blue water. But OK, we can go a bit further. But Fenn, when I say we turn round, we turn round. Deal?'

'Deal,' Fenn says, spitting out a mouthful of water.

So she is tiring, Jess thinks. Just a bit further and then we'll call it a day. It's easily within her own comfort zone and if they stop soon, Fenn will know nothing about Jess's own ridiculous disquiet.

'We can pretend we're doing a marathon,' Fenn adds, guileless. 'That's what you used to do, isn't it?'

'Yeah. In another life.' Jess wants the subject closed.

'What do you mean?' Fenn is spluttering as she talks, and that gives Jess the excuse she wants.

'Oh nothing. It was quite a long time ago.' Don't ask me any more, kid. 'Now stop talking, Fenn, and concentrate on swimming. And breathing. We've come here to swim, not chat.'

Fenn is a sensitive girl, but this time she misses the cues and ploughs on. 'What was...the last marathon...you did?'

'I was training to cross the Channel.'

'Wow! Did you swim it?'

'No.'

'Hey, why not?'

Now Jess loses her rhythm and her head dips under. She's fighting rogue tears when she surfaces, but they look no different from drops of salt water.

'You OK?' Fenn calls, seeing Jess flounder.

'Fine. I pulled out. The night before...' Jess says, treading water. Then brightly, before any more can be added, 'Now, I think we should turn back. I think all this talking means you're losing interest.'

'Aw....no....sorry, Jess,' Fenn says, clearly crestfallen, but the girl is tiring, and Jess knows this is the point to call a halt. Before there's the slightest chance of risk.

'About turn!' she calls. 'Look how far we've come.'

And Fenn doesn't argue. She spins on a sixpence and heads for the shore.

Thank goodness, Jess thinks. Whatever it is she wants out there can wait. 'OK, next time we can go further.' What a pair we are. Here's me worrying about a ghost boat out there somewhere while I'm teaching a nine-year-old to swim, and there's the girl wanting to plough on forever because.... Jess can't finish the thought. Maybe she's imagined it all. Maybe there's no more to it than Fenn wanting the thrill of being a very long way out and the triumph of having done it.

As they head for the shore, Jess can see that she has judged it absolutely right. Fenn is slowing right down, her rhythm is ragged, and her breathing is loud. The last stretch is a bit of an effort, and then Jess's feet touch the sandy bottom, and she calls to Fenn to put her legs down too.

'Wow!' Fenn says, eyes sparkling but very out of breath. 'Cool!'

'Well done, Fenn. First time out of your depth and you did just fine. We went quite a long way.' Well, comparatively speaking. Not exactly miles, but far enough. Far enough to make me worried there for a moment.

'I know.' Fenn is bent over, still getting her breath back. 'Can we do that again?'

I knew she would say that. 'Sure. Maybe another lesson or two, and then after that we'll head back out.'

They've reached the shallows, and as they wander slowly back up the beach to their towels and clothes, Jess has no idea that Fenn has another agenda and that swimming far out into the bay is not an end in itself. A glance at Fenn's face tells her the girl is pleased with her efforts, but she can't see the other hope, the other longing. She sees the girl stop, turn her head and gaze out one last time, not to pat herself on the back, as Jess concludes, but to wish herself back out there in the water, further, where she can pick up the sounds that come when she can give herself completely to listening. Today they didn't come. She was too busy thinking about swimming.

'Can we do that again?' Fenn says again, this time with a note of pleading.

'Sure. I said we could. How about we work on your breaststroke tomorrow, if it's fine, and the next day we do another swim?'

'OK,' Fenn says, and Jess hears the hesitation. Maybe disappointment.

'Listen, Fenn. The deal was I teach you to swim. Remember?'

'I know but...'

'So how come you don't sound too keen?'

'I am keen. I am.'

'But...'

'But nothing,' Fenn says, turning to Jess with a small smile. 'Sorry. I'm just impatient. It was so cool out there and I want to go again.'

'And we will. But you need to do a bit more work first. I want you to be confident and strong in the water and that doesn't happen overnight.'

'I know. Sorry,' Fenn says again.

'It's fine. I understand your impatience. Let's meet again tomorrow.'

Fenn is gathering her things and heading back towards the dunes, her mood still somewhat subdued, and today Jess simply cannot read her.

'Thanks, Jess,' Fenn calls, as she climbs the sand slopes. 'See you tomorrow.'

Chapter 20

Beached

A bird's eye view would show two heads moving across the calm, blue bay, leaving only the faintest of traces in the water behind them. One twists to one side for one stroke as an arm comes up and over, then under for three as both arms repeat the perfect arched movement. Up for one, under for three. The other head lifts and tilts back for one stroke, then ducks under for two as arms push forwards and back in a wide circle, propelling the body forwards. Up for one, under for two. You could set a musical track to either with rhythms that would barely falter, as sure as drums on a song track. The bird might read confidence and certainty. If emotions could flow in a current, they would be the colours of joy and elation. They would be a perfect match. Colour-coded for harmony.

'Hey, you're doing good, Fenn,' Jess calls across when Fenn's head breaks the surface. 'Much smoother. Stronger. Can you feel the difference?' She's shown Fenn, not told her, what she means about rhythm and breathing and not resisting the water. She's held the girl's slight body until she's felt her relax into the element and accept whatever it brings her. She's watched Fenn move softly and without resistance through calm and rough, through bumpy little waves and slow rollers. Jess can't hep but give a little nod of satisfaction. That girl has done good. She's a natural.

'Yeah,' Fenn calls back, not even breathless. I know! It's dead easy today. 'Can we swim on?'

'Sure. But let's stop here and take a breather. Tread water, Fenn.'

'OK,' Fenn says, swimming up beside Jess, plaits streaming out behind her.

The woman smiles and pats the girl on the shoulders. 'Good work!'

'Thanks.'

Their two heads bob above the water while Fenn weighs up her chances of them going further. Yeah, til now it's been all about the swimming because she wants to make amends for appearing ungrateful the other day, but the other agenda is not far below the surface. If she just can persuade Jess. Pretend it's all about the swimming and the sea, and don't give the slightest hint there's anything else.

'Are you cold?' Jess asks, always checking.

'Nope. Nor tired.'

'Do you want to go on?'

'Yes!' Yay! She didn't even have to plead.

'The sea is magical today, isn't it. Very still. Let's go just a bit further, but Fenn, we turn back when I say. Same as always.'

'OK.' Fenn gives a mock salute, ducks her head and glides away.

They swim a few metres apart, Jess keeping pace with Fenn, a smile or a nod passing over the water when their two heads break the surface at the same time. Jess switches from her slow crawl to a somewhat upbeats breaststroke so that their strokes are synchronised. Her usual style is almost slow motion, but the girl is not there yet. As one, they stretch their arms to their finger tips, then pull them back as their legs kick and curl. It's elegant, efficient, and calming. Fenn keeps swimming, doing nothing to halt their journey. They are way out now and the shore looks miles away. On she goes, checking now and again that Jess is still with her.

*

It catches Jess completely off guard. As she breaks the surface to breath, she sees a glimpse of something ahead and dread disrupts her rhythm as surely as a freak wave. 'No!' she says. 'No, for fuck's sake, not now.' She shakes her head hard as if to dislodge a troubling thought, to get rid of the thing, and looks again. It wasn't there a moment ago but it's there now, a long way further out and to the west. Jess faces straight ahead and it's gone. Twists back, glances sideways and it's there. The wood is old and pale. Reflections waver all along the gunwales. The oars are shipped. There's no-one in it. The image isn't sharp, more like a reflection in the distressed glass of an old mirror. Or something seen through smoke and flames, wavy and blurred. Jess's heart beat revs into overdrive, her head goes under and she swallows mouthfuls of salt water before sorting out her flailing limbs. This is not like her. Careful, she tells herself, when she surfaces. Glancing across at Fenn, she is thankful the girl is totally absorbed in swimming ever onwards and hasn't seen her lose it. Stay calm. Stay in control. You have a child to look after out here. It's your imagination playing tricks. It's not really there. Or have they crossed her red safety line, the place beyond which she must never go, while she was busy admiring the improvement in Fenn's style. Maybe it's not a ruler-straight line after all, she ponders, maybe something that follows the snaking contours of the waves all along the shore. Oh Jess! Stop it! There's no such thing as a safety line, red or any colour. Or a ghost boat. Your memory is playing tricks. It's grief taking you by surprise. Like a dream. Like a nightmare. Like your nightmares. Strong emotions can do that. There's no rowing boat out there in the bay. Now stop all this and concentrate on Fenn.

But that thought only switches her into another anxiety. Should I even be even out here with a child? she asks herself. Maybe I'm not a safe pair of hands any more. And that's when she feels as if the whole delicate structure of a life tentatively rebuilt comes crashing down. Debris floating in the water all around her. If she were on land, she would smell the dust. She would pick her way through the rubble. Ha, Jess. It was a good move to set up these nice little swims in the bay, but maybe you aren't up to it.

That first time, about a year after the accident, off another beach in another country, the vision of that little rowing boat on the water shook her to the core and broke down the fragile defences she had tentatively built against her grief. She was miles out, as always, swimming hard and fast to get away from her memories when the memory itself came into view. That first time, she watched it because she didn't understand what it was. Watch it and it will fade and you'll know it's not really there, she told herself. It's your imagination. Nothing else. And so she trod water and thrashed about in the sea like a beginner, cold and trembling, not from the water but from the overwhelming waves of emotion. Her ability to deal calmly with unexpected events like huge freak waves deserted her in the face of a very different kind of shock. And when the scene started to unfold, bit by bit, scene by scene, it derailed her so much that she had to turn her back and leave it with the ocean where it belonged. That time, it was a struggle to get back to the shore. It was not just upsetting, it was dangerous. In that state, with adrenaline bleeding into the sea, there was a chance she might not have made it, an experienced swimmer though she was. She knows better than anyone the need to eke out your resources, your physical and emotional stamina, because you always have the journey back and the sea can throw its own surprises. You keep something in reserve, just in case. A sudden strong gust of wind can stir up the ocean so that jagged waves knock you about like a helpless spinning top and pull you under, but she can deal with that and right herself. The vision of the boat was something else. Her confidence was punctured as surely as a nail in a car's tyre.

Knowing this, knowing her vulnerability, knowing that she is responsible not just for her own survival but that of a child, Jess turns to check on Fenn. The girl is floating on her stomach, her head under and plaits streaming out behind her, a gentle rippling on the surface a giveaway for the slow and easy swish of her legs. OK, she's fine. Jess treads water. She takes big, slow breaths until her body is quieter, her heart less skittery and she is confident she can swim back. And swim back with a child who has gone as far out as she should, maybe a bit too far. Fenn might tire suddenly or get cramp and Jess needs the reserves to tow her back to the beach, if needs must. In normal circumstances that would be a cinch. Jess chides herself that they haven't yet practised towing so that Fenn knows what to expect and can relax into someone dragging her through the sea. When she was training, she had to tow big dead-weight men and that took strength and technique, so a girl of Fenn's build is easy peasy. These rambling thoughts and precautions of the professional swimmer she will of course hide from the child. It's fine that Fenn thinks of her simply as superwoman. Fenn's growing confidence is about not feeling anxious. Jess is encouraging a healthy respect for the sea, but not a fear of it. Swimming is a quirky, psychological thing and these early stages need careful handling. Jess makes her way over to the girl, calmer now and more composed, but still shaken.

*

Lying very still, and making as little movement as possible, a few inches below the water where she can poke her head out quickly to take a breath, Fenn is trembling too but with excitement. The call came almost immediately after she ducked her head under and while she lay floating on the surface, still and quiet. Yes, she can hear it, this time louder, and more sustained. Wow! It's magical and eerie. She imagines the song carried on the current, through forests of kelp, past shoals of silvery fish, above stacks of shiny shells, a song like no other she has ever heard. No human could make that sound. It has a dreamlike quality, the sort of sound you might imagine when you are sitting alone watching the sea on a moonlit night and letting your imagination conjure up kelpies and mermaids. After some trills and clicks, comes a long-held note the colour of loneliness. It is plaintive. And it is sure and strong. It comes from the lungs and throat of a huge creature. It gives her goosebumps, and not from the cold.

Whoa! Fenn tells herself, putting her head out for a gulp of air. You're making this up. You have no evidence that the song...oh don't be silly, just call it the noise...is anything other than something on the shore or something freakily amplified on a boat. Wind can sound weird and ghostlike when it bends and blows round headlands and the edges of islands. She looks across at Jess who is treading water. Fenn is deeply lost in her own thoughts but even so, she registers that Jess looks a bit troubled. Her face is not held up in bliss to the big sky. But Fenn has more urgent things to ponder. Jess can take care of herself, that's for sure. She breathes, dives under, and waits again. And there it is. Is it really louder or is she persuading herself it is? Down there, circled and enclosed by a shimmering stream of notes that are blue and deep like the ocean, she makes up her mind after days of dithering. She surfaces, shakes her head to empty it of being sensible and stupid stuff like that, and goes down again. This time she is ready, wide open and receptive to whatever comes. The soaring notes reach and touch her and she accepts them without question or doubt. She takes them as a gift, this call across miles of water. I hear you, she says. I know you are there. I don't doubt you. I won't leave you. If her eyes weren't already wet, they would have filled with tears.

What she does next is not planned. It happens. She goes up for a deep breath, dives down as low as she dares, closes her throat, opens her mouth and calls back. She tries for the same pitch and the same long-held sound, though what comes out sounds like she's blowing down a hollow tube, only more wobbly. That won't travel very far. She hangs on to the bubbly note until her lungs are about to burst, almost a whole minute by her waterproof watch, then she heads up again for air. She is still trembling, not from the cold, though keeping still has chilled her, but from the wonder of what might be.

*

While Jess softly treads water, calming herself, one eye on Fenn, she picks up a strange noise like someone crooning or hollering under water. Surely not Fenn. But that's where it comes from. The bubbly echoes, like someone blowing down a trumpet under water, float up from the place where Fenn's legs kick in slow motion. What is the girl doing? Singing? Really? What new game is this? The singing comes to a halt and the face of a breathless girl pops out of the water, a broad grin on her face. A light in her eyes. Jess swims over to her.

'What was that?' Jess asks, very glad of the distraction.

'New way…of holding…my breath,' Fenn replies, her eyes gleaming, her fingers crossed because she's telling a lie.

'Singing under water?'

'Sure. Why not? Anyway…it's not singing…it's holding one note…for a long time. Good for the lungs.' The words come out in little breathless bursts as if she's been breathing overtime down there.

It's almost convincing, but not quite, Jess decides. This girl sure is full of surprises, and just now she's twirling in circles at her side, a fizz of jubilant energy. She can't be that excited about making blowy noises underwater. Can she?

'Hey, stop spinning and save your energy for the swim back.'

'OK.'

But Jess can't manage the upbeat mood nor join in some new underwater game. 'Fenn, we need to get back. Come on. Now.'

Fenn doesn't hear the harshness and puts up no resistance. No arguments, Jess always says. You must head home when I say. They turn for the shore, and Fenn is swimming well, as if fired up with fresh energy. Well, whatever she was doing, shouting and singing under water, seems to have pleased her. There's no accounting for nine-year-olds. But the girl does slow down about half-way back, despite her determined efforts to keep going, and Jess calls across. 'Hey, Fenn, take it easy. Not far now.'

'I'm fine,' Fenn calls back. 'Just a bit...tired.'

'No wonder. That was one long swim.'

'I know,' Fenn calls back. 'Awesome.'

Back on the shore, they wrap themselves in towels and lie flat on the sand to get their breath back. The tingling in their limbs changes to fizzing as sensation rolls back, and they know to wriggle and get warm. Jess flaps her arms. Fenn kicks her feet. The silence is long, each lost in her own thoughts. Gulls wheel over the ocean, their calls loud and shrill.

'Got the sea to themselves again,' Jess says, looking up.

Sure, Jess, if you say so. I doubt it though. She pulls herself up onto her elbows and scans the ocean. Nothing but water. Empty blue as far as the eye can see. 'They've got the sky to themselves. I'm not so sure about the ocean,' Fenn replies, a smile on her lips, but Jess is too preoccupied to see the cue.

Chapter 21

Fenn

The plates are piled by the sink. The table cleared. Hamish cradles a whisky while he pokes the peat fire. Julia has emptied the end of a bottle of red. Hero has been fed and lies curled at Fenn's feet. She has told them she wants to talk to them and that it's important. And so they have gathered.

'OK, where do you want to start?' Julia asks. 'Is this about Miss Murdoch?'

'No. It's about the whale,' Fen replies, and stares hard, daring them to question her. Which of course they do.

'Whale?' Julia and Hamish ask in unison.

'Chapters ahead of us, Fenn,' Hamish adds. 'Fill us in.'

Fenn takes a deep breath. 'OK, I heard something under the water when I was swimming with Jess a few days ago, and the next time we went swimming I heard it again, and I thought it was some sea creature or something, maybe a dolphin, except I don't think they make noises, only now I know it's a whale.'

There's a moment's silence in which Julia and Hamish don't dare exchange puzzled looks.

'So have I got this right?' Julia asks with deliberate tact. 'You think you heard something in the sea and you think it sounds like a whale?'

'I don't think. I did hear the sound. The last two times when we went quite far out. It's a whale.'

Julia doesn't argue. She knows to take Fenn seriously, but she also reminds herself that her daughter is nine and has a very vivid imagination. 'Did Jess hear it too?'

'No, she didn't have her head under the water like I did. Not for as long. I was listening out for the sound. She wasn't.'

'But you told her?' Julia asks gently. You don't set fire to a child's dreams, she tells herself.

Fenn can hear her mum treading on eggshells and would grin to herself at her choice of words if this were not so serious.

'Nope.'

'Why?'

Fenn shrugs. 'I suppose I wanted to think about it myself for a bit longer in case I was being silly. In case I was wrong.' It's the truth and not the truth.

There's another silence while Fenn dares her parents to tell her not to talk nonsense. She can almost see their brains whirring round, like one of those machines in an arcade.

'What makes you think it's a whale, Fenn?' Hamish asks.

'Because I know the kinds of sounds whales make.'

'And does knowing the sounds mean there's a whale out there in our bay?'

'Maybe.'

'Sorry, but I'm not entirely persuaded.'

Fenn isn't entirely persuaded either but what other reason can she give grown-ups? She can hardly say some weird sixth sense tells her it's a whale and she feels very very sure.

They won't believe her. 'It could be a whale, couldn't it?' she asks, looking from one parent to the other, trying to hide the pleading in her voice and in her eyes.

Hamish picks up his glass, sips his whisky, puts it down. 'First, sorry to pour cold water on all this excitement, Fenn…'

'That's a terrible pun, Hamish,' Julia interrupts, digging him in the ribs.

'Sorry. Unintended,' he says, with a twitch of a grin. 'Fenn, let's do a reality check here. We can come back to what you heard in a minute. First, whales don't swim in these waters. As far as I know, the ocean is way outside their territory. There's never been a sighting off any of the islands.'

'But one could have got lost…'

'Hang on. Hear me out. Second, humans don't easily hear their calls. Not without special equipment. And I think you would have to be much further out. I'll have to do some searching online because I've forgotten this stuff. And I'm out of date. We'll go and look on the internet, shall we?'

Fenn doesn't want to find out that humans can't hear whales. This has turned into homework about facts and information, as she knew it would if Hamish had anything to do with it. It's miles away from her what if story, a magical story about the sea and a sound, an unusual sound that drifts through oceans.

'Just supposing you did hear a sea creature, that's pretty special, even if it's not a whale,' Julia says, and Fenn hears her effort not to be dismissive but to put an end to the subject.

'That's not what this is about, Mum.' Fenn tried not to shout, but really! It's not like, 'Oh Fenn may have heard some sea creature. How wonderful. Now we can forget all about it.'

'So what is it about, Fenn?' Julia asks, trying to be more serious.

That's when Fenn blurts it out. 'The call sounded like a whale who was in trouble. His song was saying he was in trouble.'

Again, the grown-ups exchange a look and this time Fenn doesn't miss it.

'You don't believe me, do you? You think I'm just a kid making it all up. Well, I'm not! I know what a whale sounds like because when I came back from the beach that day and while you two were still busy, I listened to recordings of sea creatures on YouTube and the songs of the whales are exactly like what I heard… the same amazing sounds.'

'Hold the horses,' Hamish says quietly, a hand on Fenn's shoulder. 'We're not saying we don't believe you. What I am saying is that it's not very likely that there's a whale out there and so what you heard could have been something else. Mechanical noises from the land or noises on a boat. Sound gets distorted across water.'

'There weren't any boats.'

'You can believe that you heard a whale,' Julia adds.

'Mum, you keep missing the point! I'm telling you it might be a whale!' Fenn shouts. 'Why can't you believe it?'

'Listen, Fenn,' Hamish says, looking at her. 'We're not saying it's true or not true. We don't know. We don't have enough evidence. All I'm saying is that the chances are pretty slight. OK?'

They don't understand, Fenn thinks. They really don't believe me. She heaves a huge sigh and puts her head in her hands.

'Why do you think the creature is in trouble?' Julia asks, hearing her daughter's despair at what she has said. She's intrigued too, despite Hamish's cool reasoning.

'Because it sounds sad.' Fenn's voice is quiet and sulky.

'Whale songs do sound sad,' Hamish tells her. 'They're renowned for it. Like elegies.'

'Like what?'

'Um…songs for the dead…but the thing is…I mean you wouldn't be able to tell the difference between a whale's ordinary song and a whale's sad one because both sound poignant. Maybe a whale expert might be able to interpret emotions but…'

'I'm just a child so I can't.'

'No untrained adult or child can, Fenn. It's relatively recently that we've started to understand the language of whales and what it means.'

Fenn sighs. Hamish is unpicking her dream piece by piece. And a tiny part of her can follow him and agree. In some ways he is right. She tries one more time. 'Just supposing there is a whale out there, and just supposing he's in trouble. And we do nothing!'

'That's a lot of supposing,' Hamish cuts in, calm but firm. 'Come on, Fenn. Let's go and see what we can find out.'

At the screen, they discover, as Hamish knew they would, that with a single exception whales have not been sighted, nor found beached on the Western coast of Scotland nor anywhere on the Scottish islands. He reads the text out loud to Fenn. 'Their migration journeys take them from cold northern latitudes of the Arctic to the warmer tropical waters of the Pacific or Mexico or Hawaii where they breed and calve. During their migrations, they travel up to five thousand kilometres.'

Fenn listens, knowing he's arming himself with reason and information.

'Says here they start their migration in September,' he adds.

'That's now.' Fenn jumps in.

'That's when they start. It says it takes six to eight weeks.'

'But not exactly. Not every single whale sets off at the same time.'

'Their patterns of migration are fairly fixed, I suspect.'

'Well, just suppose they set off a week early and they've swum for four weeks…and one whale is out there and coming this way in the next days. It's the end of September. It's possible, Dad.'

What to say to this child? Hamish asks himself. It would be harsh to kill her fantasy dead but equally unkind to let her hang on to an impossible dream. No whale is swimming towards a small Scottish island at the end of September. He decides to let it hang. She's a sensitive, thoughtful child and sometimes needs time to work things out for herself. He decides to change tack.

'OK, let's check if humans can hear whale songs.' He types in 'human hearing, whale song' and up come dozens of sites. He opens the first, and reads aloud. 'Right, it says here that human hearing is in the range of about twenty hertz to twenty thousand hertz but we hear most sharply in the range of a hundred to four thousand.'

'What's a hertz?'

'A hertz is a measurement of sound. Let's look up the range for whales now. OK. Here we go…it says that the lowest sounds can last up to several minutes and they vary from twenty hertz to twenty-four thousand hertz. So calls from big whales are on the cusp of our hearing.'

Fenn takes a moment to absorb this. 'What's cusp?'

'The edge.'

'So the whale's song is lower and much higher than our hearing.'

'Exactly.'

'But there's an overlap in the middle.'

'Right again. Which means...'

'That it's possible to hear part of the whale's song.'

'There's more here, Fenn...' Despite himself, Hamish is drawn in, fascinated, wanting to read on. He is a facts sponge when it comes to birds, animals and all wild creatures. 'It says, A whale will typically repeat the same phrase over and over for two to four minutes. This is known as a theme. A collection of themes is known as a song. The whale song will last up to thirty or so minutes, and will be repeated over and over again over the course of hours or even days.'

'That's what I heard! That's what I heard!' Fenn is bouncing on her chair. 'Dad, I heard the same song every time I put my head under water.'

If it were a football match, the score would probably be Fenn 3 Hamish 2 and that's good enough for her. She shrugs her shoulders in satisfaction. Turns from the screen to face her father. 'So it's not totally impossible I can hear a whale.'

'Not impossible if you happen to live in the Pacific, say the southern corner of Australia,' Hamish replies. 'Shame you live on a Scottish island.'

'Oh Dad! You spoilsport!'

'Just teasing.'

Or is he? Hamish has to admit that it is just about within the realms of possibility that with her very acute hearing, Fenn has picked up some creature calling or singing in the ocean, but a whale...not very likely. Not at all likely.

'Wait...what's that, Dad? It says, "the world's loneliest whale". Click on that.'

He does, and up comes a page that they both pore over.

'Oh my goodness, Dad, listen…it's about a weird whale that calls at a higher pitch than other whales, at fifty-two hertz which is unusual. He is the only whale they have found that calls at this frequency. Scientists have named him the world's loneliest whale. Wow! So there are whales that have unusual songs that maybe other whales don't hear.'

'He's just one, Fenn. Poor chap.'

'Oh here's something else…it says that this whale's song is a bit higher than the lowest note on a double bass. We can hear the double bass, Dad.'

All very interesting but they are heading back to the realms of make-believe, Hamish decides. Time to stop, before Fenn decides this lonely whale has found its way to Scotland when it has only been heard in Alaska and California. 'Tell you what…I'm over at Dan's tomorrow helping with fencing. He used to be a coast guard on the mainland. He probably knows about such things. How about I ask him if whales have ever been seen or heard in these waters?'

'But don't tell him what I've told you.'

'Why not?'

'I'd rather you didn't.'

Hamish hears that Fenn doesn't want to be proved wrong and have her story crushed by a stranger. Not yet anyway. 'I promise,' he says. 'Now please go to bed, Fenn, and see if you can find the OFF switch for that very busy brain.' He kisses her flushed cheek and she wipes it away with the back of her hand. Reluctantly she gets off her stool, and walks out of the room while Hamish stays at the screen, finding more fascinating facts.

At the kitchen door, Fenn hovers and waits for Julia to

turn from the sink where her pink-gloved hands are in the frothy washing-up.

'Well?' Julia asks. 'Has your killjoy father got rid of your whale?'

'Nope,' Fenn replies, with a broad smile.

'I'm so glad. I would very much like there to be a whale out there off our beach.'

'Except he would be lost,' Fenn tells her. 'Shouldn't be there. It's not on his route.'

'Oh. In that case, if he turns up on the beach, we'll just have to rescue him, won't we? Good night, darling.'

Fenn gives her biggest eye roll. 'Night, Mum,' she says through gritted teeth. Why can't grown-ups take their kids seriously, she wonders as she heads upstairs. It's not funny saying, We'll just have to rescue him! That's gross, Mum!

Chapter 22

Fenn

Fenn is wide awake and sitting up in bed. Damn, it's raining. She rubs a hole in the misty windowpane with her pyjama sleeve but what's the point? There's nothing out there but drizzle and clouds hanging like wet washing on a line.

At breakfast, she says little. She might as well hold up a notice: No swimming today. By the time she runs for the school bus, the cloud base is so low she seems to be walking through it and the rain spits cold, sharp needles in her face.

As the eternal hours tick by, Fenn sighs and fidgets and scowls out of the streaming classroom window. Chanting silent nonsense spells, she wills the weather to change, and conjures up magical tiny patches of blue behind the wall-to-wall grey.

And then she gives up, removes herself from the classroom, takes herself far away to the beach and into the water. Remember, she tells herself. Her head was down, her breath held and that's when the sound came, stronger, clearer, louder. I know, she says to herself, or maybe to the creature who waits out there. But with sureness comes frustration as she returns full circle and is back in the classroom with the rain still lashing outside. How can the weather do this to her after the last sunny days! It's totally spiteful.But she's been brooding and plotting. And then at long last the bell goes and she cuts herself off from it all, slicing between the now and the next with an imaginary knife whose blade is clean and sharp.

The bus ride home she endures as usual on the back seat with the other kids ignoring her, and as soon as the bus pulls to a halt outside her croft, she's making her way down the aisle and jumping down the steps. The driver gives her a nod and raises his eyebrows, perhaps telling her he knows she's finding it hard. She nods back. Mustn't be rude. It's not his fault school is rubbish.

Fenn sheds her school uniform, pulls on home clothes, shrugs on her anorak and pulls on wellies and is back outside and soaked in minutes, Hero at her feet intent on tripping her and sending her headlong into the mud. She slots straight into her afternoon routine, but she is half absent and feels guilty that she is not putting her all into her chores. An outsider wouldn't notice any difference. Maybe not even her parents, should they be watching. Hero is bounding between her while Fenn runs round the croft, cajoling and herding the flapping creatures to their night-time places. It looks the same as every other afternoon but Fenn knows that she's a bit brusque and not paying enough attention to the birds. Today her mind is not on the job. Concentrate! she tells herself as Madonna does an easy runner and the geese scatter in all directions when she's looking the wrong way. 'OK, OK, I hear you, Runner Bean. You want to be picked up,' she says, unable to ignore the duck that is flapping and squawking around her ankles, but she knows that they know she is short-changing them today. The creatures that float through her mind don't have webbed feet or beaks and don't even live on the land.

Inside again, damp outer garments off and hung to drip on the pegs, Fenn runs up the bare wooden stairs. Her mum's door is ajar and there is Julia, spinning round on her stool to welcome her with a smile. Behind her, on the easel, is a fair-sized canvas with the first washes of sea and sky. A big painting, Fenn notes with quick satisfaction. That's good.

'Hey, Mum!'

'Hi, Darling. How's things?'

'I'm good. Done the birds. Have to go and do homework now.'

Fenn forces her voice to be upbeat in an attempt to hide her plans. Am I convincing?

'Fine. Hamish is outside...' Julia says.

'Planting trees,' Fenn finishes.

Julia grins. 'I was just going to say the computer is free if you want to use it.'

'Cool. I do.'

'So what's the homework today?'

'Oh just stuff.'

Julia gets up and moves to the window where the view is blanked out by the veils of rain. 'No swimming today, then, Fenn. And Jess hasn't been down either. At least I haven't seen her.'

'Hmm...I wonder why?'

'This weather's enough to even put Jess off.'

Fenn lets it lie. Rain wouldn't stop her. But Jess isn't her concern today.

'I've decided to paint something for her,' Julia says, returning to her stool. 'To thank her for teaching you to swim.'

Fenn glances at the easel again and clocks the outlines of islands rising behind the sea. It's the view they see when they sit on the sand.

'Cool. Jess will like that.'

'Do you think? I hope so. I'm enjoying painting it.'

Yup, her mum looks happier today. 'OK, see you later.' That's enough about painting.

'Sure. I'll be down to start dinner in a while. Pasta and tomato sauce tonight.'

'Great.'

'I just want to add another wash to the...'

But Fenn has gone, taking the stairs two at a time. Julia smiles. That child!

Fenn's fingers are fast on the keyboard. She clicks on Chrome and types in sea mammals, songs. Wow! There's a ton of stuff here. There are scientists all over the world doing work and making recordings. They know so much. OK, here's a summary: The sea mammals most known for their songs are whales. Humpback whales use ultrasonic sound systems to communicate.'

Yeah, right, whales sing! Thought so. What kind of a song? Why do they sing? Fenn reads on, opening page after page, scrolling down to find what she's looking for. It's slow work because there is so much small print and the words are long and difficult. So many words she's never heard of. She opens a new document in Pages and types WHALES at the top. She copies and pastes a piece from Wikipedia. It's a bit hard but she can understand enough to make her very very sure. Her face glows with the effort and her heart sings like the whales she is reading about. 'Baleen whales use sound for communication and are known to sing, especially during the breeding season. Blue whales produce the loudest sustained sounds of any animals: their low-frequency moans can last for two minutes and reach almost 190 decibels. They can be heard hundreds of kilometres away.'

Fenn sits back on her stool, takes a deep breath, and lets all this information sift down, like sand running through an hourglass. So much to find out. She had no idea. Well, why should she? She's never thought about whales before. She reads on, clicking from one article to another, taking from them what she can understand. A new window brings her this: 'Studies on the brains of humpback whales revealed spindle cells, which, in humans, control theory of mind. Because of this, it is thought that baleen whales, or at least humpback whales, have consciousness.'

Hard to follow. What is theory of mind? And consciousness? In yet another window she looks it up in a dictionary. 'Knowing, being aware, having feelings, capable of thought, intelligent.' OK! I get it. Whales can think and feel. They are clever. They understand their world. And their songs are not just noises, they mean something. So I've not been making it all up. There is a whale out there, and he is singing and calling, and he may be sending a message. Maybe a baleen. Clicking back to the screeds of URLs about humpback whales, she finds YouTube sites which play recordings of whales singing. Then she hesitates. Hang on a mo, Fenn. Supposing I listen, and supposing it's not the same? Supposing it's completely different. But she's been reading songs and moans and sighs and that's what she heard. Clicking on the first one, she inserts the connector of her headphones because she doesn't want anyone else to hear, jams the headphones on her head. Two fingers of both hands are tightly crossed. She presses PLAY.

Shivers run down her spine, icy water over a ladder of bones, when she hears the first blue and silver sounds. The soundtrack is louder and clearer, but the same. Exactly the same. The first aching, soaring call thrills her to her soul. It has a shape like an arrow rising and falling in slow motion across the sky. Like a shooting star. It contains all the violets and indigos of the rainbow. It could be a ghost wailing or a mermaid singing, but it's none of these. It's bigger, wider, more everywhere. She's never heard anything like it before. The whale's song is its very own and Fenn can think of no comparison. After the held note come clicks and trills, like teeth rattling or the kicking engine of a small motorbike fading into the distance. The song repeats, over and over, listen to me, listen to me, I am here. If she were to draw it, she would absolutely have to crayon outside the lines because this sound is not tight or contained. It spills and soars. It is huge.

*

'Dinner's ready!' Julia calls from the kitchen. 'Hurry up, everyone.'

Fenn is at the bottom of the ocean and barely registers either her mother's voice or the sound of the front door closing or the thump of Hamish's boots kicked off in the hall. Large clockwork mouse, that father of hers. That's what she would think if she were not lost in another place.

'Fenn! Dinner!' Julia calls again, adroitly tipping a mountain of tagliatelle from a pan of boiling water into a large sieve balanced over the sink before she returns to the stove to stir the thick sauce. She checks the parmesan is on the table. Yes, she did that.

'No daughter?' Hamish asks. 'Never mind, I'm here and I'm very hungry.'

Julia smiles at Hamish, kisses his cold cheek, and slips out of the door while he opens the fridge and reaches for a beer. In the study, her daughter is absolutely still, staring at a screen that has images of whales. Julia recognises the big split tails gleaming black and shiny.

'Fenn…'

Still no response.

'Fenn, dinner's ready. I've been calling you…'

'It's a whale!' Fenn announces, throwing down the headphones and twisting in her chair to say what she needs to say very loudly, as if to an auditorium. She gazes at her mother with eyes that are round and glittering. 'What I heard…is a whale.'

There's a long, breath-held silence. Hamish comes up behind his wife, looks at his daughter, looks at the screen, picks up vibes that are wire-taut.

'A whale,' he says quietly, one eyebrow raised. 'Did you just say you heard a whale?'

Fenn nods.

'On YouTube?'

'Yes. No. In the sea. Here. Off the beach.'

'OK, listen. This sounds serious. Am I right?'

Fenn nods again.

'Right. Here's a plan. We go and eat dinner. Then, we sit round the kitchen table and you can tell us about the whale.'

'Why not now?' Fenn asks, excitement colouring her cheeks cherry red.

'Because I can't manage to get spaghetti and tomato sauce into my mouth and talk about whales at the same time.'

'Tagliatelle,' Julia says.

'Pasta,' Hamish replies.

Fenn rolls her eyes and climbs down from the stool. What hope they will understand?

And so while they eat, all of them too hungry to talk about anything much, Fenn worries that she has spoken too soon. The words spilled out after she heard the songs. Now she has to face the inquisition. They won't believe her. No-one will. Except maybe Jess, and she's not here. She's not even been to the beach today. Her jubilation sinks and subsides to a forlorn dismay. Stupid of her to have blabbed. She imagines pulling a zip across her mouth, but it's too late now.

After dinner, Hamish fetches his dram and sits at the table. Julia is clearing up but turns and leans against the sink when Hamish speaks to Fenn.

'Do you want to talk about the whale songs?'

'No,' Fenn says, glaring at him.

'That's not what you said earlier.' Hamish is taken aback by this sudden about-turn.

'It's what I'm saying now.'

'But you think there's a whale in the bay?'

'I don't think, I know. And I don't want to talk about it. You all think I'm making it up.'

'I only said, last time we talked, that the chances of whales making their way to this island are very slim.'

'I'm not talking about whales. One whale, Dad,' Fenn says, 'And now I've heard the recordings, I'm even more certain. I know he's out there.'

'Your dad is just saying that it's not very likely, Fenn, but I'd like to hear more about what you heard.' Julia is trying to pour oil on the troubled waters.

'No point.'

Julia and Hamish exchange a glance which Fenn doesn't miss.

'You don't believe me, do you? And I don't care what you think. I'm the one who heard the song.' She jumps up, stomps out of the room, then takes the stairs two at a time to her bedroom. The door slams.

'She's really exercised about this,' Julia says. 'I'm not sure what's got into her. She was so content and chuffed to be swimming with Jess, and then suddenly she's in a state about a whale that might or might not be somewhere out there in the ocean.'

'Might not,' Hamish answers with a full stop. 'She's nine. Emotions run high. She has a vivid imagination.'

'But she's not normally like this. She's calm and sensible.'

'Maybe pre-teens has arrived a bit early.'

'I don't think so.'

'It will pass,' Hamish says. 'There'll be a new obsession.'

Julia isn't so sure. This worries her. This isn't like her daughter.

*

In bed, Fenn is furious and overwrought. Her thoughts tumble along the same tracks. The whale songs play on and she recalls what she heard in the recordings – the exact pitch, the shape of the sound, and the huge emotions held in the song. She has to go back to the deep basin where the same sounds flood and pool, and this time she'll take the evidence with her. She will carry the sounds she heard today, in the recordings, and compare them with the sounds under the water. Then she will be certain.

Tomorrow, she will swim out to that same spot, no matter

how dismal the weather, and anyway rain today means nothing and tomorrow may be fine. Jess may be back. Fenn wonders what kept her away when she never misses a day. And with the image of Jess waiting on the sand comes a firm decision. She will tell her and ask her to go out there and listen with her. If they both put their heads under the water.... If anyone is going to believe her, it's Jess. And if Jess hears nothing or decides the noise is something altogether different, OK, so be it. There's a weeny chance she's made a big mistake. Then so be it. But she will only give up after this one last shot.

It's a resolution and Fenn sighs her relief. She pushes her head further into the pillow and snuggles into a different, comfy shape under the duvet. Sleep comes. The plan will still be there when she wakes up.

Chapter 23

The Whale

Through days and weeks, he has swum through every shade of blue, from lightest aqua to almost purple, and now he is submerged in black water where he registers little except his muscle movements and the sloosh of water over his head and back. The traffic of fish is slight and sparse, a barely-there dash across his poor vision. Here, a vertical column of bubbles. There, the swish of a larger tail. Now a rush of clustered silver scales that swim towards him, then twist as one and retreat. For days on end, the blackness holds and encloses him, his tiny eyes sunk low on his knotted head finding nothing on which to settle as a distraction from the monotony of the hours. Down here, days and nights are not separable. Time is seamless, unmarked by dawns and dusks, not stamped by encounters of any kind. Life is no more than continuous curved arcs through water which sometimes gathers a turbulence of currents. The absence of the others has faded from a sense of loss so acute it never left his side to a resigned, subdued loneliness.

And then through the tedium comes the surprise call of

another whale, faint, yes, and far away, but without doubt the song of one of his own, and the sound thrills him to his core. He tips his bulk to soar upwards, somersaults and spins, his feelings electric-alive as they have not been for such a very long time. He follows the trills and clicks and long notes with new hope and expectation. Could it be one of his own? He surges towards the sound, picking it up and holding it like a precious gift, tuning into it with every fibre of his being. But the closer he gets, the more he understands the message not as an announcement of presence, a calling card of latitude and longitude, but as a cry of distress. And outrage. There are miles between them, but the vibrations guide him on and he closes in on the other creature.

Wait. Something is very wrong here. His first glimpse of the whale who calls makes him question if it is indeed a whale. The shape is wrong, not long and defined, but squared and lumpy. And the creature's passage through the water is not fluid and fast. There is no dipping and diving, no graceful, balanced progress through the black water. This whale is thrashing and battling, a mess of impotent movement that is getting it nowhere.

He swims on until he is circling the limping creature, a large male, and sees that he is dragging with him a ton of things that have no name among sea creatures. Again and again the creature who is tangled and bound flicks his tail and twists round to try to see why and what holds him back and makes him labour. Why am I not able to shake myself free? What is this weight I am dragging through the water with me? Why am I struggling to make progress? Inching along until he is right beside the lost whale, the burdened whale whose eyes are glazed with exhaustion, speaks of the energy he is expending, trying to swim while attached to this extra thing, this heavy, lifeless thing that holds him fast and refuses to let him go. Every thrust forward is a monumental effort. How can I soar to the surface to feed? On he struggles, inch by inch, his progress crooked and skewed. Distraught, he longs to be as he was, before his collision with something alien that fell into his ocean, and his subsequent entanglement.

He does not have words for the piles of splintered wood and rope and netting that were jettisoned into the sea from a passing fishing boat. Unlucky for him that he was swimming underneath as it fell, splayed and receptive. Caught inside the mass of hooks and holes, he was soon held fast and the more he struggled, the more he was wrapped and trapped. A ring of metal, the rim of an old tyre, circles his belly, cutting into his skin, and from it hangs the dead weight of planks stuck with rusting nails and heavy coils of rope. Across his throat, his belly and back, his skin is pierced and frayed, bleeding red into the blue. Help me, he signals. Free me. The lost whale sees the predicament of his fellow creature. He circles, nudges the weight that clings to the head and torso of his fellow creature, tries to push it away, but his attempts are futile and he is powerless. There is nothing he can do. This doomed whale who drags a tonnage of wood and metal must continue his tragic journey until exhaustion takes him down to the seabed where he will lie on sharp edges and piercing nails. Down on the sand, he will flick his tail in a feeble, pointless rhythm until, all hope gone, he lies motionless, waiting for death. And that comes slowly, agonisingly slowly. Small fishes flick past and gaze on an ending.

The whale twists to send a look of pity and sorrow, and continues on his way, his next long call through the ocean coloured darker with the pain he has witnessed as he sings of another tale of unnatural death. He does not know yet that there will be more. There are always more. On this journey, he will collect a compendium of the saddest stories.

Way off beam now, thousands of miles away from his pod who have reached their breeding grounds in another ocean, the whale turns away from the islands, his repeated call echoing back the data for the map he needs to keep away from the shores. With sure instinct, he knows that closeness means shallow water and danger. He has not yet given up on self-preservation.

*

Staying closer to the surface, he picks up some of the sounds he heard in previous seas, many days ago, the staccato sounds that warn him that he has arrived in another place populated by that other species that rides across the water surface on things that buzz. They speak with tinny voices. From the noisy vessels that hold them, they throw discarded nets, not that he knows that name. And there's a never-ending stream of other stuff that comes tumbling down into his space, so many pieces of hard and soft shiny stuff that he can't name as plastic. Bottles, containers, boxes rain down and fall to the bottom. For the whale, these objects are unwanted, of no use. He hates to see them drop into the clear waters, dead things that serve no purpose. Sometimes they float along in the current, sometimes they plummet and collect in piles on the seabed.

What happens next comes too soon. The memory of his encounter with a fellow whale close to death is still dragging him down as he continues on his way. The blue that colours his calls has not begun to fade when he picks up another thin, pain-encrusted song and gathers himself for the possibility of more sorrow. It is not long before he locates the creature, a young female, an emaciated whale who lists badly and vomits blood that feathers misty red into the water. She moves through a halo of scarlet. Coming close alongside her, he looks into her eyes and acknowledges her excruciating pain and fear. This whale's predicament is not so obvious, apart from the poppy-red fluid that floods from her stomach to her mouth and seeps into the sea.

My belly is painful, she tells him. It is heavy and hurting, like I have swallowed rocks and stones.

I can see, he answers. From how you move, from how you look.

What is inside me?

I don't know.

I located food, the echoes bounced off and reached me. There was a lot of it. I ate my fill, my mouth wide. I fed trustingly. I swallowed everything.

As we do, he replies.

And then my belly hurt. And hurt more.

You have eaten something that is making you ill, he says.

I know. But what?

Neither whale knows that her belly is full of compacted plastic, part of it so hard and heavy that it has calcified. She swallowed plastic bags, water bottles and nylon rope when she fed open-mouthed after her echolocation bounced off solid matter. The trash sounded like food and she moved towards it. Each time she opened wide her massive mouth, she took in sea water containing the thousands of small fish and plankton she needed for nutrition, but she also swallowed floating and half-sunk garbage, her filter feeding system not equipped to separate and discard food from rubbish. As her stomach swelled and grew taut, so her body wasted.

She does not know any of this, only that the pain is intense, that she cannot feed, that her energy is draining away.

The lost whale stays at her side, his own body streaked with her blood, but what can he do? How can he help? Young though he is, he understands that the weak and the injured must always be left behind. His elders taught him that rule of survival. In the end, saddened but helpless, he swims slowly away in search of a place that is safer and where there is less distress.

When he scans the acoustic memory of his previous migration, he does not recall events like these. Images of hurt and dying whales do not litter his recollections. This is new. This is different. He asks himself if his ocean, his playground and feeding ground, is changing. He fears for the future.

*

Days pass, maybe weeks because he isn't counting, and another expanse of ocean is left behind. The whale's acoustic detective system again picks up not a vast stretch of vacant water ahead but the shapes of land rising from the ocean and rooted below it not far away. He needs more information, but he is desperately tired, wearied by everything that has happened, and his instinct speaks to him of the futility of setting off in yet another random direction. His energy is sorely flagging. His mood is sombre. Emitting clicks from the front of his nose, he listens hard to the echoes that resonate in the fatty sac beneath his mouth. He pulls up the images of land masses, layer upon layer, small and close together, the water all around. Whether from exhaustion or dismay at what he has seen on his journey or simply a fatigue that can sustain no further travel, he sighs long and hard, slows down, and continues in the same direction. It is a risk he will take.

Chapter 24

Jess

Jess takes her mug of cold coffee to the sink, tips out the liquid, washes and dries it, puts it back in the cupboard. Straightens the other mugs in the cupboard so their handles face the same way. Then plumps up cushions that are already plump, tidies a pile of books that are already tidy. Like a pacing tiger in a cage in a zoo, she walks from the living room to the kitchen and back, repeats the circuit, then goes upstairs to straighten a duvet that's already perfectly straight. She sits on the bed, puts her head in her hands and sighs in exasperation. With herself.

There was no rowing boat, she tells herself.

There was, she replies. I saw it.

Figment of your imagination.

Sure, and as real as I am real.

Stop thinking about it.

Can't.

Up she gets and takes herself downstairs again, stopping to hang an anorak that's fallen to the floor and to line up her boots and wellies.

Stop it!

What else do you suggest I do?

Something useful.

Can't. I'm thinking about the boat. Why did it appear where I least expected it? Fenn and me were swimming contentedly and there's the bloody boat.

Stop dwelling on it.

And now I can't swim there.

What? Why?

In case it comes back.

That's pathetic.

Fine. I'm pathetic.

Standing at the window, tears brimming, she spots a wavy black line of Canada geese flying away from the ocean, so many of them in a perfect v shape, making their way as surely as if their route was drawn in the sky. Watching their progress, she tells herself that there was no boat in the bay. If there was, it was only a weird projection of her grief that one day will go away. But no matter which words she uses, the sight of that little boat coming towards her with Dan holding the oars breaks her into pieces that she has to pick up and put back together. Every time. With another deep sigh, she follows the pattern of birds. The geese are on their own journey, an arrow making its way across the grey sky. With a shrug she goes to the cupboard, takes out the same mug, makes fresh coffee and this time drinks it at the window while watching the geese until they become a line of dots and are then out of sight. The boat that is burnt on her retina is fading too. How many more times do I have to go through this heartbreak?

This morning is all messed up. She was going to start digging the ground around the cottage ready for planting spring bulbs. In brown paper bags, she has crocus in every shade of mauve and purple and deep-pink, tulips spiral-petalled like peonies. The locals she has chatted to, to pass the time of day and to act like a friendly neighbour, have told her she's wasting her time, that the bulbs won't come up, nothing comes up, not in the blasts of winter wind, but she's ignoring them. They may well be right but she has to give it a go. Life without plants to nurture is not an option. Yes, she knew this when she chose to come to the island. It was part of the deal. So she should be seizing this long, end-of-summer break in the weather to bury her hands in the damp, infertile ground and to dig in the seaweed she's been told is good for the soil. On fine days, the air here has a glass-like quality: squeaky-clear and clean without the filter of city pollution. She should be outside, getting some colour into her cheeks.

The weather won't stay kind like this. Soon, October and November will blast across the island with raging rain and stinging sleet. The gales will be ferocious. No gardening then. She'll hardly be able to stand upright some days and walking along the beach will be a draining, ferocious battle into gusts that will howl off the ocean and roar across the beach, sandblasting her face and filling her eyes with grit. She'll come back red-cheeked and panting. The locals will wonder why on earth she ventures out.

Neither can she be bothered making sculptures out of her bits of driftwood and shells and stained glass. No, Jess, not sculptures. You just mess about and make things to stick in the garden. Things to hang from the one scraggy, wind-bent tree and to plant in the earth. Fragments of stained glass fascinate her with their infinite colours and shades. There's something satisfying about the shoulder-bent graft of cutting and grinding the glass, and edging the pieces with copper foil then soldering them. It's physical work and it takes concentration or you cut and burn your fingers. Hours pass. Sometimes the results surprise her. Today, it is of no interest.

She had been doing so well with the shutters pulled down hard over her past. Not just pulled down but locked with the key thrown away. The image of the boat on the ferry crossing had been a blow but she persuaded herself it was an aberration. A final farewell. It would stay behind on that stretch of water. Don't go there, she told herself, once she had taken refuge on this island. Don't look back. Stare straight ahead and don't even turn your head. Place one foot in front of the other. Leave the past on the mainland, in another country, and let it fade, as it will. Slowly. Very, very slowly. She had been managing. Swimming with Fenn helps because she has to be so very much in the present, making sure a nine-year-old doesn't drown.

Wrong word, Jess. Freudian slip. What has *drown* got to do with it? Why didn't you say, 'making sure the girl learns to be a strong, safe swimmer' or 'enjoying the ocean with an eager-to-learn child'?

The guilt hits her hard. So does her selfishness. Yesterday, she didn't go to the beach because the vision of the past in that precious place had knocked her for six. It felt like a violation. She chides herself for putting her own emotions before Fenn's enthusiasm. Yesterday, the weather was pretty awful but Fenn is increasingly impervious to it and once they are in the water, a bit of rain is no hindrance to their pleasure. The girl may have been on the beach by herself, waiting and wondering, staring out to sea, looking back at the dunes for Jess, wanting to swim to that point where she sticks her head under the water and emerges looking wildly excited. Jess has seen her do it twice. What is it she sees or hears down there? What fantasy is she conjuring up? Jess knows Fenn will tell her when she's ready. It looks like too big a secret to hold inside, though the girl is fiercely independent and strong. Fenn will have sat on the sand, Hero digging holes at her side and covering her in sand, and then perhaps she went for a walk along the beach by herself. Jess imagines the girl's disappointment. The afternoon ritual has become important for both of them. It's their way of being together in the sea and being together on the island.

She should go. The kitchen clock tells her there's still time. It's unkind of her to let the girl down again.

Before Jess can move, the flashback is up and running, wobbly as if made by a hand-held camera and slow to move from frame to frame. She turns her head and looks away but the images run on as if projected on her kitchen wall. Oh for christ's sake! Not again! For the first time, anger and resentment replace upset as she sees the rowing boat, oars shipped. No, she is not going to watch. She doesn't have to put up with it. Up to now, she hasn't had the courage to turn her back nor the sense to let it go, as if refusing to acknowledge the imagined boat is the same as refusing to acknowledge her grief and loss. They are not the same, she tells herself now. You are not powerless, Jess. You don't have to be sucked into this charade anymore. You don't have to watch this day-time nightmare. She makes a quick decision and decides to stop it in its tracks before it moves on any further. It was at exactly this same point in the story when she snapped at Fenn, too brusquely, to turn back and head for the shore. Without understanding why, Fenn heard the insistence and obeyed. Did it carry on playing behind her back? Was there a man in the boat, the oars shipped? On

202

her kitchen wall – or is it only on the canvas of her mind – the film plays on but Jess is not watching.

Wait. She has to do something more decisive. Turning her back is such a pathetic, passive response and all it does is press the pause button and invite the thing – whatever it is – to return and haunt her again. It doesn't get rid of it once and for all. The only way to stop the film is to change the reel, Jess decides, playing along with the metaphor and doing just that. Imagining herself really doing it, she lifts out the one with the wrong ending and inserts the reel that plays the good stuff. Or better still, why not cut the bad film at that moment when everything goes belly up so that the ending is erased? She fetches a razor blade, slices the film and lets the cruel part of the reel fall to the ground. Yeah, yeah, she knows, nowadays it's not reels and projectors, it's videos and technology. Hard luck. This is all she can imagine in her current hyper state. Reels and razor blades. Like that film, Cinema Paradiso.

So she's switched reels and now she's watching the good days, the training days, because you can't watch two films at once. The cruel images lie tangled and impotent on the floor. She fast-forwards the very early stuff from their life in the Adirondacks and stops at the more recent, sometimes good, sometimes dispiriting, days of training off flat, grey English beaches. Not that she and Dan found them disheartening. They had a purpose. They were there for a reason. How could they be depressed when she was about to swim the Channel? Nothing she had done before came close to the challenge it offered.

She looks up at the film playing on the wall. Of course there's no projector and no screen, and yes she knows her technology is wildly out of date, but it's as vivid as if a reel is winding past the lens. These scenes contain only the good times. There's the rowing boat, a hundred yards from the shore, not a nightmare vision but a familiar, welcome sight with Dan shouting at her through his megaphone, telling her to slow down or change her stroke or take a rest or have a gulp of hot tea. And sometimes she does as he says and sometimes she takes no notice because her instinct tells her to do otherwise and ignore him because she's the one in the water. Now he's yelling at her to stop and pack it in for the day, but she heads out once more before swimming effortlessly back to the shore.

Afterwards, in an empty seaside cafe, at a formica-topped table, their cold hands round mugs of coffee, he admonishes her, half serious, half teasing.

'Why have a coach if you take no notice of him?'

'I'm the swimmer. Sometimes my body knows better than my coach.'

'Then I'll stay at home and not sit in a freezing cold boat in a freezing cold wind while you pay not the slightest attention to my wise instructions.'

'I do take no notice of you.'

'You're a stubborn pupil.'

'You're a bossy husband.'

'I'm not your husband in that damn rowing boat, I'm your experienced and very patient coach.'

His arm is round her shoulders and he's kissing her cold cheeks, finding her still-icy lips, and telling her he loves her and admires her, but she can be damn difficult.

'It's two days before the crossing. Are you ready, pupil of mine?'

'More than ready.'

'It's been a long, hard road, Jess. I don't know how you've

stuck at it. Fucking masochism, swimming in England.'

'Water under the bridge, Dan. We said goodbye to the Adirondacks. Goodbye, deep lakes and pine-covered mountains and black bears. Hello, English beaches. Hello, grey sand and grey skies.'

'Don't you mind? Leaving all that?'

'You've asked me that so many times. No. You were head-hunted and here we are. It's a great job that gives you time to coach your stubborn wife. And she is excited about crossing the Channel. Couldn't have done that on the other side of the pond. New opportunities all round, Dan. And one last long-distance swim before I hang up my bathing suit.'

'Last long swim, Jess? Truly?' He needs to know, though she's told him a hundred times before.

'The last one.'

'No more hours and hours ploughing through cold water.'

'I like cold water.'

'No more marathons? A stay-at-home wife?' There's laughter threaded through his words. And a small grain of doubt.

She kisses him again. 'A mother, I hope. A mother who swims and who teaches her daughter to swim.'

'And if he's a boy?'

Jess shakes her head. 'She'll be a girl. A girl who loves the sea as much as I do.'

'And grows up to swim marathons?'

'Oh that will be her decision, not mine.'

They each look into each other's eyes that are the exact same shade of deep-water blue and acknowledge the ending, and the beginning. The completed journey across an ocean. The journey across the Channel that is to come. It has been planned for a long time.

'Have another piece of cake, Jess. You need more blubber.'

'I've put on six kilos while training and have been eating cake like it's my birthday every day.'

'You'll lose more than that on the crossing.'

'No. Maybe four or five.'

'Twenty-one miles, Jess.'

'Sarah Thomas from Colorado swam the channel four times non stop. Once is a doddle!'

'Sarah Thomas is something else. One hundred and thirty miles and fifty-four hours in cold water.'

'Once will be fine.'

'Eat your cake. Let's call it a day and go home and warm up. Watch a movie. Tomorrow we do some gentle training and you rest up before the big day.'

'OK, skipper.'

Jess stops the film there. That reel contains her happiness and her hopes. The next reel, the one she pulled out of the projector, the one she cut with a razor blade, contains the ending. Not the ending she and Dan spoke of as they drank coffee and arecake and planned their future together. The other ending.

With a shrug of her shoulders, Jess looks at the kitchen clock again. Time plays tricks, as well as her imagination. What feels like an hour has only been ten minutes, but it's slowed her heart beat and she's calmer. There is still plenty of time to join Fenn. Do it, she tells herself. Remember those happy times, turn your back on your morbid thoughts and go to the girl who likes and admires you. Don't dent that trust.

Perhaps it's because she is already finely tuned and receptive as she allows herself to soak up the memories. Perhaps it's her hyper emotional state that leaves her wide open to signals of another kind because she senses a call that is nothing to do with her and nothing to do with her story. She leaves the house and walks to the boundary of her garden and looks out at her rocky beach and the unsettled sea. It comes on the wind and in the notes called by the circling gulls. It reaches her in the irritable rattle of water over pebbles. It comes in the sigh and splash of the waves. What felt only a minute ago like a mild duty to a girl on a beach now feels like a necessity. Jess hears urgency and danger. This isn't a matter of her making a decision. It's not a matter of choice. Go. Go now. Fenn is in trouble.

The sky's the colour of seaside rock, palest blue with thin pink stripes. It won't be so long before the sun starts its slow summer descent down the sky. Jess runs to the kitchen, switches on the kettle and finds the flask. Next, into the bedroom where she undresses and pulls on her swimsuit, her wetsuit on top. Needing warmth, she piles on a t-shirt and fleece, and at the doorway pulls on her boots. She shoves her underwear in her rucksack with a spare t-shirt, joggers, towels and a thin blanket. Back in the kitchen she makes a pot of sweet, milky tea and pours it into the flask. Too bad there's not enough time to make it good and strong. She shoves it in her rucksack with cereal bars and chocolate.

Then she runs.

Chapter 25

Fenn

The clouds are thickening and there's a bit of a wind, one of those unsettled, overcast days when the weather can't make up its mind. Fenn has sighed her way through the hours at school, barely concentrating, and worrying that by the time she gets home, there'll be an almighty downpour. But her mind is made up. She has to do what she has to do.

The coast is clear. Hamish is down by the loch, planting saplings. Where else? She sees him wave and nod after the bus drops her off and as she races along the path, then he goes back to his digging. Fenn knows he will labour on, the herculean task demanding his full attention as the days, very gradually, begin to draw in. She notes that he has gone up a gear. How can he do that?

Julia isn't home. Over breakfast, she told her daughter she needed to go to the arts centre during the afternoon to stock up on paints and she wouldn't be there to welcome her home from school. The centre opens odd hours, she said, as if it were a problem. So? Fenn thought. I can probably manage for once without you in your studio, Mum. And today her mother's absence happens to suit her perfectly well.

She's quickly changed, back outside and into her after-school routine with Hero and the birds, a bit brusque and not stopping to chat to Jemima Duck when she presses against her ankles nor to Runner Bean when she squawks and fusses, wanting to be picked up. Her mind is on another creature who is not of the land and who doesn't have webbed feet. With the birds safely housed, she runs inside, collects her swimsuit and towel, and jogs away to the sand dunes. Hero is left behind, whining in protest.

By the time she reaches the dunes, the wind is brisk, lifting and blowing clouds of sand into her eyes. There's a biting edge and quickening gusts. The sea looks much as usual, grey, the long rolling waves carrying some extra foam, but out in the bay the surface is only a bit rippled. If there are signs of wind and currents building, Fenn chooses not to see them.

But where is Jess? Why isn't she on the beach? She's always here. Why, today of all days, is she not down on the sand? It can't be the weather. They have been out in worse than this and Jess has said she doesn't want Fenn to be a fair-weather swimmer because that would certainly limit her scope. Once in the sea, rain doesn't stop you because you're soaking wet anyway, and it's fun. They've been out in squalls and Jess taught her not to fight the turbulence but to slip through the middle of the bumpy waves, otherwise you get slapped in the face and that's not pleasant. Go under and through, she told Fenn. The chances are you'll come out in flatter water on the other side. If you hit a lumpy stretch, hold your breath a while longer until you reach that calmer place in the water. They practised riding bigger waves, using their bodies like surfboards to climb up, stay on top, and fall down on the other side. Jess is a water-conjurer with the tricks that she plays.

But her not being here is a major blow to Fenn's plans. This is what was going to happen. They would sit on the sand and Fenn would tell her everything and risk being made to feel very small and very silly. She can imagine Jess throwing her head back and laughing, especially when she explains why she was singing underwater. Fenn will tell her what she heard out there. She will say she sure it's a whale, and lay out all her evidence and all her reasons for thinking that. She will describe the evening of fact hunting with Hamish, and her mother's dismissal of the whole thing as a lovely made-up story. Then she'll ask Jess to swim way out with her and lie with her head under the surface. Clear your mind and listen hard, she'll tell her. As if she needs to. Jess can concentrate like no-one she's ever met.

And this is what will happen once they have swum out and lain like a pair of flat fish beneath the surface. She has it all worked out, but as if to make the plan solidi, she finds for three large pebbles and lines them up in a row.

Stone Number One: this is what will happen. Fenn hears nothing and will have to let the story go, a dream that washes away with the next wave. After all, what can you do if a sound, however beautiful, however heart-wrenching, comes and goes? There's no proof she ever heard it, let alone that it's sung by some creature. OK, it was a random squeaking noise that travelled underwater for a few days and disappeared again. In the story under Pebble Number One, Jess will ask just what they are supposed to be listening for because she can't hear a thing. And that will be that.

Stone Number Two: this is the outcome. She hears the whale, or whatever it is, but Jess hears nothing. Again there's no evidence other than from her own ears. And so unwillingly, reluctantly, Fenn will chime in with whatever Julia says, that there's nothing there, that it's a lovely story, but it ends here. Maybe she just has bizarre hearing. People do go on about her hearing. She and Jess will go back to swimming. Fenn will have to get over it.

Stone Number Three: this is what it says. Fenn and Jess both hear the same sounds, and Jess agrees that it could be a whale calling, then…Fenn can't continue because it means there is a whale out there and it may be in trouble. Well, it is in trouble because it shouldn't be there. Whales don't swim in seas around Scottish islands. It means it is lost. Perhaps alone. That truth is dizzying. That truth needs Jess, and Jess isn't here.

Fenn waits another twenty minutes. With impatient sighs, she twists her head backwards to the sand dunes, but no spiky-haired figure waves and comes dashing down, apologising for being late and explaining why she was delayed. C'mon, Jess! Fenn is starting to shiver while her impatience is reaching boiling point. Her step-by-step plan is hanging in mid-air, a balloon of an idea that could fly high or pop and die. When you are nine and have worked this hard to hold on to your hopes and your maybe mistakes, a lot is at stake. Fenn needs an answer now. Why on earth is Jess not here?

She doesn't actually take a decision. She finds herself undressing, and pulling on her costume and laying a big stone on top of her clothes. Ooh, it's cold. Somehow splitting herself into two separate people, one doing and one watching, Fenn walks towards the sea. One Fenn says, Don't be stupid!

Don't even think about going out there by yourself! You promised never to do that. The other Fenn says, It will take less than fifteen minutes and I'll be back before anyone knows and nothing dreadful will happen. Neither Fenn says, There's actually no point in doing this because without Jess, you won't have her word to back yours. You're doing something very risky for nothing.

Fenn does say, I'm coming. Wait for me. I'll be with you soon and I'll hear you. If you are in trouble, I'll work out what to do. Or words to that effect.

Unlike Fenn, the weather has made up its mind. Heavy, rain-laden clouds are blowing in on a wind that is gusting hard. The few bright patches of sky are covered by an ominous grey. Out in the bay, the sea looks black beneath colliding white crests. All of this Fenn ignores. She winces when she stumbles on the pebbles at the shore's edge, grits her teeth through the cold shallows, then plunges in and heads out. At first she swims smoothly, pushing through the waves, but she slows down sooner than she usually does. Is it because Jess isn't at her side? Are the waves really that much bigger? Or has she already burned up too much energy worrying about Jess not coming, worrying over the questions that have no answers? About half way to the point where they stopped last time, swimming starts to feel like really hard work, but she pushes on. And soon after that, her sturdy breaststroke fragments and falters. Her arms and legs are all over the place. She stops. Shakes the water from her eyes. Treads water as Jess has taught her when she's tired. She's very cold and her fingers and toes are numb. At this point, anyone looking down from the dunes would be able to read the speech bubbles written in capitals over her head.

I AM GETTING INTO DIFFICULTIES.

I SHOULD GO BACK WHILE I CAN.

But Fenn has left her sensible self on the shore so ignores the warning, flips back onto her stomach and carries on. Anyway, there is no-one on the dunes to see a girl struggling through a sea that is turning ugly.

It takes an almighty effort to reach the place that she remembers. Oh my goodness, it's a long way out. She's breathing hard. Her lungs ache. She has swallowed a lot of water. But she's made it. It is now or never. Never mind that she feels shivery and tired to her bones. Ignoring all of that, she flattens her body and ducks her head under. In a way it's easier below the surface because she's out of the wind and she's not battling the colliding waves that soak her face. She steadies herself, lies still, and waits.

The short wait feels like forever but only in stillness, and while giving herself to the sea, will she hear the sounds in the depths. And they come, faint at first, notes as thin as filigree threads and still without colour, but they are there. They come blowing through the reeds and the shoals of tiny silver fish. 'The same,' she whispers, but not out loud. Motionless, apart from the gentle peddle of her feet, Fenn tunes in to the whale call – yes it is a whale call – that grows colours from palest blue through to violet and a colour that Fenn hears as a shade of sadness. The same. The volume increases until the long arching chord, metallic and mystical, rings clear and sharp and ends in a flourish of clicks and trills. The same. And the sounds come from somewhere not far away. Somewhere in the bay.

And they are exactly what she heard in the recordings. 'I know you're there,' she sings back on a ragged breath when she goes back under. 'I'm sorry I doubted you, even for a minute.' She needs more air. None left in her lungs. Hard to breathe. Up to the surface, and straight back down to finish her message. 'I know you are in trouble. I won't leave you here alone.' Surfaces again. This is hopeless. Can't say more than a few words at a time. Why is it so hard to get air into my lungs? But Fenn is determined. Her sense of duty to this creature is unshakeable. Down she goes again, only for a few seconds to send an answer in her own song, bubbles of quavery sound, and she keeps singing until her lungs are about to burst.'

I'll get help. Hang on. Please hang on.

Where are you?

Are you in trouble?

Do you need help?

With a twist she surfaces, gasping for air. At first it's hard to see anything because she's dizzy and the annoying waves burst over her head and slap her face. She has to wait for a brief hiatus. Spinning round before the next flurry of waves knocks her under, she searches the water for a sign, any sign, of another creature. She looks for tell-tale ripples on the water. A patch of sea that is churned a different colour. A fin. A tail. Shadows. There is nothing, only the darkening sea. And the threatening sky.

A rogue wave knocks her under again. Her limbs flail and her mouth is full of salt water. When she rights herself, she notices how strong the wind is and how dark the sea. And how spent she is. It's quite an effort to keep her head up as the rain begins in earnest.

She turns for the shore, but her arms won't do as they're told and her legs are jelly. Breathing in and out takes so much effort. Euphoria deflates into fear. And then panic. She calls, but what on earth is the point? OK, she tells herself, do one stroke at a time and take it very slowly and you will get back. Jess has shown you how to swim through a choppy sea. You can do it. Fine words and good intentions, but the reality is that she is making no headway. In her last ironic comment to herself, before sheer terror takes hold, she asks, 'How can I help the whale if I go and drown out here?' And then she goes under. Black closes over her. So hard to hold this breath. Down. Down. Jess, why aren't you here with me? Jess, I need you.

On the shore, the waves thunder in before they foam fast and furious up the beach.

Chapter 26

Jess

There was never any other option.

A quick glance out of the window tells Jess that the weather is turning ugly. That's not a squall that's on its way, but a front bringing heavy rain and wind. Only an hour ago the waves were breaking on the shore in long, soothing runs of three and four, but now they are chaotic, crashing on the sand, a formidable energy in each break of foam and froth.

It would take too long to get to the beach along the road so she clambers down to the rocks on her small beach and holds her rucksack high above her head to wade thigh-deep round the headland. Only by a squeak does she make it because the wind is whipping up the waves, spray thrown against the rocks. She is soaked but the bag stays dry.

And her instinct, or whatever one might want to call it, is right. The vibes that reached her are real. There is Fenn, way out in the bay, a dot in the darkening water, ploughing on and on away from the shore. My god, what is she doing? What has got into her? She looks dogged and determined, but even as Jess races along the first stretch of the beach, she can see her smooth strokes falling apart and she can imagine the energy draining away, left behind in the water. And yet Fenn presses on. It's not difficult to guess where she is heading. And even if she makes it, will she be able to get back? The stupid girl! What on earth is she doing! I thought she was far too sensible to attempt a stunt like this. The struggling, slow-moving swimmer has stopped fighting the waves and is treading water. Thank god for that. No, wait, now what? She's diving under. Up comes a streaming head, and goes straight back down again. Jess runs across sand spotted with rain drops.

Jess puts her demons into an imaginary box and slams shut the lid. Compared with what's happening here and now, they are of no consequence. A child's life is at stake. Please, please don't let there be another drowning. Jess strips off, dumps a rock on her clothes and rucksack, and runs. Switching with ease into competition mode, her dive from the shingle and ankle-deep water is arrow-straight. Then she's powering through the waves, muscled shoulders and strong legs performing a perfect crawl. The sea is bumpy, turbulent, but nothing compared to other waters she's swum. She covers the space in no time.

Under the water, Jess sees the sinking form of a child. She dives deeper, places her arms under ice-cold shoulders, and drags her back up.

'OK, I've got you.' Jess says, when both their heads break through the surface. 'Breathe slowly, Fenn. Don't do anything else. Let me take your weight. Relax, Fenn, and don't fight me.'

It takes a minute for Fenn to understand. She struggles, fights the constraints with flailing limbs, then her head is above water, being held, and she can take raw, choked, painful breaths and spit salt water. When she opens her fear-filled eyes, she sees Jess's face right beside her.

'Don't talk,' Jess preempts. 'Save your energy. Just listen to me. We're going to stay here for a minute while I tread water and hold you while you get your breath back, and when you're ready, I'm going to pull you back to the shore.'

Fenn leans against Jess. Trembling from cold and fear, she flops like a rag doll. She is spent and shaken. Frightened and ashamed.

'I'm saying nothing about why you're out here,' Jess says, as if able to hear Fenn's thoughts. 'Not now. We're going to do one thing and one thing only. Get you back.'

'Yes,' Fenn says, and then bursts into furious tears. Jess feels the sobs that shake the skinny shoulders she holds in her arms. Fenn's face is already streaming with rivulets of rain and sea water.

'It's OK. You're OK. I got here in time. You'll be fine.'

'Thank you. I was just...' but more sobs drown out her words.

Jess waits for Fenn to calm down, then speaks slowly and firmly. 'Listen to me, Fenn. This is what we're going to do. I want you to float on your back while I put my arm round your neck and head. Like we practised. Let me take the weight of your body.'

Fenn can do it, and lies on the water, her head cradled. Her breathing slows. The terror lets go, just a notch or two. The panic washes away as she feels herself pulled along without making the slightest effort. She knows she has been very stupid. And yet, despite all of that, the whale's song soars in her memory, persuasive and plaintive. She has to tell Jess. She must listen too.

'Jess...' she begins, needing to say something now that she doesn't have to swim back alone.

'You're OK, Fenn. Don't talk.'

'Yes...No...just a moment...before we go back. Jess...stop a minute...please put your head under...tell me...if you can hear it...the whale...' Fenn's words come out in tiny staccato bursts, through chattering teeth. Her eyes are pleading.

Jess can hardly believe what she's hearing. 'No. Absolutely not.'

'But... it's right here...'

'Listen to me, Fenn. You have just put yourself in real danger.' Jess is speaking loudly and firmly, as if to a small child. 'You might not have made it back to the shore. You are close to getting hypothermia. The bottom line is that you could have drowned. Do you hear me?'

'I'm OK now...just need to get my breath back and...'

'You're definitely not OK. And I am not going to listen to whale songs. We're going straight back and I'm going to get you warmed up.'

Fenn looks absolutely stricken but knows she hasn't a leg to stand on. No legs and nothing to stand on, to be exact. Still she doesn't give up. One last try. She must give it one last try. 'I won't go back until you listen too. I'll be fine for two more minutes. No-one believes me. I wasn't going to drown. Please, Jess.'

This normally sensible girl is in shock, and no wonder, and not thinking straight, Jess concludes. She doesn't mince her words. 'For heaven's sake, what's got into you? Listen, Fenn. Conditions are deteriorating. And if you struggle while I'm trying to help you, you're putting my life in danger too.'

There's no arguing with that. Fenn's small forlorn hope sinks. The shame returns.

'Listen to me,' Jess continues. 'I don't want to hear another word. Lie back again against me and don't even think about trying to stop me. Hold your head above the water while I swim with my legs.'

They've done this before, part for fun, part practice for a situation exactly like this one, not that either of them imagined it would ever happen. They continue on their way, a strong woman towing a light child who has finally given in and is silent. With their faces held up to the sky, the rain dumps on them, rapid fire and bullet hard. Once safely in the shallows, Jess hauls Fenn up, a shivering, trembling wreck of a girl, and supports her across the stones and wet sand. They sit, not far from the sea's edge.

'Wait right there.' She runs for her rucksack and Fenn's clothes and runs back. Unloads towels. 'OK, get out of that costume.'

Fenn has gone limp. She is colder than she's ever been in her life. Jess helps tug off a swimsuit that stubbornly clings to goose-bump flesh, and rubs her hard with a towel. Heavens, this child hasn't a centimetre of fat on her. Handing her the joggers and t-shirt, she helps Fenn to put them on, a tricky set of movements because Fenn can't stop shaking. She wraps the blanket round the bony shoulders. All this Jess does while still in her swimsuit, and while the rain comes down in sheets. Jess's hands are steady as she pours hot tea and helps Fenn hold the full flask lid so as not to slosh the liquid all over the sand. Or herself. She fishes in her rucksack and hands the girl an energy bar and some chocolate.

'OK, here's what we're going to do. Are you listening?' Jess is still speaking in that school-mistress voice. 'Eat. Then we'll walk back to the dunes and I'll settle you somewhere a bit out of the rain and wind, if that's possible. Then I'm going to run home and fetch the car. I can drive it along the farm track. It will take me ten minutes. Will you be all right if I leave you?'

Fenn nods.

'Then we'll climb the dunes and we'll drive to my cottage.'

Fenn nods again. 'Are you going to tell my parents?'

'One thing at a time. OK, let's move back up the beach and find you somewhere to wait.'

They do it, Fenn supported by Jess because her legs are jelly. It goes to plan. With a quiet, white-faced Fenn and all their stuff stowed in the relative shelter of the dunes, Jess rolls off her swimsuit, her own body icy cold now and grainy with sand, towels herself quickly, and pulls on her underwear, shorts and t-shirt.

'Stay right there,' she calls, as she races up the dunes, her rucksack on her shoulders.

Seen from above, the picture is utterly forlorn. A sodden child sits huddled in driving rain. Her wet head is bent against the wind, and heavy with the weight of the dawning reality of what she has just done.

Chapter 27

The Whale

There is one story which he doesn't carry to the others, wherever they might be, because he is the story and it is still playing out. From an outsider's perspective, and of course there's no way he can see this, it's a story about the survival of his species and the heart-breaking possibility of its extinction. The story is paused halfway, between its long-ago beginning and its end, just as the whale is part-way through a journey whose starting point is almost lost to him and whose destination he cannot see.

For most of the journey, every day, every hour, over and over again, he has accelerated up through shoals of fish with enough momentum to ensure that every mouthful is a full and plentiful one. There's no point cruising along and collecting a few because he needs a ton of nourishment in every gulp to sustain and power him onwards. He feeds low in the food chain, the small fishes and zooplankton. And so, repeatedly, he readies himself in the depths before he soars upwards. If he were an engine, he would switch to turbo. He opens his mouth wide. He pulls back his tongue to block his throat and lets the water rush in together with whatever krill and codepods swim in with it. With the fish caught in the thick ropey strings that hang from his palette, he quickly swallows the food and presses his tongue against his palette to push out the water. It's fast. It's efficient. It is a perfect filter system. On he goes, his mouth a sieve that collects and strains his food for him.

On this long journey, without his pod and without landmarks, far from familiar and remembered feeding grounds, he has encountered long stretches of ocean where he has had to work hard to catch enough fish to not go hungry. Feeding himself in those depleted waters became an endless, thankless trek to the surface to get his fill. Where are the massed shoals of fish? Where are the clouds of plankton? The time will come soon when going hungry is the norm. While he registers this hunger as a failure on his part, a feebleness and listlessness, a loss of drive to push on strongly enough to find nourishment, he is only half correct. If his fellow whales were at his side, they too, as a community, would register this lack of food, these empty waters, and call and signal to one another that food is in short supply. The fish aren't here to be caught. The sea is emptier. Move on, they would call, to seas that are fuller. As it is, by himself, he only knows that he is burning energy and not filling his stomach nor his tanks of adrenaline. How can he know that the supply of fish is hugely depleted? He is confused about the geography of his journey, feeding where and when he can, and he is hungry. The further he travels, the more hungry he becomes. And weary and defeated. His strength is fading. His call is less loud. He calls less often. The notes have taken on the grey colours of indifference and resignation.

That was then. This is now and conditions have worsened.

It is summer and his search for food should be urgent and continuous. He must eat a lot more, enough to lay down blubber as reserves for the lean winter months ahead. But feeding himself has become draining and has demanded too much. Instead of cranking up through the gears, he does the opposite and slows down, making do with what he can catch without bursts of exertion. Yes, he is of an almost unimaginable size with the strength and stamina to match, but chasing quick-darting fish has changed from the simple and familiar to a chore that requires more than he can give. He feels depleted and dull. Soaring to the surface requires too much adrenaline so instead he rises slowly, catching barely enough fish to sustain him today, let alone into the future. There are hours, perhaps days, when he coasts, floats, barely rises from the seabed, twists and turns on the surface with barely a glance to right or left and goes without food.

If he were still with his pod and if he had arrived safely in the breeding grounds of a warmer ocean to lie still and recover, and to live off his blubber, he might also notice that there are fewer calves this year. He has experienced the shortage of food and of having to work harder to catch what there is, but he would not make the link between the shortage of food and the shortage of babies. The shoals of rich, nourishing herring have swum away, the seas too warm for comfort and survival. The females in his pod can't find herring and they too go hungry. They mourn when their babies are born dead. They are perplexed when, having carried their babies to term, they can't feed them because they have no milk. Their babies suck on nothing. The anxious mothers lick their calves as they die of hunger.

But the whale knows none of this, worn down as he is by an exhaustion so profound that it stops him from hunting and gathering what diminished nourishment does remain in the seas.

There is something else that is amiss in the once plentiful, well-stocked oceans, something other than diminishing supplies of fish and insufficient food. He is unaware that the beautiful blue ocean through which he swims is no longer pure and clean and safe. Even if he manages to avoid swallowing plastic bags and bottles, plastic wrappings and plastic boxes, spat out after they are caught in his fringed palette, he is still absorbing tiny particles of the same man-made material. The zooplankton and small schooling fish he eats are toxic because they, before him, have carried on feeding in their usual way and swallowed the invisible particles. And so the whale adds poison to his diet, bit by tiny bit as he eats fish poisoned before him. On a contaminated diet, he lacks the strength and vigour he once had. He blames his malaise on his endless journey, on his loneliness, on his yearning for his pod, on the pain of the creatures he has met along the way. It is all of that, but something more.

The hopeful, eager bursts of travel that characterised the start of his journey and took him across a hundred miles every day, have slowed to a resigned, dispirited onward push far below the surface as his hope of finding the others fades to a shadow. The discord built from futility and failure finds expression in the sombre colours of his infrequent calls. Rainbow hues bled away long ago. His will to carry on is fraying and he sings in greys and blacks and darkest blue.

He is defeated, exhausted and lost.

Chapter 28

Everyone

At Jess's kitchen table, Fenn sits silent, head bowed, white-faced, shoulders hunched. Her hair hangs in long, damp strands even though Jess has towelled off the worst of the salt water. She's wearing Jess's thick joggers, a long-sleeved t-shirt and one of her fleeces, all miles too big with sleeves hanging down over her hands. Through excess inches of cuff, she cradles a mug of hot, sweet tea and is working her way through a packet of chocolate digestives. Jess checks her out, again and again, sending quick glances her way while trying to conceal her worry. As a bit of colour returns to the girl's cheeks, she begins to relax. Fenn will be alright. She's taken a beating and she'll be weary to her bones, but nothing worse. Thank god. And she'll be mortified.

'Are you warming up, Fenn?'

'I'm fine.' The lie is barely veiled.

From the expression on the girl's face, and the wilted droop of her body, Jess decides it would achieve nothing to give her a row. Fenn knows what she's done, and is abject and ashamed. This sensible girl has made her first big mistake. Jess decides to make her point once, quickly and simply, then leave it with her. She knows Fenn will take it to heart and go over it, and over it, until the worry stone is rubbed smooth.

'I hope you've frightened yourself enough never to do anything that foolish ever again. You risked your life out there. You do know that, don't you, Fenn?'

Fenn nods. Tears well up and slide down her cheeks. 'I'm sorry,' she says in a very small voice.

Jess lets it go and turns to the practicalities of getting Fenn home.

'I'm going to phone Julia and tell her you're here. She may be worried.'

'Will you tell her?' The question was waiting.

'No. Not yet.'

Their voices are quiet against the rain that rattles the windows like someone throwing handfuls of small pebbles. The wind has built to a gale that batters the walls of the cottage and bends the branches of the one tree.

'Wait. Please wait.'

'What?' Jess asks.

'I have to ask...'

'What, Fenn?'

'I know I've been stupid. And I know you think this is not important and that I'm being silly, but please...will you go back out there and listen. Just once.'

She's still not letting it go, Jess thinks, seized suddenly by a desire to shake the girl hard and make her see sense. Whatever it was, she's hanging on to it like a terrier with a bone. Even after almost drowning herself. Goodness! But Fenn is looking at her with such a pleading expression that Jess's common sense and good judgement waver, and she waits that extra beat. Perhaps she really did hear something out there otherwise why did she stay when she could have swum back safely? Against her will, Jess is back on the same see-saw of maybe and maybe not that they have played out for days.

'You really think there's a whale out in that bay?' Jess says, capitulating because the girl's earnestness is hard to resist.

'Yes.'

'So after rescuing you, you seriously want me to swim back out there and stick my head under the water?'

'Well…not now…but later…yes. Please.'

'Don't you think that's pretty unreasonable?' Jess can't hide the slightest twitch of a smile, and sees that Fenn sees it.

'I do think it's unreasonable. But I wouldn't ask you if I wasn't certain. Almost certain.'

Jess caves in. She puts out a hand and rests it on Fenn's arm. 'OK. I will go out tomorrow, by myself, and listen for a soundtrack under the water. Yes?'

'Yes.'

'Once. The one and last time.'

'What if the weather is horrible, like now?'

'I've swum in worse.'

Fenn manages a faint smile. Her eyes shine and not with tears. 'Promise?' The word is very tentative.

'I promise.'

'Thank you.'

'Now finish your tea while I phone your mum.'

On the phone to Julia, Jess speaks loud enough for Fenn to hear, so that the two of them will tell the same story. She makes up some half-truths about them setting off in somewhat uncertain conditions and having to turn back as the weather deteriorated. Fenn beams across glances of gratitude and relief.

'Is Fenn OK?' Julia asks.

'She's cold and tired. I shouldn't have taken her out.' It's a blatant lie but her loyalty to Fenn overrules her need to tell the truth. The girl would be grounded for weeks. Perhaps not allowed to swim by herself again. Or even go to the beach alone. And then Jess would miss her, she admits. White lies, she tells herself. The girl is here. The girl is safe.

'I bet she twisted your arm. I know how keen she is,' Julia is saying, swallowing the story hook, line and sinker.

'I know how to say no. Anyway it didn't look too bad when we set off. But can you come and get her? An early night might be a good idea.'

When Julia arrives fifteen minutes later, she picks up nothing amiss and nothing out of the ordinary, except Fenn's attire.

'Wow! You look quite something! Thanks, Jess, for lending her those. I'll wash them and get them back to you.'

'Her wet things are in that bag,' Jess replies, keeping to the safe and the practical.

'So it was a rough swim, was it?' Julia asks, noting her daughter's paleness.

'A bit,' Fenn says. 'We had to turn back.' Jess notes the slightly worried glance Fenn throws her way and gives her the smallest nod of agreement. Yes, Fenn, we are in this together. God help me.

At the door, while Julia is bundling stuff into the back of the car, Fenn turns and wraps her arms around Jess, hugging her tightly, her eyes speaking of shame and gratitude and maybe hope. A lot can be said without words and Jess hears it all.

*

That evening, round the dining table, Fenn says not a word while she attacks her venison stew and moves seamlessly on to apple crumble. Hamish and Julia are chatting about trees and sheep and other croft matters that require nothing from her.

'Nothing like a cold swim to give you an appetite,' Julia comments. 'Good job I did some cooking today. Cheese on toast wouldn't have hit the mark.'

Fenn looks up and smiles.

'But you look very pale, sweetheart. Are you sure you're OK?'

'I'm fine.'

'I'm a bit surprised you two went out today. The weather took a definite turn for the worse when I was in town. I got drenched.'

'Jess swims in all weathers,' Fenn replies.

'It's you I'm worrying about, darling. Not Jess.'

'I've spoken to Dan,' Hamish says, his interruption perfectly timed. 'Not that I needed to because the subject of whales is all over the news.'

'What?' Fenn asks, rising above her exhaustion, suddenly alert.

'Odd timing with our daughter going on about whales.'

'What, Dad?' More loudly.

'Aye...well...I didn't need to ask Dan about previous sightings because a sperm whale was washed up on one of the other islands yesterday. Sixty-six foot male.'

'Goodness, Hamish. How awful,' Julia says.

'Was the whale alive or dead?' Fenn asks, at the same time.

'It had been dead for at least six hours by the time the folk from the Marine group got there.'

A cold shock trembles down Fenn's spine. It could be her whale. Grounded on a different island. It's too late. It's beached. It's dead. Her eyes swim.

Hamish sees the look on her daughter's face and reads it correctly. 'It's no' your whale, Fenn. If there is one. Timing's wrong.'

Fenn takes a deep breath and works backwards from hearing the song today. Of course. Her dad is right. She's not thinking straight. She lets out a huge sigh.

'It's a bad deal,' Hamish continues. 'When they cut it open, they found two hundred pounds of plastic in its stomach.'

Now Julia's face blanches. 'Oh my god, how awful.'

'Aye...coils of rope, netting and tons of plastic. Nasty way to die.'

'I've been reading a lot about plastic polluting the oceans. But that much...' Julia tails off.

'Aye, it's happening more and more. Fish stuffed to the gills with plastic.'

'Where was it swimming?' Julia asks. 'I missed the story on my phone because I was out buying paint and then picking up Fenn.'

'They think it crossed fishing areas between Norway and the Azores. It got into difficulty somewhere near Inverness.'

'Chucking plastic in the ocean shouldn't be allowed,' Fenn says loudly, fighting her way through the exhaustion that is closing in on her. 'Why is it allowed?'

'Because people are stupid and ignorant,' Hamish replies. 'And the English government doesn't give a fuck about wildlife.'

'Hamish!'

'Sorry.'

'We should do something!' Fenn is aghast.

'Aye, well how about you sit outside the school with a placard like that lass from Sweden?'

'Her name's Greta Thunberg, Dad.'

'Aye, her. I'm no' good with names.'

'Maybe I will.' And with the news of the whale's death comes another thought. 'So it's not impossible that there are other whales…near other islands?'

Hamish and Julia exchange looks. And a question mark. Yes, they acknowledge their child's exuberant imagination, but could she possibly be right about a whale in their bay? They will speak of this later. When she is in bed.

'Do you no' think one whale washed up on a Scottish beach is enough, Fenn?' Hamish asks her.

'Your jokes are totally stupid, Dad. There could be another whale swimming towards our island.' And with that parting shot, her head drops onto her arms, and her eyes close. Today has been way too much.

'Go to bed, darling,' Julia says. 'I'll fill a hot water bottle.'

Fenn nods.

She says nothing more, but hope flickers as she climbs the stairs. The story isn't over yet.

Chapter 29

Jess

She promised, and she won't break a promise, especially to a child, especially to that rather unusual and rather wonderful little girl with a large bee in her bonnet. Wrong metaphor, she thinks. Wrong size of creature. Wrong element.

Better get it over with early, she decides, in the morning when Fenn is safely in her classroom and can't even think about following me into the water. Jess doubts she would, not after the fright she got yesterday, and she expects a subdued Fenn for a while yet. The other reason for going, and going soon, is to put this long-running story to rest. It's time. But here she hesitates because she too read about the sperm whale that was washed up on a beach on one of the other islands with a stomach full of plastic. Not far away. And only yesterday. Not for the first time, she considers the possibility that Fenn's absolute assurance is not pure fantasy. Her dogged insistence that she has heard something can't be signed off just yet.

First, Jess has to have a firm talk with herself and she rather dreads it. Her decision, after the rowing boat floated on the horizon that last time she swam with Fenn, was to stay out of the sea. Sure, there was no boat out there yesterday, but her mind was totally occupied on one thing and one thing only, getting a cold, exhausted girl to safety. But before that, before Fenn took leave of her senses, Jess had made up her mind not to go back for long, gentle swims until she feels strong enough to face the sea again. To be honest, that last appearance shook her to the core, bad enough to stop her wanting to swim, and that's serious. So, she asks herself now, what happens if the boat pops up while she's out there hunting down a whale? So be it, she replies. Deal with it. Fenn has conjured up a whale in distress that eats away at her and worries her sick. I have conjured up a boat that makes my heart sink. What a pair we are.

While changing into her swimsuit and packing her rucksack, Jess thinks about the endings that she and Fenn need. For Fenn, the simplest answer is for the sounds to be nothing to do with whales or other lost creatures of the deep. The child is preoccupied and anxious, trying to save a creature who may live only in her imagination. She might be freer, lighter, without it. And her? She wants never to see the damn boat again. But is that the whole truth? Is she in some perverse way clinging to the boat as the last image of the man she loves? Is it her own need that brings it back over and over again? Is it because she can't let it go? The word they use is closure. That's what they called it in the counselling sessions she tried and abandoned as unhelpful. Sitting in a hushed circle with other miserable people made her even more wretched. Grief piled on grief. No. Only she can work out how to deal with what happened and find a way to accept the sea without fear and dread.

Fortunately, the gale has blown itself out. Jess leaps down

the sand dunes under a clear if slightly uncertain sky. The water, marbled and crested yesterday, is simmering down to its habitual state of untroubled blue. The waves seem to be in no hurry to wash up the beach. She imagines the ocean breathing softly again, its mood benign and welcoming. Jess strips off, stretches her arms high above her head, touches her toes, twists and turns to wake up her muscles, breathes in the clean, wind-washed air. She tells herself she is mad doing this, but carries on anyway.

The tide is in. Three steps and a dive, and she is under, then streaming away with a strong, elegant crawl that takes her quickly to the line that's drawn in invisible ink on the water. Today, out here, she is at ease, her worries left like a pile of stripped-off, folded clothes weighed down with a rock on the shore. Which is why she so resented the intrusion of the boat. This is her playground, her joy, her world. This is where she belongs. The damn boat tears her in two, her longing to be in the water at war with her dread of it. Don't think about it, she tells herself. She swims on, blissful, enchanted, glorying in her easy buoyancy, her supple strength. At the place where the child instructed her to stop, she stops, flips onto her back and floats, the water all around her. This gentle pause is her gift to herself.

OK, time to put your head under, Jess! Feeling rather ridiculous, but telling herself she can't renege, she takes a huge breath and dives down. Holding herself very still, she waits. And waits. And feels her heart quicken. Her skin is all goosebumps and not from the cold because she can hear something. No, no, she tries to tell herself. You're easy prey to someone else's imagination. You're hearing what Fenn wants you to hear. But no, it's nothing to do with Fenn, and nothing to do with clouded reasoning because she can hear something, a continuous vibrato which isn't anything like the familiar creaks and squeaks and bubbles of the alive underwater world she knows so well. This long-held note pierces all those smaller, familiar noises, like someone running their finger up and down a taut wire with the volume turned up full. The sound travels to her across horizontal lines. It's melodic and metallic and shrill and tubular. Wow! Jess feels shaken, like the most unlikely thing has happened after all. Against all the odds.

Surfacing for air, she notes that her heart is pounding. Down she goes again, and straightaway she picks it up like this player hasn't stopped playing while she's been away. Lines of music stream through the ocean. The song is heartbreakingly beautiful. It is mesmerising and haunting. So this is what the child has heard. My goodness, no wonder she is so worked up about it. And there I was not really believing a word she said. That poor girl, no-one believing her when she has heard this poignant, surging call.

So what is it? Jess asks when she reluctantly comes up again for air. A whale, comes the whispered answer. Treading water so as to barely disturb the surface or the sounds that sing down there in the depths, and thinking hard, trying to put reason before wish fulfilment, she asks herself a flurry of questions to which she has no simple answers. How come she can hear the call? And Fenn too? Humans can't hear whale songs, can they? Unless this whale is different from all the others. And is there really a whale somewhere in this bay, as Fenn thinks? It contradicts all Jess knows about patterns of migration, and feeding and breeding areas, but then she remembers the whale that was washed up on the other island beach. Well, you're not going to find the answers bobbing up and down here, she tells herself.

Once more she goes back down because this underwater song pulls you and holds you. Yes, it is still playing on, coloured with an emotion that Jess might call yearning or longing if that makes the slightest sense. It contains a twist of notes that are haunting and beautiful. So very beautiful. She shakes her head down there. Reaching for words to describe it is pointless. There are no words. The song is itself and Jess accepts it. With gratitude, With gladness. With humility. She will tell Fenn. And then what should they do? One answer, and more questions.

She's only just turned back, stretching her limbs in a satisfyingly slow breaststroke whose rhythm matches the thrilling arcs of sound that play on in her head, when she sees it. For fuck's sake! This time, her mood is defiant and furious, perhaps because she's just heard a whale sing and she's thinking about a creature who is out there calling, perhaps in trouble. The rowing boat is of no interest. It's redundant. An intrusion. Hey, Dan, this time you've got the timing all wrong. Turn around and head for the horizon.

'Go away!' she shouts. She ducks her head and switches mid-stroke to a fast crawl. She lifts one arm then the other over her head, kicks hard, and knives through the water. 'Leave me alone. I've had enough. I've grieved for you for two years. Bloody hell, isn't that time enough?'

Jess turns her head to face the shore and swims on, angry with herself and her own sick imagination that brings the hauntings. There's no boat. There's only a whale.

Chapter 30

Jess

Having vowed to look straight ahead, to ignore the boat, to swim on and reach the shore and run as fast as she can go, Jess finds herself slowing, turning her head, glancing back. Always, always, the pull is too strong. With a weary sigh blown out as bubbles through the water, she halts. She can stand here. It's just shallow enough. The song of what might have been a whale fades as the boat comes further into view. There are two stories here. One kills the other.

Before, all those other times, the ghost images played in slow motion, frame by frozen frame, and that gave her time to look away. And she always did so at the exact same point in the story, like she's shouting, Stop! Stop right there! I'm not looking. I'm not watching any more of it. Self-defence, self-protection, call it what she will, it amounts to the same thing. She is unable to watch it through to the end.

This time, the image on the water is more like a cinema film: clearer, sharper and spooling out in normal time. Dan is already there on the thwart, oars resting in the rowlocks, looking at her to check if she needs anything. The megaphone is in the bilge so he's not about to shout at her to change stroke or alter her pace or take a rest. Good, she thinks. My beloved trainer finds my progress satisfactory today. And here she catches herself slipping straight back into her part, as if it were yesterday, and there's nothing she can do about it.

Back she goes, back in time. It's not the day she hears the whale, but that final day of training in a cold English sea off a cold English beach, before she makes her attempt to cross the channel. She's practising an arms-only crawl in case she gets cramp in one of her legs. It's usually her calf muscles that seize up and that's both agonising and destabilising. She swims on, a few yards from the boat, switches to breaststroke, using arms and legs, and lifts her head. She and Dan exchange a nod and a smile of satisfaction. They have worked so hard for this, both of them, and they are confident she can do it. She has swum across lakes on another continent but now a grey sea beckons. She will get out of this stretch of water in France.

Jess is right back there, both taking part in the scene that plays out, and at the same time watching it. Inside and outside. Dan's position in the boat has shifted. What is he doing? He was upright and laughing a minute ago, but now he's hunched over, one arm flung across his chest. His face looks strained and very pale. He's not looking at her any more but staring, glaring at some other invisible point beyond her. Then he's folding over...folding over...

This is the moment when Jess always stops watching, her face wet with tears. Cut! Cut! Cut! Dan folds over and Jess looks away. Every time, Dan folds over and Jess looks away, not wanting to see any more. But this time she is in the film as well as outside it and has no choice but to carry on.

Dan is doubled over, arm still flung across his chest. Leaning. Top heavy, he is keeling over and unbalancing the boat so that it rocks like crazy. My god, he is going over. He's going over the side of the boat and into the water. He rolls into it head first in an almost perfect tuck dive and black water closes over him. During the seconds that Jess waits, and holds her breath, he does not reappear. Christ, why doesn't he come back up? Where is he?

'Dan!' Jess yells. 'Hang on. I'm coming. I'm coming.'

Jess swims as hard as she's ever swum in her life. It's only twenty metres and she's there in seconds. Dan is still under. She dives, sees him going down, a big bundle of a man sinking, not struggling. She grabs hold of him, an arm, a piece of anorak, then they're both heading for the bottom, tangled together. Jess frees her arms, gets them under his armpits and tries, with desperate frog's leg kicks, to drag him back up. He is utterly limp. The layers and layers of clothes, worn to keep warm when sitting still in a small dinghy while his wife powers through miles of water, are impossibly heavy with water. Her lungs are bursting and she cannot pull Dan up. Christ, she must do it because he needs air. It's taking far too long. Panic kicks in. Despite her skills as a lifeguard, despite having practised similar manoeuvres with men pretending to drown, she can't move him. They are both going down. She lets go and surfaces and maybe the boost of oxygen jump-starts her brain because she knows that of course she can't drag his weight straight up. The only way to do it is on a diagonal, slower, but so be it. Down she goes again, and this time she kicks at Dan's legs to tilt him onto his back so that he is partly floating. Now they are moving through the water, but too slowly, and all the time she's thinking it's taking far too long. He's taking in water. Oh christ, he's taking in water. Hurry up, Jess! Dan needs to breathe. With nothing left, she gets them to the surface, breaks through and takes great gulps of air as she battles dizziness and nausea. But now she's having difficulty keeping Dan's head above the waves because it flops sideways, his neck useless. She treads water until her breath steadies, but she must carry on.

'Dan, I've got you. Hang on in there,' Jess says with what little breath she has.

His curly hair is dripping rivers down his face and his eyes are closed. Refusing to listen for a breath because of course he's breathing, she struggles to keep his head out of the water as she sets off again, dragging him inch by inch towards the shore. God, he's a dead weight. She catches herself thinking that word. Stupid thing to say. Of course he's not dead. He's fainted. He's collapsed. He's taken in water but he'll be fine. It's slow progress. Jess can do it, she's been trained to do exactly this, but it's taking a lot out of her. With everything concentrated on keeping Dan above the water and getting him back to the beach, she has to shut out thoughts about what's wrong with him.

It seems like forever but she's only gone a short way when she hears voices but she can't turn her head because she's locked in a life-saving embrace with her husband. Then a voice is close. Hands and arms reaching out. There are others in the water.

'OK, you can let go. I can take him now.' The man at her side sounds calm and confident. He says it again. 'Let go. Let me take him.'

She trusts the voice and so they play pass the parcel and extricate Dan from her arms and into his. Free of the weight, she stretches her aching neck, and looks around. There are several people close to her, the one who spoke swimming Dan steadily back to the shore. With one glance she is confident he knows what he's doing.

'Are you OK?' Another voice.

'We were on the beach.' A different voice. 'We're all swimmers.'

'Yes,' Jess replies. 'I don't know what happened out there. He... '

'Don't talk. You can explain later. Do you want some help getting back?'

'I'm fine,' Jess says, and sets off after the man who is kicking backwards with her husband hanging in his arms.

Two others swim close on either side of her, like guards keeping watch in case she falters, but Jess powers on and walks out of the sea and across the pebbles in time to help take Dan's weight and carry him up to the dry reaches of the beach. None of it makes sense, none of it is clear, but she's aware that others are supporting him. Four of them lay him down and roll him into the recovery position on his left side. Jess is on her knees, pushing away his dripping curls with one hand, the other hand inside his sodden anorak and jumper and shirt as she tries to find his heartbeat. A man is kneeling next to her, his fingers searching for a pulse in his neck. He glances up at the others.

'Are you...?' He turns to Jess.

'His wife.' Jess answers as an ice-cold finger draws a line right down her spine. She's shivering and trembling as the situation, bit by shocking bit, starts to sink in. Yeah, this is real. Dan was drowning out there. Incomprehensible and impossible but it happened. It has happened.

'I'm a medic.' It's the man who had his fingers on Dan's neck. 'I'm going to start CPR.'

They move as a team, rolling Dan onto his back. A different man tips Dan's head back and holds his mouth open. Then the jump-starting begins. Over and over and over.

'I've phoned for an ambulance,' says one of the others. 'Five minutes.'

'He'll be OK, won't he?' Jess asks.

No-one answers.

From afar it must look like a strange slow-motion dance performed by five wet people in swim gear who move about on their knees, leaning over a man who is prone and still on the grey sand.

And after that, the film goes into fast-forward with people taking turns to press on Dan's chest and someone wrapping a blanket round Jess's shoulders and putting a paper cup of brandy in her hand and a crowd gathering on the beach and being told to keep away and a police woman bending over Jess and telling her she can go with her husband in the ambulance that's waiting on the promenade and Dan is being lifted onto a stretcher and people in uniform walking with him and Jess jogging at his side holding his hand and telling him he will be all right and that she loves him. Loves him so much.

It's a blur, then, of being inside a speeding ambulance with sirens ringing and a paramedic pressing down on Dan's chest until they get to the hospital where the ambulance doors open and people are running with a trolley, running back with Dan on the trolley, a clutch of white-coated medics at his side, a doctor doing CPR in A & E while Jess is led away and told to sit on a chair in the corridor and wait because there's nothing more she can do. Some time later, a senior doctor arrives at her side. And she knows.

'Let's go into the side room over there,' he says, taking her elbow.

He closes the door. And Jess knows.

'He didn't make it. I'm so sorry.'

Some time later in a fog of days and nights, the phone rings and Jess hears a voice speaking as if from far, far away. The voice says he's a doctor from the hospital, and something about having the results from an autopsy. The words fall out of the phone in small pieces.

It was a heart attack

Massive

Hypertrophic cardiomyopathy...we call it HCM...the walls of the heart muscle thicken...disrupt the heart's electrical system...fast or irregular heartbeats...can lead to sudden cardiac death

A cause of death in young athletes

Like a time bomb

Would have known nothing

Could have happened any day

Nothing to do with falling into the sea

A very fit man but the plumbing of his heart was flawed

Kind words but Jess rubs them out with an eraser. She has relived those minutes so many times that she knows the script by heart and she knows the doctor is saying these lines just to comfort her. Dan drowned. He felt dizzy or had one of his migraines, maybe passed out and fell overboard. It was an accident. And it was her fault. She didn't reach him in time. She didn't get him to the surface in time. She had to come up for air and leave her husband sinking. Her slowness cost him his life. All those years of training and lifting weights and swimming across miles of ocean and she wasn't strong enough to pull her drowning husband to safety. It's ironic and improbable as hell, like a really bad joke, but it's absolutely her fault that he drowned when a moment earlier she had been swimming beside the rowing boat while he waited for her to clamber aboard. He was about to hold out his hand. Like he always did. She carries the guilt like an albatross, its claws sunk deep into her shoulders. No wonder he comes back to haunt her. To chastise her. Yes, Dan, I deserve your mockery and your fury.

Back in the ocean that laps the shores of an island almost a thousand miles from the accident, Jess blinks away the past as her focus returns to the present. She seems to have continued swimming without registering any movement because she is close to the shore. Tears pour down her already wet face but she feels a quiet relief along with the sadness. This time she saw it through all the way to its ending. The sea is quietening after the gale. The boat is gone.

*

Who is that waving on the beach? It can't be Fenn because she's at school. It is Fenn. The girl has jumped up and is running hard towards Jess who walks out of a sea that holds so many stories. Jess swipes at her face to wipe away the tears.

'Hey Jess! You're early.' Fenn calls. It's not a reproach. Maybe Fenn has done enough swimming for now.

'I fancied an early dip,' Jess lies, and gets the predicted eye-roll response. 'Why aren't you in school?'

'Mum decided I could have a day off. I was dead tired last night.' Fenn raises her eyebrows, waiting for a reprimand that doesn't come. 'Thank you for not telling.'

Jess shrugs her shoulders. 'It's history. Am I right in thinking you won't try that again?'

Fenn nods, shamefaced. Then shakes her head. Nod or shake, which is the right response?

'I just worry that Julia thinks I'm totally irresponsible,' Jess adds. 'And may not look so kindly on us two swimming together.'

'I told her it was my fault...that I begged you to coach me even though it was a bit stormy because you go out in all weathers.'

'Hmm. Let's hope.' Jess is not convinced. Julia probably isn't either.

A comfortable silence settles over them as they make their way slowly up the beach but in Fenn's fidgeting, Jess senses the barely contained and unspoken question. It explodes as they reach the dunes.

'Jess, did you hear it?' Fenn holds her breath. Behind her back, her fingers are crossed. Her body is rigid as she waits. And hopes.

'I did, Fenn. I did.'

Fenn's mouth stretches in the widest of grins. She jumps up in the air. Does a handstand that covers Jess with sand. 'Oh cool! Oh hurray!'

Jess smiles too.

'And what did it sound like?'

'Amazing and magical and very moving.'

'I know!'

'Now I understand your obsession.'

Fenn shrugs her slim shoulders, as if a weight has fallen off them. 'So what shall we do now?'

'Well, we could talk to the coastguard down by the harbour. There's usually someone on duty. Let me find out,

Fenn. Or we could talk to your parents first? Your dad might know what to do.'

'They won't believe us. Mum will think you've gone batty and Dad will laugh at us. Let's tell the coastguard,' Fenn says. 'I have to go back very soon because Mum said half an hour and no longer. She's keeping a careful eye on me after yesterday.'

'How about we meet after school tomorrow here on the dunes? We can go together in my car. But, Fenn, I doubt anyone is going to do anything.'

Fenn considers this. 'Well, at least it's not just a child telling them.'

'OK. We can try. But listen, don't get your hopes up. I mean, what can anyone do about a whale singing a sad song in our bay?'

The humour is lost in a child's need for action. 'Take a boat out and see if they can see anything? A fin? A tail? You never know, they might see it.'

'And then what?'

'Um...find a way to turn it round and head it away from the beach.'

'That wouldn't be easy.'

'Maybe with several small boats they could form a kind of barrier and persuade it back into the ocean?'

'And afterwards? When the boats leave?'

'Well, we'll have tried.'

'Yes, we'll have tried.'

Fenn gives a tight little smile. And Jess understands how very much this means to her, to have someone else who backs up her story, someone else who has heard the whale. May have heard the whale, Jess corrects herself. The girl is at her side, her arms wrapped tight around her waist, her head resting on her shoulders. Jess can almost hear her words, Someone understands. And then she's off, exuberant, exultant, very much Fenn.

While Jess gets changed, Fenn races up and down the sand doing cartwheels, Hero barking round her ankles. He's picked up the mood of excitement and it doesn't matter that he hasn't a clue what it means. This is fun. His mistress is happy.

And Jess thinks about how she has told only one story. There was another.

'Yes, Fenn, I think I heard your whale. And I watched Dan die.'

But this she says silently. Who to tell it to?

Chapter 31

The Whale

He has been listening keenly for that infrequent and intermittent sound, delicate and sweet, faint and unfamiliar, not the call of another whale, but something calling because it comes again and again, though he cannot predict when. In its soft ripples he hears no hint of a threat, rather kindness and caring. Sometimes he reads more into the calls, perhaps there's a wish to find him, a wish to be at his side. With that thought, he leaps to the surface and crashes his great tail from side to side to make his presence felt. And seen and heard. After the weeks without whale song, he treasures the new song that unexpectedly trembles towards him. He twists and turns, making sure he doesn't miss it in an ocean that is awash with splashing, streaming, slapping sounds. He waits expectantly. And with hope.

Then there is nothing. It stops. Was it his loneliness that changed a meaningless, transient ocean noise into a song that promised something more? He had almost persuaded himself, for a few days, that another creature was trying to reach him. It came from under the water, the call liquid and built of bubbles. And so he swims on through a double silence. No whale calls. No silvery ribbons, as thin as strands of seaweed that bend in the rush of a fast current. Sound tracks from the past and from the present fall silent.

His stomach is empty, his energy depleted and, close to defeat, he dips and arcs through the sea without purpose and without a point ahead which marks his destination. He swims without the chords that used to ricochet from whale to whale in his pod, a constant guide and reassurance. He has almost forgotten what those calls are like. For a very long time he hung on to the possibility of finding his family, but that hope has been rinsed away in the miles of crossed water. The rhythm of his arcs slows and becomes laboured. The silence, more present since the second soundtrack also stopped, feels ominous.

Where should I go?

Which way shall I turn?

What is the point in carrying on?

Because he is exhausted, his echo-location calls to pinpoint his position are too infrequent and too weak to give him the information he needs. The clues are there, but he misses them. Worse, his strong instinct to survive is eroded by weeks of solitude and makes him careless. He swims on, barely paying attention. After all, what's the point? What will be, will be.

On he goes until he is close enough to land to pick up a weak electrical signal and for a while his interest is piqued. It's something. It's not more miles of empty ocean. But whereas once he would have been all critical attention, now he is listening with senses dulled by his gruelling journey. So while he can feel the tingling lines of static that streak through the water, he doesn't have the energy, or perhaps the will, to use them to construct the precise contours of the place that lies somewhere ahead. Anyway, does it matter? Tuning in and out, not concentrating, he misses the clues and half-heartedly constructs a small mass, flat and rimmed by water. It's not a danger, he thinks, and switches off his receivers, and in doing so makes his first serious mistake. Had he tuned in for longer, he would have worked out that the land is not far away. Mistaking its modest size as an insignificant land mass, maybe rocks, he carries on, perhaps in the belief that he can easily swim around it. If he had encountered these echoes sooner, when he was stronger and more alert, he would have picked up dissonance and danger, and queried it. He would have heard the equivalent of bells ringing on red alert.

Hey, is this really right?

Am I not heading for land?

And isn't that land too near?

And so he crosses an invisible line and chances into an area of water that hums with complex magnetic activity. If he had been surrounded by his pod, they would have called a warning to one another to turn around and swim the other way. Alone, what he feels is this: a sudden fizz of energy zipping through the water and catching the tips of his sensitive whiskers. He knows this pull to be the earth's magnetic field, a criss-cross of electric signals easily picked up in places like this where it runs strong and clear. After swimming to the surface, he rotates his head to collect the signals, tunes in to the vibes and stores them. There's a hazy, inexact memory of other whales doing this when the magnetic field was strong, when they headed upwards, bodies rotating, heads held high, senses acute. Afterwards, they would swim with the vibrations, dipping and diving in and around the magnetic lines that pulled them parallel to the coast into deeper, safer waters. When he rode the magnetic lines with his pod, and listened as they listened, they all moved as one, a constant distance from a shore. This is good, they sang to one another. Keep swimming onwards. We can trust these signals.

But they would have been ready for a rogue signal and a wrong turn. In another time, in another place, older whales would have called to the others to be wary. Take care, they would call. These lines are good for us to follow, but stay on guard because they can be fluky. They can also be wrong. Dangerously wrong.

As indeed they are here. Instead of running reliably parallel to the shore, one of the magnetic lines bends inwards towards land. This is his second drastic mistake. He fails to pick up a freak change of direction. A sharp ninety degree turn. The whale alters course towards the shore.

Is that what happens? Is it a mistake born of exhaustion and a growing indifference to his own safety? Or, after three thousand miles of ocean, is anywhere that promises other life better than pushing on alone? Or is it the whisper of a promise that ahead he'll pick up the seaweed bubble sounds of that creature whose call promised an end to loneliness.

For whatever reason, distracted, the lost whale misreads the vibrations as long straight lines and relaxes into the equivalent of a helping hand that pulls him through the depths of the sea. Here at last is the security of a humming trail that he can follow and he clings to it as to a life raft. He turns off his receivers and enjoys the companionship of electric sparks that are flicker and fizz over his skin.

But luck is not on his side. He fails to note that the line he is following turns inwards towards land, a sharp kink, in exactly the wrong direction. There have been others before him, single whales and even pods who followed a freak magnetic line and were beached. Like him, they may have been tired or struggling. Or confused. No-one knows for sure. Certainly the lost whale is blithely unaware that he is riding an errant signal and is on a doomed course.

He's drawn ever closer to land. It's a cruel stroke of fate. Unaware that he's making a catastrophic error and still relaxed and at ease, he swims the remaining miles with an easy confidence, rising and dipping in arcs that hold the residue of his former grace, and heads for the Atlantic-lapped shore of a small Scottish island. Here the faulty magnetic line comes to an abrupt end and dumps him.

Shock waves tremble through his bulk as he registers the inadequate wash of shallow water over his long back. The skin of his belly is scraped and scratched by pebbles and gritty sand as he bumps and grinds over the seabed. And it is far too late to alter course. There is no way he can turn his heavy, sunken body around and hump himself back into the deeper water. With a terrible sense of the inevitable, he feels his bulk being dragged wave by wave through the shallows and onto the hard-packed sand where he is beached with a tide in retreat. Out of water, he senses his massive size and weight as a calamity that presses on his internal organs and inflicts pain. His taken-for-granted buoyancy and improbable lightness when riding the waves are gone in seconds as his contours spread into a shapeless mass of blubber. Already he is drying out. He is immobile. His great tail gives a last sway, side to side, then that too lies still on the sand.

Chapter 32

Beached

It's 10.30.

The tide is half-way up the beach, not quite at the seaweed line. Men and women from the marine centre have arrived. Oxygen tanks and dive gear, coils of rope and webbing lean against the dunes or are propped up on the sand. In their uniform navy wetsuits, they stand in a tight group, talking to the islanders who have led the rescue and those with diving experience. The bucket line came to a halt when it was made redundant by the tide. The bucket-bearers are further up the beach, some rubbing arms that still ache.

'It will be difficult,' the leader, Duncan, is telling the others. 'If he were further out, deep water could give him buoyancy and help us push him but he's too far up the beach. So here's the plan: we form a ring around him. Some of us will be on the seabed...you know who you are... and if he starts to move, with luck a wobble from side to side, that's when we go for it. Try to get straps and ropes under him, dig into the sand if it helps. But be very careful not to get hands and arms caught. That creature weighs more than you can imagine. And we have a very short time window.'

'What if we can't get him afloat?' It's the question no-one wants to ask, but James says it.

'Then we fail. He's totally inert and if he isn't rolled by a bit by the water, it will be hellish hard to budge him. Can you tell all these people to go further back up the beach? A noisy crowd doesn't help. And those bloody journalists. How did they get here so quickly? OK. Let's go get the equipment, then every hand on deck.'

James grabs the megaphone. 'Will you please move back up the beach. I repeat, move right back up the beach. Thank you to all those who helped with the buckets. There's no more you can do. Nothing is going to happen quickly so you might as well go home.'

There is some shifting of positions, some movement towards the dunes. A few mothers take their children's hands and set off home. Older people leave too, their joints stiff from sitting too long on the sand. The crowd thins. Julia walks back to the croft to fill a rucksack with food and hot drinks. She notes the chill in the air and smells rain on its way.

Jess and Fenn had to retreat when the water reached the top of their wellies, but not before Fenn stroked the whale's head and whispered more quiet words. Hamish, in his wetsuit, is with the group by the whale.

Jess turns to Fenn. 'I'm going to race home to get something to eat and get my wetsuit. 'I should have thought of that.'

'Mum's bringing lunch.'

'I know. But I need my heavy-weather gear. Won't be long.'

Her words bounce off the girl whose eyes don't leave the whale.

'Do it,' she says. 'Please do it.'

It's 11.30.

The whale, surrounded by abandoned piles of ropes and straps and spades and helmets thrown down on the sand, lies exactly where he was, enormous mouth agape as if in a frozen cry for help. Men and women, clearly spent, sit on the damp sand, shoulders stooped, heads bowed. The crowd has dispersed because there's nothing new to see and hope is fading. The disappointment is palpable. Who wants to stare at a dying whale?

When the tide rolled further in and covered the whale, they had moved into action, a well-briefed, well-organised team of about twenty people who set to with a calm but almost superhuman energy. It was a careful, coordinated series of movements as ropes were dragged over the creature and across the surface of the water. Divers' heads appeared from the shallow water to pull ropes down, ready to tuck under his bulk if he lifted, even for a second. They waited for that one chance.

There was a moment when the whale rocked, pushed by strengthening waves and a shout went up. Under the water, divers struggled to push ropes under him. In the moments that followed, all went to plan and the whale lifted off the seabed. For a few more moments he rolled from side to side and the divers got more ropes under.

'Pull! Pull!' Duncan shouted.

And they pulled, but the whale subsided and sank back down. It was excruciatingly close.

Fenn leant her head on Jess's shoulder. 'Is it all over?' she asked.

'No. Not yet.'

It's 12.00.

The situation is grave but the team has decided to give it one more go while the tide is in. While the whale is still alive. A steady drizzle darkens the sand. The horizon is a black line which predicts a squall. Further out, the waves are building and frothing.

Julia has trudged back to the croft several times to fetch more blankets, more hot drinks and Fenn's wetsuit, a request she couldn't refuse. She appears again now on the dunes and looks down on her daughter with love and worry before jumping down and crouching at her side.

'Fenn...sweetheart...please come home and warm up. You'll be frozen.'

Fenn shakes her head.

'You can come back.'

'No. I'm staying.'

'Just ten minutes to get warm.'

'No!' Fenn glares at her mother. How can she even think about dragging her away.

Julia sighs. Knows it's hopeless. 'You must be frozen too, Jess,' she says.

'I'm used to it. Done a lot of this in my time. Being cold and wet was a way of life.'

'Even so....' Julia forgets what she was about to say.

'But now you're here, I'll go back and join in.' Jess doesn't say she's been itching to join in again, to use her expertise, but she stayed on the dunes with Fenn.

'Fine. You go down. Looks like things are happening again.'

Jess walks away to join those who are standing up and stretching before gathering ropes and heading back into the water. The wind is up and sandblasts their faces. The sea looks troubled. The whale is half submerged.

Back at the sand dunes a girl peels off her wet clothes and, shivering, drags on her wet suit.

It's 14.00.

The onlookers who have stayed to watch the last act are on their feet. The whale is afloat, its body lifted first by ropes but then held by the water. He isn't moving. His fin sticks up rigid and redundant. But his eyes are open. Jess is right there with the other divers in wetsuits and helmets, hoods and goggles. Some bob along the seabed on tiptoe and at a signal all push at once against his mighty tail. Others swim alongside him and nudge him with their bodies, inch by inch, further out to sea. They know to keep their movements slow and even. Each and every one is aware that this is their last chance. And as they urge the whale on, the wind roars in, marbling the water and chucking it in their faces. The storm is not far away. But this is in their favour.

Duncan has waved the flotilla of boats away because they aren't needed. People are less threatening than motors. The skippers have chugged towards the headlands, ready to fire up again if called. As the divers reach the underwater cliff edge, they allow themselves a fizz of excitement at reaching deep water. Cautious, hesitant excitement. Jess is swimming near the front when a small person in a bright blue wetsuit and cap appears at her side.

'Fenn! What the hell are you doing here?' Jess yells, aghast that the child has ventured into the sea. Why didn't someone stop her? 'It's too cold. Too dangerous. He might dive or roll.'

'I know. I'll be careful.'

'It's not safe. We don't need a child out here. We have enough to worry about.'

'I'll swim by you.'

'You're cold and tired. For christ's sake, go back!'

'No. I want to help him too.'

And because Jess is too busy, too determined, too involved, too anxious, she hasn't the time or the will to argue. Not out here in the sea where a whale may live or die. Side by side, they swim alongside his floating body, hands on skin that is rough and dark, gently nudging it forwards. Further. And further. And then, perhaps fifty metres from the shore and in churning, choppy water, the whale shudders. The swimmers quickly move away, Jess pulling Fenn by her arm. The whale squirms, a corkscrew twist. Shudders again. As if running through tests to see if everything is still working, he makes small movements and adjustments, swings his tail, moves his fins. Like a plane before take-off. His first dive is careful and cautious. He surfaces, and dives again. He is in slow motion but he is swimming. Of course the divers want to shout and scream, but they limit their rejoicing to splashy high fives and quiet laughter. And tears.

Jess grabs Fenn's arm. 'Back!' she commands. 'Now. Hang on to my shoulders and I'll pull you.'

Fenn doesn't argue. She's spent.

One by one, the swimmers drop away, leaving a few hardy swimmers to see it through to the end. Conditions are nasty. Squalls rip across the surface. Waves buffet and boil, their white crests rising and breaking. Fenn puts one hand on each of Jess's shoulders, secretly glad of the ride as waves break over her head and knock her under. Too busy and preoccupied before, others have noticed a child amongst them, and two swimmers stay close, one on either side, ready to grab her or the woman towing her, if either falters. Fenn spots her parents waiting at the water's edge. No swimmer,

Hamish retreated when his contribution on dry land was done. Fenn lets go of Jess, stumbles over the pebbles and rushes into Julia's embrace. Her mother's arms are open, holding out a towel. She rubs her shivering, white-faced daughter and wraps her in a blanket. Fenn looks from one to the other. There is no scolding.

Jess is at their side. Nudging on a whale that is barely breathing while making sure a child stays alive in deep water has left her a bit winded. The toll is more emotional than physical but she bends over to catch her breath. Fenn notices, despite being done in herself. It's a novelty to see Jess puffed.

'He's…on his way,' Jess says.

'That's wonderful,' Julia replies. 'It was touch and go.'

'It's go,' Jess smiles, already recovered. 'He's quite a long way out…in the right direction…and going steadily.'

'We're heading home,' Julia tells her. 'Fenn's done in.'

'I'll stay on,' comes the expected reply.

Two very tired grown-ups and a child so exhausted she can barely put one foot in front of another, trudge up the dunes for the last time. Back in their field, Hamish lifts an uncomplaining Fenn onto his shoulders where she folds up, limp as a rag doll. At the croft gate, she rallies one last time as squawking geese and pecking chickens gather crossly at their ankles. Where have you been? they squawk. Why hasn't this girl taken us to our night places?

'I haven't put the birds to bed, Dad,' Fenn whispers.

'Dinnae worry,' he says. 'It's my turn tonight.'

In the morning, Fenn won't remember sitting at the table, eyes glazed, eating a bowl of chicken soup. She won't remember being put under a hot shower nor having her long hair washed and dried, nor being tucked up in a bed warmed with a hot-water bottle and piled with an extra quilt.

She sleeps for fourteen hours, a sleep filled with dreams of being under the deep blue ocean where she sits astride a whale who dips and dives, a ride as exciting as any fairground wurlitzer. As he powers onwards, he sings a song that soars with notes of joy and freedom. He is going to try again to find his pod, his family of whales.

Chapter 33

Jess

It's 16.00

Not many people linger on the beach. The curtain has fallen on the drama that unfolded over the course of the day and there is nothing left to see. Rain is falling hard from clouds that will soon tear apart to dump their load in puddles on the sand. The wind is gusting from the east, nasty and freaky. The team is all packed up, their job done, ready to catch a plane back to the mainland. Islanders and divers exchange congratulations and heartfelt thanks. They pat one another on the back. And when all is done and dusted, the group sits on the sand and passes from hand to hand not buckets of salt water but bottles of whisky. My god, they deserve that dram. Or three. Some eyes still turn to the water, but the whale is no longer their responsibility. He has been returned to the place where he belongs.

A few hardy swimmers, too euphoric to call it a day, are still mucking about in the shallows doing handstands and opening their mouths to drink the rain. After all, not a lot happens on this small island. But one by one, they make their way back, climb wearily up the deserted beach, gather their stuff and head home. They fail to notice that one swimmer, who waits until the coast is clear, is walking in the opposite direction and stepping over stones into an ocean that is disturbed, as if it's just witnessed something unnatural.

Jess is fast. This is what she does. What she did, she reminds herself. Puttering with Fenn barely counts as exercise. Some days since coming here, alone, she swam hard and fast, but that line on the water rose up like a physical barrier to halt her. Now, she doesn't give a damn about any of that. There is something more important to do. She needs to follow the whale and to reflect on all that has happened, not just today, but all of it. From the accident to the present. Her breathing is easy, her crawl light and rhythmic as she swims over the line that haunted her and on, out towards the horizon. Her swimming is so powerful, so streamlined, that the strengthening wind barely bothers her and her pace doesn't falter through increasing turbulence. She swam in far worse conditions.

About a mile from the shore, not that she's measuring, she flips onto her back, floats motionless and stares up at clouds. She accepts the lashing of rain on her face. It will be hard work out here in another hour or two, she knows that, but for once the challenge of fighting an unruly sea is of no interest. Been there, done that. In another lifetime. The point is to convey to the ocean that she accepts it in all its moods and she will ask it to accept her as she is now, unsure and unsettled, and without Dan. The day has been momentous and full of portent. On the beach there was a communal holding of breath. For the stranded whale, the scales of fate tipped one way, then the other, life and death in the balance. It was touch and go.

Jess has not reached her own ending. She has one further step – or rather one further stroke – to take, and she senses it is very close. A single rod of zig-zag lightning shoots down the sky, away on the horizon,a blue-white strobe illuminating the bay. There will be more of that soon but she has time first to deal with what awaits her. She knows it's there.

The boat is not blurred nor does it come slowly into view like a mirage made of sorrow. Sharp, clear, real, Dan is rowing steadily towards her across the bumpy sea, the little boat rising and falling as it rides the white-crested waves. She can see the lovely grain of the larch and the dent in the prow where Dan hit a rock while chatting to her instead of concentrating. He's smiling at her and his eyes glint with his trademark mischief. In minutes, she is beside him, touching the boat, hanging on to the gunnels, reaching for Dan's hand as he slips the oars into the rowlocks.

'Jess, darling Jess, why do you keep running away from me?' he asks, his hand tight in hers.

'Because you're a flashback. A ghost.'

'I'm not a ghost now.'

Nor is he. She knows this hand, rough and calloused from rowing, always toasty warm even in the coldest conditions. She knows this weathered face as well as she knows her own. She feels his pride in her. And his love.

'I miss you,' she says, tears flowing down cheeks already sea-soaked. She reaches in to touch him, to make sure he is real, even as the sea tries to throw her against the boat and knock her under the surface.

'I know,' he says. 'Listen, Jess. It may help if we say goodbye.'

'There was no goodbye. I lost you.'

'That's why I've been trying to reach you. To put that right. But you always turn away.'

Jess looks at his beloved face. Could that be true? 'Perhaps I wasn't ready,' she says quietly.

'And now?'

'I'm ready.'

Their silence is loud yet tender as the banshee wind howls around them.

'OK, let's go back there, Jess. One last time. To the grey sea where one minute we were fine, and the next minute, my heart stopped. Not a word of warning. Inconsiderate of it, I reckon.' Behind the lightness is a depth of sorrow.

'Don't spare me, Dan. You drowned. I didn't save you.' Jess is sobbing again.

'I didn't drown, Jess.'

Their eyes meet, the same blue, and she knows it's the truth. Dan is folding over again and for a moment she panics, but he is only leaning over to place his hands on her wet shoulders and to touch her mouth with his. It's a goodbye kiss of exquisite poignancy that speaks of their life together and a love that will endure long after he has gone. Then he pulls away, straightens, picks up the oars, and rows. Tears and rain and salt water blur her vision and she lets go of the boat to swipe at her face. When she opens her eyes, he is far away. How did he row that fast? He is waving. She waves back. And he is gone.

The second rod of lightning is multi-forked and lights up the sea, the beach and the sky in neon white. Jess is swimming back, straight past that pesky line on the water that has been erased as surely as if someone has taken a giant eraser and rubbed it out. Maybe Julia sneaked out here and painted over it. The rowing boat has vanished too. Jess imagines

Dan following the whale towards the horizon, each of them parted from those left behind on the land. Fenn will miss the underwater singing, Jess thinks, as she scrambles out across shifting stones and is pelted with driving rain. As I will miss Dan. She runs up the beach, head down, limbs weary and heavy. When she has rubbed herself dry and tugged on her clothes, she stands and looks long and hard one last time at the ocean on this prescient day of departures. There is the sense of an ending.

Chapter 34

The Whale

Slow and stiff from his ordeal, the whale swims on in deep cobalt blue, choosing the water's middle path, a half-way depth that demands less of a body that is bruised and a soul shocked by an almost deadly mistake of his own making. He monitors his energy because he knows the extent of the damage done by his wrong-footed migration, by the bleak stories he has carried with him, and by that long stretch of time out of his element. To run on empty now would take him down, down, down where he would lie immobile on the seabed as he lay stranded on the sand. After the hours of pain, after the agony of feeling his body as a crushing weight and his silent struggle to stay alive, he has nothing in reserve to thrust him back up to safety. If he sank, it would be to a slow death. Watching all of this as if from the corner of his tiny eye, he harnesses his last small bursts of energy to take him further into calm, miles-deep water where the ocean is as it should be with its soundtrack of skittering silver fish and trembling seaweed and cold colliding currents. Mouth open, he eats, the broom in his palate still working well to expel the sea water and push the nourishment to his throat. There are fish here. Krill and algae in plentiful supply. He eats and floats. Eats and rests. Sunshine filters through weeds whose green fingers touch the surface and he catches sight of his own soft shadow moving below him across the seabed. That image reflects back to him exactly how he feels. I am an echo of the creature I once was. Remembering the sights that troubled him, that frightened him, he knows he can take on board no further trauma. Looking up, he sees the light break into a thousand glittering stars that dance on the surface of the sea and he gives thanks that he has, by chance, stumbled into this haven.

Silent for all those hours on dry land, he tests his voice because a whale can't travel without calling to his pod, wherever they might be and however long it's been since he heard them. He calls. Instead of liquid notes that pour into the water, there is rust and sand. A gravelly sound sinks down to the seabed. For a while he is disheartened, but can't countenance defeat, not now. He travels back in time to that place where the sea ran dry and spat him out on to hard sand like a great big stone. Exposed and vulnerable, he was waiting to die. And then, all around him, there had been a flurry of activity. He smelt and heard the care and the striving of those other creatures who did not leave him, not for a moment, but moved together to tend to his needs. Those creatures poured water, spill by spill, onto his cracked and parched skin until the burning eased. Voices spoke with authority and tenderness and concern. When his element washed over him, trickle by trickle, then wave by rolling wave until he was half-immersed, they stayed close by him, seeming to know that he could not move by himself. And finally those helpers sent up a mighty roar when he wobbled and swayed and was lifted, and was held light and alive by the weight of water. Still they stayed, swimming alongside him, reaching out with a touch that said, We are with you. Fully afloat, of course it crossed his mind that he might not have the strength and stamina to swim and their efforts would be in vain. Tired to his bones, he trembled. He snapped his tail and angled his fins. A meagre arch inched him onwards. Then another.

Thinking of that blessedness from creatures who could have killed and eaten him, he draws their colours into his song, the sun yellow of kindness, the tidal pool blue of care, the moonlight silver of compassion. Next time he calls, his song is brighter, and he hears the new palette of colours splashed over his vocal chords. The sound is very fine, he thinks, but not quite complete.

There are other notes he has yet to add. It takes longer to turn these into whale sound because he clings to them in all their purity, wanting to keep them close to his heart. Their origin is the sweet hum he heard when he lay on that hard, dry sand, his body collapsed, heavy, useless. One of the other creatures lay beside him, a hand on his head, a small body curled close to his. Only once did he dare open an eye and look. It was one of their young, a female calf, and she was gazing straight at him. The sound she made was like the rippling of reeds in rain-washed rock pools. It was so full of love that it contained many of the palest and rarest colours of the ocean. The whale waits until he is ready, then he weaves them through the other vivid tones, adding the opalescence of an oyster shell, the palest green of sea glass, the almost-yellow of a limpet, the white of foam. These are the gifts she gave him.

He calls. His song is a taut, wire-strung twist of tones

that peal out like church bells and organ chords. He hears its strength and fullness, and rejoices in its reach. Its journey through water is fast, like lightning across a night sky, but its echo lingers, filling basins, twisting through sea grass and sea oats, and rolling in and out of turbulence.

Will it find them? Will they hear his call of bold, lucid colours? Will he pick up the water music of his pod as it pulses back? With a flick of his tail, he travels on, his senses alive to an answering call.

Acknowledgements

Unlike Linen Press authors who have a gremlin on their shoulders (me) who edits and mauls their prose, I have none. I wish it were otherwise. I sent this novel to the usual suspects – agents and publishers – who all rejected it, and so the writing journey has been as solitary and unguided as that of my whale.

But throughout that journey, my writer-friends have sent me encouragement and love, and picked me up when I was down and almost out. Avril Joy, winner of the Costa prize, whose lyrical writing I adore and admire, believed in this story and believed in me. Avril has been at my virtual side through the years and the drafts, positive, creatively constructive and unfailingly wise. Derek Thomson has cheered me on in emails, and in our podcasts, *The Truth About Fiction*. While his spy thrillers roll out effortlessly, my literary fiction falters, and so we talk in circles about genres, blocks, obsession and success, all punctuated by his ridiculous jokes. Thank you, Jess Richards – you who have come lately with your exceptionally fine antennae for prose and your understanding of the outsiders and misfits who occupy my novels. Thank you, Rebecca Pitt, for your daily contact and support about all things Linen Press, about donkeys and dogs, about needing time alone. I turn to you in times of calm and tempest, and always you are there.

Thank you to my sister, Trish, who has put up with me obsessing about writing and books for about forty years. Our family genes split – she is numbers and I am words –

but she is a keen reader and heroically keeps tabs on the precarious finances of Linen Press. To quote her: 'Linen Press seems to be where our worlds collide.'

And love and thanks to the family who do live on a croft on a small Scottish island and whose admirable, tough, amazing way of life is the bedrock of this story. All inaccuracies in my portrayal of crofting are mine. I apologise for not changing Runner Bean's name but who could resist? Of course the characters here are not you, though one of you did plant three thousand trees all by himself.

9 781739 177775